DEAD AND BURIED

A DCI HARRY MCNEIL NOVEL

JOHN CARSON

DI FRANK MILLER SERIES

Crash Point

Silent Marker

Rain Town

Watch Me Bleed

Broken Wheels

Sudden Death

Under the Knife

Trial and Error

Warning Sign

Cut Throat

Blood from a Stone

Time of Death

Frank Miller Crime Series – Books 1-3 – Box set

Frank Miller Crime Series - Books 4-6 - Box set

MAX DOYLE SERIES

Final Steps
Code Red
The October Project

SCOTT MARSHALL SERIES

Old Habits

DEAD AND BURIED

Created with Vellum

ONE

Dan Foley had just dropped his cigarette into the frying pan for the second time when Mike Black walked into the quiet hotel kitchen.

'Sake,' Foley said, chasing it around the pan, managing to scoop it up on the third try.

'This is the reason I don't eat out anymore,' Black said, coming further into the large room. It smelled of old grease and burnt chips.

'It's not like I gob in it,' Foley said, putting the cigarette back in his mouth. It was greasy and barely smokable, but he gave it his all.

'I thought the restaurant closed at eleven?' Black said, looking at his watch.

'It does. It did. This is for some sod in their room. Ordering a full Scottish at this time of night. I told that prick on night duty I was finished, but he said he would throw me a fifty for doing this.'

'Fifty for flicking ash into somebody's scran? It's a wonder you don't get five years.'

'Och away. What they don't see, they won't puke over.' Foley was a big man with a big temper and big fists, both of which got to see the light of day on a regular basis.

'Rather him than me.'

'Did you get them?' Foley asked.

'Aye, they're under the table.'

'Good. Wait till I serve this pile of shite onto a plate and get one of those daft suitcase jockeys to come and take it upstairs, then we can be off.'

'Hey, *I'm* one of those daft suitcase jockeys.'

'You can take it upstairs then.'

'Will I fuck. I'm off duty.'

Foley began the same journey he'd just started a few moments ago with the cigarette, chasing black pudding and sausages round the pan. 'Fuck's sake,' he said, the manky cigarette bobbing up and down in his mouth, ash falling down into the grease.

After the food was out, he took the two fried eggs out of another pan and added them to the plate.

'I bet prisoners get better food than that,' Black said. 'Which you're about to find out.'

'Which *we're* about to find out if we get caught,' Foley answered.

'It's harmless. We're just making a point, showing those arrogant –'

Foley held up a hand. 'Save your voice for the demonstration.'

Black looked at the clock. 'It's already started, so our timing is perfect. Nip in, do the biz and then away.'

'His nibs still knows we're coming then?'

Black laughed. 'He's counting on us being there.'

'Good.' Foley picked up the wall phone and spoke to the front desk. 'That's the scran ready. Get that wee plook to come down here and pick it up right away. And I want my fifty by the start of my shift tomorrow.'

He hung up and slapped a metal cover over the plate, which he'd placed on a tray. Then they picked up the small white buckets that had been hiding in plain sight under one of the steel prep tables.

Foley took two empty backpacks out of his locker and handed one to his friend. 'They'll fit in there. I made sure.'

'They look a bit small,' Black complained.

'What do want? Five-gallon bins? Get a grip. They'd weigh a ton.'

'We haven't got far to go.'

'Do I look like the sort of guy who works out?' Foley said, patting his ample gut. 'No. And I'm not about to start now. Plus, you're a skinny bastard. You get the wind knocked out of you opening a can of beans.'

'Let's just go. If we're too late, he'll go off his nut.'

They walked out of the kitchen and into the darkness of the lane that ran behind the hotel.

Foley was sweating like a pig when they got round the corner and went through the archway into Royal Exchange Square. The crowds had gathered in front of the Gallery of Modern Art, but there were still a lot of people at the side.

Foley and Black walked through the people and saw the police uniforms near the front. They strolled casually past and saw their esteemed leader belting out his rhetoric.

'Men like this man here!' he shouted, pointing to the statue of the Duke of Wellington sitting atop his horse. This statue was known the world over as The Man with a Cone on His Head. Only tonight, he was going to have something very different on his head.

'This is capitalism at its finest!' the man on the top step was shouting. Clifford Dunn had everybody's attention. He was well away from the statue, and no doubt he'd chosen this position to make it easier to point up to the cone that sat atop the statue's head. 'We need to rip these statues down and make them disappear! Never again shall human beings suffer at the hands of other men!'

The crowd exploded with applause and shouting and cheering.

Cue Foley and Black.

They took the small buckets out of their backpacks, prised the lids off and, hiding in amongst the crowd, threw the blood over the statue. It hit the stone and sprayed back onto some of the onlookers.

Then they ran as people screamed, but the screams were indistinguishable from the fevered chants and shouts of the demonstrators.

Then one girl looked down and saw what was amongst the red liquid dripping off the bronze horse.

That scream brought everybody else to a halt.

TWO

'What do you think hurts more, a man getting a punch in the bollocks or a woman giving birth?' Detective Sergeant Robbie Evans weaved the unmarked patrol car through the late-morning traffic.

'I don't know. Why don't I punch you in the bollocks now and we can find out?' Detective Chief Inspector Jimmy Dunbar popped a Tic Tac into his mouth. 'Why are you asking anyway?'

'I was just wondering. I'd like kids one day.'

'And you're worried that they're going to punch you in the bollocks?'

'No. I'm thinking of taking it to the next level with Vern.'

'What? You might actually put your hand in

your pocket and pay for a meal on your own instead of asking her to go Dutch?'

'No, I mean I might ask her to move in with me. Then we can progress to getting married and having kids. She's on the fence about kids. She says she's heard it hurts too much. And why are you eating so many of those things? Didn't you say they make you fart?'

Dunbar had already cracked a window, just in case. 'I did, but I'm having a notion of taking up smoking cigars again and Cathy isn't happy. Tic Tacs take my mind off smoking.'

'Happy wife, happy life,' Evans replied.

'How would you know? Have you secretly married your old mother?'

'That's not even funny. That's borderline psycho talk.'

'Don't talk pish. You took me by surprise, talking about married life when the only woman you've ever got close to taking down the aisle came in a plain brown box with a bicycle pump.'

'I'm still going to ask Vern. Nothing you can say will put me off.'

'How about the fact you live with your maw, who launders your skids with a bottle of sulphuric acid and does everything else for you?'

'Not everything, boss. I can look after myself,' Evans said, pulling up behind a bus.

'Look after yourself? Take this quick test to see if you really are ready: do you make your own bed?'

'No.'

'Do you cook?'

'No.'

'Chip away at your Ys with a hammer and chisel?'

'Och, away with yoursel'.'

'Nil points for doing the washing. How about paying the bills?'

'I give my ma some dig money.'

'What, you toss her twenty quid a week and expect room and board for that?'

'You make me sound like a miserable bastard.'

'Listen, son, you have less points in this quiz than Britain gets in the Eurovision Song Contest. I think you might well want to give that lassie a break. Wait until you get your own place.'

'I've been looking for places, but prices are through the roof. The pay we get, I'll be lucky to buy a dug kennel.'

They moved forward.

'Seriously, though, do you think she'd say yes if you asked her?' Dunbar said.

Evans was silent for a moment before answering. 'If I'm being honest, she was the one who was hinting.'

'You mean she actually wants to move in with you and your maw?' Dunbar popped another Tic Tac. 'Watch the fur fly if that happens.'

'No. Nothing like that. She owns a wee flat, but she said if we moved in together, then she'd rent it out. She'd rather we get another place together first. Sort of neutral ground.'

'Smart lassie, keeping her options open in case Romeo turns into the Hunchback of Notre-Dame. But that still begs the question, where would you live?'

'We could move in with you and Cathy, since your kids are grown and have left the nest. You'd rent us a room, wouldn't you?'

'Aye, fucking watch me. It's bad enough having you honking the car out with your bogging aftershave without having to use the lav after you've been in it recycling a Ruby.'

'God Almighty. Last Saturday night was a one-off.' Evans shook his head. 'I hadn't been feeling well, then I had the Ruby Murray and it shot right through me.'

'In my house. Not your own. While we were

having a party. I had to tell Cath that a rat had died in the sewer pipe. She almost called a bloody plumber. I used three buckets of water to clean the lavvy, dirty bastard. I hope you shat your pants that night.'

'It was a close call. Did Cathy think you'd flushed the rat away?'

'Something like that.'

Evans pulled into the side of the road behind the fire engines that were parked in front of the art gallery. The scene was cordoned off with police tape and a uniform lifted it for them as they showed their warrant cards.

'You have to get suited up first, sir,' a forensics officer told them, and pointed them to the forensics tent. They got the suits from the forensics van and began putting them on.

'I mean, Muckle McInsh and his missus are really getting into this buying-flats-and-houses lark. They bought a wee flat not that far from the station and it's not too far from their shop,' Evans said.

McInsh, Vern and a friend of theirs, Shug, ran a private investigation business out of a shop on the Southside.

'You reckon he'll give you a good price?' Dunbar asked.

'I'm sure he would. It's a one-bedroom and in good condition. We'd be as good a tenant as anybody.'

'Just remember to take plenty of air freshener.'

'Finbar O'Toole rents a place from Muckle. It's a temporary place until he gets the insurance money from his house that was blown up.'

Finbar was an ex-pathologist who was working as an investigator with McInsh.

'I heard Calvin Stewart is finally going to accept retirement,' Evans said.

'Aye. They made him a great offer, especially after what happened when they tried to get him out the door already. He'd be a fool not to take it. He told me that's what's on the table, but it's a one-off. If he rejects it, they'll just make his life a misery until he can retire and there won't be half the compensation that's on offer now, so he's keeping his head down.'

'I'll miss him,' Evans said.

'You're kidding, right?'

'Of course I am. You think I'm daft or something?'

'As a matter of fact...'

They saw a figure in a white disposable suit waving them over. Dunbar didn't recognise the person at first, until he saw some of the blond hair peeking out of the tight hood round her face.

'I have to say, this isn't the most flattering outfit I've ever had on,' Detective Superintendent Lynn McKenzie said.

'Oh, I don't know, ma'am. That tartan sweater you had on last week was a real belter. Jimmy Shand called and wanted his kilt back.'

'You're hilarious, Jimmy. Now over here and have a look.' She led them over to the statue, where the grand old Duke of Wellington sat atop his horse looking down at the peasants before him, his cone now sitting loud and proud at the side of the plinth.

Another forensics tent had been set up further back. Uniforms were at the entrance to the gallery, but there was no sign of any member of Joe Public.

'There was a major incident last night. It sparked off a right stramash, so it did.'

'There was a demonstration here, I read,' Evans said.

'There was,' Lynn said, turning to look at him. 'But somebody decided to up the ante: they threw buckets of blood on the old duke and Trigger there.'

'That must have been a crowd-pleaser,' Dunbar said. 'Sticking it right up the Establishment.'

Lynn blew out her rosy cheeks. 'It created a bloody mess. Pardon the pun. Because blood is considered a biohazard material, the area had to be cleared. The fire service were called in and a hazmat team were directed to do the clean-up. People scattered after the blood was thrown so we don't know how many were contaminated, and they probably won't show their faces. But it was what was *in* the blood that was cause for concern. Let's go inside.' She stopped before entering. 'Oh, and DSup Stewart is here.'

They went into the white tent. The temperature inside wasn't any better than outside, but at least they were out of the wind.

DSup Calvin Stewart was standing next to the pathologist. 'Here they are, our two superheroes: Sewer Man and Jobby Boy.' He looked at Evans. 'What was that all about last Saturday? Invited along to Jimmy's wife's birthday party and you stink the fucking hoose out. You should be ashamed of yoursel', ya dirty bastard.'

'I'd had a curry with Vern before I got there. I think it was a bad batch.'

'Bad batch? It's a wonder you didn't blow a hole out the back of your fucking troosers. Don't think you're getting invited along to any party I have. I don't want to call out a hazmat team to hose down my fucking lavvy.'

'Duly noted, sir. Not even your leaving do?' Evans said.

'Shut your hole.'

A table had been set up and there were bagged exhibits sitting on top. Dr Fiona Christie, one of the city's pathologists, was there.

'Hello, gentlemen,' she said, after Stewart had calmed down from his little rant.

'Doctor,' Dunbar replied. 'Good to see you again.'

'You too.'

'Fingers,' Lynn said.

Evans held up both hands.

'I think she means the contents of the bags,' Dunbar translated. He pursed his lips and gently shook his head in a *fucking halfwit* way.

'I did,' Lynn confirmed. 'These were in the blood. Four of them. Or more accurately, a thumb and three fingers. We have forensics combing the immediate area to see if we can find the fifth.'

Dunbar and Evans moved closer to the table as if they were about to pick out a flavour of ice cream.

'No nail polish,' Fiona said. 'Looks like they've been cut off with something sharp. Very clean.

Decomposition has kicked in. Hard to tell if it's a man or a woman because they're on the smaller side.'

'Could it be a child?' Evans asked.

'I'm not ruling it out, but if I was to hazard a guess, I'd say adult.'

'Can you tell how long they've been detached?' Dunbar asked.

'I'd have to inspect them more closely.'

'If you were a betting woman?'

'I'd have to roll the dice on two to three days. We'll get the prints off them in the mortuary and send them over right away.'

'Thanks, Fiona,' Lynn said. They left the tent again, stepping into the wind, which was getting stronger.

'Has the CCTV been checked yet?' Dunbar asked Lynn.

'It has. Clifford Dunn was at the podium giving his speech when two figures took out two small buckets, popped off the lids and threw the blood over the statue.'

'Could you identify them?' Evans asked.

'No. They had scarves round their faces, which didn't stick out because everybody had winter-wear on. Hats, scarves, gloves. It looks like they might have got some blood on themselves, but it was difficult to see.'

'What about Dunn?' Dunbar asked. 'Have you talked to him?'

Lynn shook her head. 'No. He's not at home and nobody knows where he is. We're still looking. We just want to know if he knows who those two were, but you know what he's like – ex-professor at the university and full of himself.'

'Exactly,' said Dunbar. 'Now we want to see if he has blood on his hands too.'

THREE

The CID office in Leith police station smelled of fish suppers that had foregone the brown sauce and been splashed with Old Spice instead.

It was a far cry from what Detective Chief Inspector Harry McNeil's office in Fettes station had been like. That had been when he had led a Major Investigation Team. Before his detective wife, Alex, had died of a ruptured brain aneurysm. Before he had taken a leave of absence and gone to live in the south of Scotland. And his team had been disbanded.

He had been placed back in CID until a new team was formed, but it was taking time to find the right detectives to become part of the new MIT.

Now, in a cold, wet December, he was looking

out of his office window onto Queen Charlotte Street. Christmas was coming up fast and he wasn't looking forward to it. On the one hand, it was his daughter Grace's first Christmas, but on the other it was the first Christmas without her mother.

Alex's sister, Jessica, lived in Harry's house in Murrayfield and that had been a blessing. Though he was worried that his daughter would grow up thinking that Aunt Jessica was Mummy. It was stupid to worry about it just now, and he knew she would be told the truth when she was growing older, but it bothered him.

He turned to look into the incident room, at the other detectives, none of whom he could call a friend. He had previously worked in Professional Standards, investigating other cops, and they all knew it. They looked at him as if he had burned down an orphanage and thrown petrol on the flames, even though he had never investigated any of them.

He watched as a lanky detective sergeant called Ian Pierce walked over to his office. The man opened the door without knocking and Harry saw DI Ray Walker grinning over at them from across the room.

'We got a call,' Pierce said.

'First of all, this is not your first fucking day at primary school,' Harry said. 'You knock before you come into my office. And second, you address me as *sir*.' He looked over at Walker again and saw he was grinning even more as Pierce got a dressing-down.

'Sorry. Sir. But we got a call about Lenny Stafford.'

Harry mulled over the name for a moment, then he caught up with himself. 'The guy you've been looking for?'

'Ten out of ten, Captain,' Walker said, appearing in the doorway. 'The guy we've been looking for.'

Harry stared at him for a few seconds, trying to control his temper while picturing taking a Samurai sword and ramming it through his gut. 'Get out, Pierce. Walker, close the door behind you. From this side.'

Walker made a face at the younger detective as the man left and he closed the door.

'You know, Chief, you really don't have to have such a thin skin. We're all mates in here.'

'This isn't the seventies, Walker. You show me respect when you come into my office. Boss or sir, not Captain, Chief or Willa-fucking-Wonka. Do we understand each other?'

'Of course, sir. I'd like to apologise if I stepped out of line. But most of us get along in here without taking offence. Our old DCI was one of the boys.'

'DCI Thompson has retired. He's not coming back, so you're stuck with me for the foreseeable future. And I expect respect from my team. Is that clear?'

'Crystal, boss. So, we got a tip about Stafford. He's hiding out in an empty flat up at Dumbiedykes. I can send Pierce round with a couple of guys if you like?'

Harry looked out the window at the team and wondered if anything but a doughnut run would be above their competency level. There was only one detective in the department that he trusted, one of his own old team members, DS Lillian O'Shea. Besides, he had just watched Pierce put his coat on and leave.

'I'll go. I'll take DS O'Shea with me.'

Walker's face fell. 'I have her doing some other work, sir. If you could take Elvis, that would be good.'

Colin 'Elvis' Presley was a man of small stature who gave the impression he was only there to make up the numbers.

'Fine,' Harry said.

Walker opened the door. 'Oi, Elvis, look lively. You're going out with the boss.'

Presley looked up from his computer on the

other side of the room and stood up as Walker watched him. He grabbed his jacket from the back of the chair as Harry entered the main room.

'You're with me,' he said. Then to Walker: 'Have you written the address down?'

Walker handed over the Post-it. 'Ian did. That's it there. Call us if you need back-up.'

'Get onto uniform and have a patrol meet us there.'

'Right away, sir.'

Harry didn't know how old Walker was, but he was willing to bet the man wasn't going to go far up the career ladder.

He left the office with Presley and stepped out into the cold air. Darkness had descended on Leith now and it was freezing. The rush-hour traffic was just beginning to gain a stranglehold as they got into the car.

'Dumbiedykes,' he said to the younger detective as Presley got in behind the wheel.

'How do you like working in CID, sir?' Presley asked as they set off.

'What's not to like? Working with a bunch of fine, upstanding detectives like you lot.'

'Ah, the sarcasm. It happens to every one of the

DCIs who comes here. If you don't mind me saying so.'

'I don't give a toss, to be honest.'

'That's the spirit. Not one of the DCIs we've had has ever started a shift by singing "Oh, What a Beautiful Morning". By the time the end of the shift comes round, they're all dishevelled and playing with matches, looking for something combustible to burn the station down with.'

'It's safe to say that morale is low, then.' It was rhetorical. Harry had never been bothered by what other officers thought of him. He'd investigated quite a few in his four years with Professional Standards, and had met many liars and cheats and officers who should have been wearing a prison uniform not a polis one.

'Oh, yes. Not for the little team in there, but for any officer who comes in to join them. They're like a pack of hyenas. Pierce, Walker and some sleekit DC who never seems to be there much. Ricky...Christ.'

'Ricky Christ?' Harry asked, his voice tinged with scepticism.

'No, I mean: Christ, I can't remember his name. No, wait.'

'Wate?'

Presley took his eyes off the road for a moment

and looked at Harry. 'I get the distinct feeling you're yanking my chain here, sir.'

'Who, me? I'm just trying to help you finish your story, son.'

Presley took one hand off the wheel to snap his fingers. 'Dawson. Ricky Dawson. He works under-cover a lot. Then there's me and Lillian O'Shea. She's solid.' He looked at Harry. 'Sound as a pound,' he added, in case Harry wasn't up to speed on what 'solid' meant.

They drove up Easter Road, over Abbey Mount and up to Dumbiedykes.

'Viewcraig Gardens,' Harry said, reading the address off the Post-it note. He stuck it to his finger, keeping it on standby should Presley prove to have the attention span of a fruit fly.

'What was it again?' Presley asked, turning off Holyrood Road.

'Sake,' Harry said, sticking the piece of yellow paper in front of the fruit fly.

'Nice to see Pierce can write using a pen sticking out of his arse. Would you mind transcribing that into English for me, sir?'

'Add secretary to my already long list of skills and be done with it. Viewcraig Gardens.' Harry said it slowly, like Presley was daft.

It didn't help that the interior of the car was in darkness, illuminated only by the dull glow of the street lamps. The right side of the street was lined with trees and bushes, and with a long stretch of the imagination, Harry could almost believe they were driving in the country. Although if he *was* going for a drive in the country, he could think of a better companion than the moody little detective who was in the driving seat.

He looked out the window at the passing flats, most of them with a light on in a window. 'Up there, on the left,' Harry said.

Presley looked at the trees on the right-hand side before looking at Harry. 'Left-hand side, you say?'

'Don't be so jaded, Presley. All DCIs aren't dicks.'

'I never said they were, sir.'

'I could tell you were biting your tongue when I said up on the left and there's just a jungle on the right.'

'That's your prerogative to say where we're going, sir.'

Harry put the Post-it into his pocket. Twice. Like Post-its the world over, it didn't want to let go. 'Bloody thing,' he muttered, looking out of the car into the darkness. 'Where's that bloody patrol car?'

'We could always go and have a look ourselves. Scout the place out before the patrol car gets here,' Presley said, turning off the engine.

'Aye, why not?' Harry thought they'd been sent out on a wild goose chase, but there was always that one per cent chance.

They got out of the car and Presley was careful to lock it. Harry had one more look down the road they had driven up, but there was still no sign of a patrol car. Several other cars were parked, but nothing with a light bar on its roof.

They walked through the cold air and Harry wondered if the wind coming off Arthur's Seat in the background drove the residents of these flats to keep the heating on for longer. He had a friend who had lived in Frogston, a short distance away from the Pentland Hills, with fields in between, and the man had kept his heating on all day, it was so cold with the wind rushing off the hills.

He looked up at their destination: a maisonette-style flat on the first floor which had boarded-up windows. If Lenny Stafford was indeed holed up in there, he wasn't looking out the window.

'Let's start pushing buzzers,' Harry said, approaching Presley, who had got to the communal front door first.

'No need, sir. Some kindly gent has done us a solid and dismantled the lock.'

There he was, using the word 'solid' again. 'Could have been a woman,' Harry said, stepping past the DC as he held the door open. A flight of stairs led them up to the landing.

'Who's going to try the door handle on the flat?' Presley asked.

Harry took out a twenty-pence piece. 'Call in the air.'

'Heads,' Presley said before Harry had tossed the coin.

'Maybe I should make it heads, I punch you in the bollocks; tails, I kick you in the bollocks.'

'You caught me off-guard. I might have jumped the gun, but to be fair, you were a bit slow.'

'In the air,' Harry said, tossing the coin.

'Tails.'

Harry caught the coin, slapped it onto the back of his hand and peeked at it. 'You lose,' he said without showing Presley the coin.

'I bet you're good at winning pints in the bar with skills like that, if you don't mind me saying, sir.'

'I don't mind at all. Now, look sharpish. I want to get a fish supper for my dinner if this radgie Stafford isn't here.'

Both men took out a torch and Presley put a hand on the door handle and found no resistance. He pushed the handle all the way down and pushed the door, expecting to hear creaky hinges announcing their arrival, but they were keeping mum.

They walked into the hallway and were introduced to smells that usually belonged to something ancient and putrefied. Junk mail lay on the carpet, mixed in with free newspapers and regular mail to make a concoction that would help a fire gain hold. A fire that would redecorate the whole flat in under twenty minutes.

'I'll check upstairs,' Harry said, and he shone the light until he found the carpeted stairs. Actually, 'carpeted' was being kind; 'floor covering of indeterminate origin' better described it. He put a foot on the first stair and was surprised it didn't squeak. None of them did.

After Harry made his way up, Presley shone his light into the living room as he entered. The room was as clarty as the hallway, with a couch covered in mildew and stacked with old newspapers. Litter lay around the carpet like a plastic bug infestation. What wasn't covered in mould was covered in dust.

Presley took a step forward and swung the torchlight around the room. Unless Stafford was hiding under the cushions of the settee, the room was empty. He was about to turn round when he was roughly shoved in the back. He went sprawling on his front, thinking that Stafford had come charging out of the kitchen.

But it wasn't Stafford. Unless Stafford had taken to wearing all-black clothing and a ski mask.

Presley rolled onto his back and watched as the figure advanced on him. His torch had gone flying and lay near an old coffee table, illuminating the underside of it and the manky wallpaper beyond.

He was about to shout for Harry when the boot swung at his face.

Presley rolled and caught the boot, twisting the leg and kicking out the other. The man yelled as he fell, then Presley let go and both men clambered to their feet.

Ski Mask rushed the small detective, throwing a roundhouse punch. Presley ducked and slammed a fist into the man's gut, which doubled him over for a second, but he batted Presley away and stood facing him, fists by his side.

Then a second man appeared, dressed exactly the same way, only his mask was a knitted balaclava. 'Got him fucking sorted yet?' he said.

'Shut up,' Ski Mask said, then they both rushed

Presley. The detective got a punch in, connecting with Ski Mask's face, and he felt cartilage being manipulated by his fist. But they overpowered him and dragged him to the front door. Ski Mask opened it and Balaclava threw Presley out onto the landing.

'Look who just left the building,' Balaclava said, laughing.

'My fucking nose,' Ski Mask said as blood gushed out.

Balaclava closed the front door and locked it as the detective hit the railings. Presley tried to get his phone out of his pocket, but he realised it was gone. And Harry was now inside by himself with two thugs. Stafford and a friend? Maybe. But why were they dressed like that?

FOUR

Harry knew that life was good for him, despite his wife dying a few months earlier. He still felt numb at times, but life could be a lot worse. He could be living in this shithole, for example.

Upstairs, the landing turned to the right. The door facing him led into a bathroom. The torchlight bounced off the mirror on the medicine cabinet. He moved the cabinet door and caught his reflection: five o'clock shadow; hair in need of a cut; eyes tired and carrying too much baggage. If his face was an airline, it would be charging an excess fee.

He turned and shone the light into the hallway landing, before moving forwards and shining it into a bedroom. Hardly the honeymoon suite: it had peeling wallpaper, the remains of a fast-food meal and possibly some disease formerly unknown to man.

'Good God,' he said out loud. He checked the room: no wardrobe, built-in or otherwise; nowhere to hide.

He stepped back onto the landing.

Harry had been in many a situation where somebody had suddenly appeared and his training had kicked in, so that instead of jumping back he had instantly controlled himself. Which had been good practice for now, as his torchlight picked out a hulking man dressed in black and wearing a ski mask.

Hulk instantly moved forward, drawing a fist back at the same time. Harry countered the move by turning sideways and blocking the punch with his right arm, then he rammed the man's face with an elbow. Hulk let out a grunt but quickly launched another attack.

Harry once again moved sideways and shoved the man. Hulk was at the top of the stairs and now Harry saw that he was outnumbered three-to-one, as two other masked figures were advancing up the stairs to be with their friend.

Hulk had other ideas: as he fell back, arms out in an effort to save himself and avoid breaking his neck, he hit the other two men, and they all tumbled down the stairs and landed in a heap. Hulk lay on the floor, moaning, but the other two men, Ski Mask and Balaclava, recovered quickly.

They saw Harry coming down the stairs just as the front door crashed inwards.

Ski Mask took a swing at Presley, who easily countered the measure and threw a punch at the man's face. It connected with his eye socket, knocking his head sideways.

Then Harry was down the stairs. Balaclava took advantage and threw a punch into Harry's privates which would have been enough to stop a rhino, and it was certainly enough to stop Harry.

Presley stepped forward and kicked Balaclava on the side of the thigh as Harry landed on the floor.

Ski Mask and Balaclava looked at Harry, Ski Mask still bleeding through the nose hole in his mask. They grappled with Presley as he threw another punch at Balaclava and shoved him into the living room, where his torch still lay. Then they grabbed their friend, Hulk and dragged him out of the flat.

Presley got to his feet. He had to choose quickly: either chase after them or help Harry. He chose to stay with the DCI in case there were others.

'I'm not going to ask if you're okay, sir, because you look like shite,' Presley said.

'Bastard got me in the bollocks,' Harry said, his hands cupping the family jewels.

'I got a good few smacks in,' Presley said, not bragging but trying to assure his boss that the assailants hadn't got off scot-free.

Harry looked at the smaller man to see if he was jesting or not, but apparently he wasn't. Presley had found his phone and was about to call it in when Harry put a hand on his arm.

'Don't,' he said simply.

'Why, sir?'

'Just...don't. I'll explain later. Just help me up and out of this shitehole.'

Presley offered Harry a hand. 'A joiner will have to be called to board this place up.'

'Why? In case somebody comes in and chories the curtains? They'd probably get fucking typhoid off them. Just leave it, son, and let's get out of here.'

Harry got to his feet and stopped for a moment, bending over, making a conscious effort not to put a hand on a wall to steady himself and instead relying on Presley to keep him balanced.

'I think I'm going to be sick,' Harry said, taking in deep breaths. It wasn't the first time he'd been punched in the balls. He'd even been punched by a five-year-old before, and this time wasn't as bad as that, but a close second.

He stood that way for a few minutes until the feeling that his genitalia were going to explode subsided.

'If I ever see that bastard again, I'm going to give him a size eleven right round the fucking goolies,' he said, standing up straight.

'You're going to take the law into your own hands and inflict violence on somebody?' Presley said.

'Aye. You got a problem with that?'

'Nope. I'll be right there with you. But I did get a few good punches in.'

'Me too. And a good elbow into the bastard's face.'

'I think we did some damage to two of them at least.' Presley looked at his boss as they left the scabby flat, Harry giving the impression that he was walking barefoot over Lego bricks.

They put their torches away and heard boots running up the concrete stairs to their level.

Presley stood with his fists bunched until Harry nudged him and they looked over the wall of the balcony to the blue flashing lights on the roof of the patrol car in the car park.

'Now they show up,' the smaller man said.

'They're not our back-up. They wouldn't have announced their arrival.'

The first uniform shot onto the landing and saw the two men standing facing them, looking dishevelled.

'Stay where you are!' he barked.

Harry and Presley both reached into their pockets.

'Keep your fucking hands where I can see them!' the uniform said as his partner joined him.

'Relax,' Harry said as he and Presley pulled their warrant cards out.

'Oh, right. Sorry, sir.' The uniform managed to look sheepish, even if he wasn't quite at the 'pulling a beamer' level. 'We got a call saying there was a break-in and disturbance at this address.'

'We were on a follow-up call and there's nobody here. Nothing to report, son.'

'Very good, sir.'

'It's just an abandoned flat that could do with a lick of paint and a wee hoover,' Presley said.

'Okay, sir. Thanks. Probably some kind of misunderstanding.'

Harry and Presley walked back downstairs behind the uniforms and got back into their car.

'Why didn't you tell them, sir?' Presley asked.

'Same reason you didn't contradict me.'

'It was a set-up.'

Harry looked at him in the dark as the engine began building the heat up. 'Tell me why you think that.'

'There were two of them waiting downstairs. I got shoved by the first one and fell; then he tried to put the boot in, but I defended myself. Then the other one appeared. I was fighting them, but they manhandled me to the door and threw me outside. One of them said, "Look who's just left the building." You know, the reference to Elvis: "Elvis has left the building." They knew who I was, because of my nickname.'

Harry nodded in the dark. 'They were waiting for us. Two downstairs, one upstairs waiting to come down or attack us if we split up, which we did. Maybe they thought you were a pushover.'

'Because I'm not as tall as you? Maybe. But I was a boxer, and I continued boxing in the army, something I don't brag about. They think I'm a midget in there, and they can take the piss all day if they feel like it.'

'Do you see the patrol car that I requested as

back-up?' Harry said, looking around. The other one that had turned up was gone.

'No, I don't.'

'That's because it wasn't coming. There *was* no back-up.'

Presley looked at him. 'You don't think Stafford was here at all?'

'Do you? Why here? Why would he be in that craphole of a flat? Nobody can live in there. The council will no doubt have it on their list for gutting, but I'm sure even Stafford isn't that desperate. Somebody knew that place was empty and sent us there.'

'You don't think DI Walker sent us there on purpose, do you?'

Harry was silent for a moment. 'I'm sure. But people in Leith know I was with Professional Standards before I was asked to lead my own MIT. People who wouldn't shed a tear if I got my arse handed to me.'

'I wasn't in Standards.'

'You're collateral damage. You were with me so it wouldn't look like I was being singled out. They were going to kick the shit out of both of us, but they didn't figure on us fighting back. They saw us as an older bloke and a wee man.'

'I'm not *that* wee. Five-eight.'

'And I'm in my forties, but they couldn't see the woods for the trees. They might know us, or they might have been working under orders.' The wave of nausea was passing now and the pain had subsided to the level where Harry felt like his balls were only being clattered between two bricks rather than run over by a steamroller.

'I think I broke the nose on one of them,' Presley said proudly. 'I've broken enough of them to know.'

Harry knew what the other man was inferring: the guy with a broken nose would have to go to Accident and Emergency if he wanted it set right.

'Right, this is how we're going to play it. We get back to the station and tell Walker that Stafford wasn't there. The place was empty. Nothing happened. Understood?'

'Absolutely.'

'I'm trusting you here. They used you, so I'm guessing you're not one of their inner circle.'

Presley scoffed. 'Inner circle? I have more respect for my granny's cat than I do for Walker. Besides, I'm going to put in for a transfer through to Glasgow. I have a mate who works there and I heard it's quite good.'

'It is. I have friends Glasgow Division, and my son's in uniform there.'

'It's better than working with that back-stabber. I've never worked with a superior officer who thinks less of his men.'

'Right. Let's go.'

They drove back down to Leith and parked outside the station next to a patrol van.

Upstairs, the incident room was winding down for the day. DS Lillian O'Shea was gone. Only DI Walker was there, sitting on a chair and talking quietly into his phone. He cut the call when Harry and Presley walked in.

'Dead end,' Harry said before the DI could speak.

The man looked like he was trying to pass a kidney stone the size of a pineapple.

'That's the breaks,' he replied. 'Sometimes the intel is a bit shaky at best.'

'Where are the others?'

'They've gone for the night. I was just finishing up on some paperwork.' Walker stood up. 'Goodnight, sir. See you in the morning.'

'Goodnight.'

Walker walked out after grabbing his overcoat.

'Well, DC Presley, time to knock off for the night. See you tomorrow.'

'Goodnight, sir.'

They had agreed not to discuss anything in the station. Maybe the place was bugged, maybe not, but best not to take a chance. They both left at the same time.

Outside, there was snow in the air.

'You have your own car?' Harry asked.

'I take the bus.'

'Get in. I'll drop you off away from here. Just in case.'

'This isn't over, is it?'

'Nope.'

FIVE

Flora zipped her jacket up as she walked down the front steps with Harry by her side. 'There's really no need, Harry,' she said, pulling her gloves on. 'My car's only along the road.' The housekeeper smiled at him.

'Nonsense. This is Murrayfield, and I'm sure none of my neighbours would mug you, but people travel.'

His adrenaline was going again. He had arrived home five minutes ago and a car had pulled in to the side of the road further along from his house and he'd thought that maybe it was the uninjured one out of the trio coming to his house for a follow-up fight. Truth be told, he would have welcomed it.

'I'm just here,' she said, taking her key fob out

and opening the door to her little hatchback. Snow had fallen with a promise of more, but it wasn't anything the windscreen wipers couldn't take care of.

'Thanks again, Flora. I don't know what I'd do without you.'

'Starve, maybe?' she replied with a short laugh.

'I'd be living on sandwiches.' He smiled at her as she climbed in and watched as she drove off.

He walked back to the house. It was a terraced house, one of four in the block, with a driveway up the side that he shared with his immediate next-door neighbour, an old boy called Rupert. He was an officer in the army, long-retired, and Harry had wondered if Rupert was his actual name or the slang term for an officer that had stuck and he'd never been able to shrug off.

Harry's house was on the end. His home, which he had run to back at the end of the summer after his wife's death. The house had been left to him in an ex-girlfriend's will, just like the nursery business she had owned and run. The nursery that Jessica Maxwell, Alex's sister, was now in charge of. She was a blessing and he was glad that she had decided to stay in the big house with him.

He climbed the short flight of steps and looked

around again, just as the headlights of the car came on again. The driver pulled away from the side of the road, did a three-point turn and drove away. Harry watched the red taillights until they disappeared.

He opened the front door into the heat and locked it behind him.

Jessica was in the living room on his left. 'You eaten yet?' he asked her. When he looked at her, he could see certain elements of his wife; Alex had had a similar smile, a brightness around the eyes that drew you in. He loved Jessica, but only in a family way. She had been his rock while he mourned, and she had stepped into the role of mother to Grace like she was born to do this.

He wondered when his bubble would burst and she would leave them to fend for themselves, and then he would be left to sink or swim. She hadn't mentioned leaving, and he had given her a good life too: she had a good-paying job, a roof over her head and nothing to worry about. But she was two years younger than her sister had been, about to turn thirty, and he knew she would want to spread her wings one day.

'Flora made a terrific stew,' she said. 'I wanted to wait for you. Grace is away to bed, so we can eat in the dining room or have it on the folding TV tables.'

She smiled at him, indicating that having dinner and watching TV wasn't above her.

'I'll get the trays set up if you want to start dishing up,' he said. He took his coat off and hung it up in the hall as Jessica went through to the kitchen. The tray tables were on standby against the wall, hidden behind a drinks cabinet. He placed them in front of the couch at each end before joining Jessica in the kitchen.

'I'm sorry I'm late tonight,' he said to her. He stopped and looked for a moment, at the blonde hair falling past her shoulders. If he didn't know better, she could have been Alex. He mentally shook himself and opened the cutlery drawer.

She turned and smiled at him. 'When you were away, it was me, Grace and Flora. We got on just fine. Now that you're back living here, being a little late is no biggie.' She reached out and rubbed his arm. 'I'm just glad you're back home, Harry.'

'Me too.'

They served the food and took it through on their plates, then Harry went back for two bottles of Coke.

'News?' Jessica asked, holding the TV remote.

'If I wanted to watch some clowns, I'd go to the circus.'

'Sceptical.' She looked at him with raised eyebrows. 'There's *Are You Being Served?* on BritBox.'

'Sounds good to me.'

Jessica navigated her way through the menus with all the dexterity and skill of a fighter pilot until she found what they wanted.

'Stew's good,' Harry said.

'Flora's a godsend.'

They watched the show and Harry sat back when he'd finished his meal. His thoughts took a sideways turn, to the masked men and how they were out to hurt Harry. That angered him, but what really pissed him off was the fact they were prepared to hurt the young DC as well.

Harry had stepped on the toes of many officers in the four years he'd been in Professional Standards, and there were too many to single out any one individual who would want to harm him. The attack had taken planning, and he thought DI Walker had something to do with it, but proving it would be another matter.

He would wait and watch, and hope that Presley was who he said he was and wasn't in cahoots with the DI. He didn't think so, but he'd met some pathological liars in his time, and they were good. Presley might be one of them, and if he was, he'd get what was coming to him too.

'How was work today?' Jessica asked.

'Same old. Except I got intel about somebody who has a warrant out for his arrest, and when Presley and I got there, it was a set-up.'

'What? Are you kidding me?' Jessica's face fell and Harry could see the genuine concern in her eyes. 'What about Elvis? Is he okay?'

'Well, I don't think they stepped on his blue suede shoes, but he gave them what for. Did you know he was a boxer and kept up boxing in the army?'

'I have to ask you how you think I would know that.'

'It was rhetorical. But he was and he did. He fought off two of them.'

'Why were they after him?' she asked.

'They weren't. He just happened to be with me when it happened. They were willing to give him a skelping too.'

'How many were there?'

'Three.'

'That means if you'd gone there yourself, it would have been three against one.'

'They knew I wouldn't be alone. The guy we're

after has a penchant for violence, so they'd make sure there was at least two of us. To keep up the pretence.'

'Bastards. Why are they going after you?'

Harry smiled. 'Because of my time in Standards. I made a lot of enemies.'

Jessica reached across the divide of the cushion between them and put a hand on his. 'Be careful, Harry. You have two girls at home who need you to come home in one piece.'

'I know.'

'Do you think they'll try again?'

'If I was a betting man, I'd say so.'

They both ate in silence after that.

SIX

It wasn't exactly a high-octane lifestyle, crocheting; it was more a form of escapism. Maggie Parks was head of the Edinburgh forensics team, dealing with death and all sorts of thrilling stuff. People who had taken their own life and were sitting in their house waiting to be discovered. She and her team would be called in to have a look around and see if there were any signs of foul play. Then there were the times they were called to a scene and the manner of death left no doubt that it was indeed foul play.

She lived with DCI Paddy Gibb in her basement flat in Claremont Crescent on the edge of Edinburgh's New Town. Right next door to the church. She'd seen a poster on the noticeboard one day advertising a knitting club where they knitted and crocheted and did all sorts of crafts.

'You're too young for that nonsense,' Paddy had said in his thick Irish accent. 'You've only just turned fifty.'

'You for one should understand the horrors we see every day, Paddy,' she'd said. 'I just want to escape to some mundane wee club where I can forget it all for a couple of hours. You go drinking with your pals, escaping it all.'

'We talk shop, love. It's hardly a flower arranging club.'

'But you choose to do that. You're not telling me it isn't a distraction for you, even though you talk about your cases.'

'Aye, right enough,' he conceded. 'Have fun.'

And she did, every Wednesday evening. In the garden room at the back of the church. She and a group of around twenty women would sit and knit and chat about their lives. Maggie almost never talked about the gruesome sights she witnessed, only occasionally mentioning some of the less traumatic cases. At the end of the day, she didn't want the ladies pissing themselves and not with laughter. A few of the older ones looked like they would vomit into the baskets they hadn't quite finished weaving if she'd gone at it with a full description of how a body looked after sitting in a room for a week with a three-bar electric fire going full tilt.

She'd thought about bringing along a nitrile glove filled with watery jelly until it was stretched out and then popping it with a pin. Give a bit of a visual demonstration. Then she thought her team would be called out after half the club keeled over.

Tonight, at the end of the session, the minister came in and smiled. 'I hope I'm going to get my new sweater before the end of winter,' Tom Michaels joked.

'I did say before the end of winter,' Maggie said, 'but I didn't say which one.'

'That's true. Maybe as a retirement present then?'

'I'll do my best.'

'You're not retiring, are you, Reverend?' one of the older ladies asked.

'Not for a while,' he answered. 'But I'd better get my order in for my sweater.'

The women packed up their stuff, got their coats on and shuffled out of the back door of the garden room. Maggie was the last one to go, leaving the minister to close up.

She walked up the pathway and reached the gate to the steps that led down to her flat. She turned round, stopped and looked down. Then screamed.

SEVEN

'Fall apart indeed,' DI Frank Miller said, sticking a tablet in the dishwasher. Okay, so he'd forgotten to put it on earlier, but he knew how to use it. Kettle, microwave, dishwasher. He wouldn't starve or not have a coffee in the morning. If he forgot how to use the dishwasher, then he could go old school and use the brush and detergent.

Besides, his dad lived along the landing with his girlfriend, and if Miller struggled with something, there was always those two. And Google. And if it was something really technical, like how to unblock the lavvy, YouTube.

His wife had taken their daughter, Annie, and his step-daughter, Emma, to see Emma's father in London. Kim thought that Miller would be pulling his hair out without her for a week, but she forgot he used to live on his own.

He looked at his watch; almost seven-fifty. He was meeting Andy Watt, one of his DSs, and DCI Paddy Gibb, his boss, at eight o'clock.

He put a jacket on and went downstairs. The main entrance to the flats was on North Bridge, a stone's throw from The Inn on the Mile. He crossed over the slick road and walked into the bar.

Andy Watt was sitting at a table talking to a woman Miller didn't recognise. She smiled at Watt and gave him a peck on the cheek as she stood up. Then she smiled at Miller as she walked away.

Miller ordered two pints, seeing Watt was already down to the dregs on his first. When the pints arrived, he sat down.

'Not introducing me to your new girlfriend?' he said, taking a sip of lager.

'Oh, here, that's enough of that talk, Frank. Girl-friend? Kate would have me shoved into a body bag before you knew what was happening if she heard you talking like that.'

Miller looked at Watt and waited. 'Well?'

'Well what?'

'Are you going to tell me who she is, or am I just going to speculate?'

'She's an old friend, that's all.'

'God, Andy, you're playing with fire,' Miller said.

'Playing nothing. I knew her a long time ago and she just happened to be in here. Don't worry, I'm not messing about on Kate.'

Miller looked at his watch. 'Paddy's running behind, isn't he? I thought he would have been in here sucking a bottle of Jameson's dry.'

'Aye, it's not like him to be tardy. I tried calling him a couple of times, but it went to voicemail. And you know what some of the older generation are like – not tech savvy.'

'That's you, though, Andy: older generation. Don't know how to download apps on your phone, think a MacBook is a novel about how kilts were invented.'

'Och, don't talk pish. Paddy's a few years older than me. He's the one you should be slagging.'

'Don't worry, he'll get slagged off too.'

They drank some more.

'How's Kim and the bairns enjoying their wee break in London?' Watt asked.

Miller nodded. 'She's doing well. Eric asked to see his daughter, Emma was excited about going to see her dad, and it was actually Eric's new wife who suggested Kim come down with Annie as well.'

'It's good you don't feel jealous,' Watt replied. 'To be honest, I don't know how I'd feel about that. I might want to put one on his chin.'

'Eric's ex-SAS. I don't think I'd ever get near his chin. Not that I would want to. We get along well and I'd like to keep it that way.'

Miller had only drunk a third of his pint when his phone rang. It was a number he didn't recognise.

'Hello?'

'Frank? It's Maggie! It's Paddy! He's fallen down the steps outside our flat! God, Frank, he's in a bad way. The ambulance is coming. Oh God, he's bleeding, Frank.'

'I'm with Andy. We're on our way.'

Miller hung up and jumped up from the table.

'What's wrong?' Watt said, standing up.

'I'll tell you on the way.'

An ambulance was outside Maggie and Paddy's place in Claremont Crescent. A patrol car too, and a couple of uniforms were standing at the gate at the top of the steps. Miller parked outside the church, a large stone affair with six huge columns supporting the front.

But it wasn't this that Frank Miller concentrated on as he parked his car. It was the woman who was being comforted by another man as she stood back from the steps.

He and Watt got out into the cold night, where the remnants of snow hid in the shadows. Miller walked over, and Maggie saw him approach and let go of the man and threw herself at him.

'Oh, Frank. It's Paddy. They think he fell down the steps. They're working on him now.'

Miller looked down to the bottom of the steps where an ambulance crew was working on his friend. Maggie was holding on tight to him and he gently prised her off but held on to her arms. Her face was streaked with tears and her eyes were red and puffy.

'I'm not supposed to be like this,' she said, her voice thick. 'I'm supposed to be a professional. Trained to deal with terrible stuff. But I just can't bear to be standing here, watching.'

'They're the experts, Maggie. Tell me what happened.'

She rubbed her eyes before answering. 'I was at the knitting club next door in the church. Paddy was meeting you and Andy for a pint, but not until eight, as you know. The club starts at six o'clock and finishes at eight, because we're an older generation.

The club ended, and I was the last one out because I was talking to the minister. I came up here and saw Paddy lying at the bottom of the steps.'

'Did you check him before you called for an ambulance?'

'I screamed, Frank. I froze. It was like electricity shooting through me. I couldn't move. Oh my God.' She gripped Miller's arm and her mouth started trembling again. 'The minister came running across. He was locking the front door of the church. He went down to check on Paddy while I called for the ambulance. They were asking me questions and I was asking Reverend Michaels. He relayed to me that Paddy was breathing but unconscious.'

More uniforms arrived in a patrol car and Miller turned to look at them.

A uniformed sergeant walked up to Miller. 'Sorry to interrupt, sir, but the ambulance crew requested back-up to help lift the stretcher up the stairs.'

'Okay. Get down there and help him. You know who he is?'

'Yes, sir. One of ours. We'll give an escort down to the Western General.'

'Good. We'll go down there after he's been transported.'

Miller turned to see Watt talking with the minister. He asked Maggie, 'Do you know what time Paddy planned to leave to meet with us?'

'He sent me a text saying he was leaving. Around seven-forty, I think.' She took her phone out and opened up the text messages and saw Paddy's. 'Seven thirty-eight,' she said.

She showed Miller the screen and he read: *Leaving now. See you later. xxx.* Then the reply: *Have fun. Love you.*

'Andy couldn't get hold of him when he hadn't turned up at the pub,' Miller said. 'Now we know why.'

'We're ready to move him,' one of the paramedics shouted up.

The sergeant ordered two younger, fitter uniforms down the steps to help carry Gibb up on the stretcher. A few minutes later, the DCI was in the back of the ambulance with Maggie by his side. It took off under escort, and sirens screamed as they headed down towards Canonmills.

Miller walked over to the minister, who was still with Watt.

'This is awful. I'm Reverend Tom Michaels,' he said, offering no handshake.

'Maggie told me she came up here and found

Paddy at the bottom of the steps,' Miller said, with-holding judgement on the minister.

'Yes. I heard her screaming and came running across. I thought she was being assaulted, to be honest.'

'You can look after yourself, then?' Watt said.

'I'm sorry?' Michaels said, turning to him. His eyebrows furrowed and he looked like he wanted to go boxing.

Watt was a bigger man and didn't take kindly to the man of the cloth's attitude.

'I would think that question was self-explana-tory: you can look after yourself in a fight. If you heard her screaming and ran over, maybe thinking she was being mugged, then you would have been prepared to take on an assailant.'

'I didn't see anybody else standing next to her.'

'You just said you thought she was being assaulted.'

'I had my back to her. Then I turned and looked.'

'Ah.' Watt nodded, the one word implying that Michaels wouldn't have run over if there was anybody with Maggie.

'What are you suggesting?' The minister was getting angrier by the minute while Watt stayed calm. Let the man work himself into a frenzy to see how quickly he could turn from innocent reverend into the Yorkshire Ripper.

'I'm not suggesting anything,' Watt said, keeping eye contact with the man.

'What happened next?' Miller asked.

Michaels paused for a second, like he was going to throw a punch at Watt. 'I rushed over, saw Paddy down the stairs and hurried down. I told Maggie to call the emergency services. I checked on Paddy and found he had a pulse but his breathing was ragged.'

'Do you know Paddy?' Watt asked.

Michaels rounded on him. 'What's your problem?'

'From where I'm standing, sunshine, you're the one with the problem. I'm only asking you a simple question, but you're suddenly combative.'

Michaels took a couple of deep breaths, like this was an exercise that a therapist had taught him. Watt kept his hands in his coat pockets, either because he was cold or to stop one of them landing on the minister's chin. Miller thought that would be a first for him, seeing a minister engage in a street fight. If he'd been a betting man, he wouldn't have given Michaels very good odds against the older detective.

'Do you know him?' Miller asked again.

'Yes, of course I do,' Michaels replied, spittle flying through the cold air.

'There, that didn't hurt, did it?' Watt said.

'Oh, fuck off. Seriously,' Michaels said, turning on his heel and walking away.

'Was it something I said?' Watt growled at the man's back. Then he looked at Miller. 'I've never had a man of the cloth tell me to fuck off before.'

Miller took his phone out as they walked back towards the car. 'I need to call Paddy's daughter, Kelly. Paddy gave me her number a long time ago in case he was killed on duty. I never thought I'd be calling her for that, never mind an accident at home.'

They got in the car and Miller talked to the young woman.

Watt watched as Michaels walked round the side of the church and disappeared.

EIGHT

Harry sat with his iPad on his lap, the cover turned into a stand, and typed on the digital keyboard. He hated using this as sometimes it didn't want to follow his directions. Nothing to do with his having sausage fingers.

He was writing to his mate in England, a crime writer who was trying to get published. James Barr and Harry had 'met' on a forum for a well-known writer. Barr had asked if there were any police officers on the forum, especially from Scotland, and Harry had answered, intrigued by Barr's question. Alex had encouraged Harry to write to Barr, especially since the man was a retired police officer himself. After a quick check by Harry to make sure

Barr wasn't a knife-wielding serial killer, they were up and running.

Comparing stories on the forum had progressed to writing emails. Barr had told Harry that he'd been writing detective novels for years, and despite getting interest from a few agents, hadn't quite hooked one. He'd asked Harry if he'd ever thought about writing a detective novel, and Harry had admitted he'd given it some thought years before but wouldn't know where to start. Barr had given him lots of encouragement and had told him he would give him any advice he wanted, but Harry hadn't pulled the trigger.

Barr had said he was writing a detective novel set in Glasgow and had asked about Scottish police procedure, and Harry was happy to help. Barr was also writing a thriller, and was excited to share the details with Harry. They were just talking about abseiling out of a helicopter when Harry's phone rang.

'Hello?' he said when he saw it was Frank Miller's number.

'Hi, Harry. I have some bad news. DCI Paddy Gibb has fallen down the steps outside his flat and he's been taken to the Western with a head injury. You remember Paddy, don't you?'

'Of course I do. God, that's terrible. He lives with Maggie Parks, the head of forensics, doesn't he?'

'He does. She's pretty cut up about it.'

'You want me to come down?'

'You could. That would show support for Maggie; plus I want to talk to you about somebody we met tonight.'

'I'll get my coat.'

Harry finished his email quickly and sent a text to Jessica, who was in her room.

She came downstairs.

'One of my colleagues has fallen and he's got a head injury. I was going to go down to the Western, if you're okay with being with Grace.'

'Of course I am. We'll be fine. Do what you have to do.'

'Thanks, Jess.'

'I won't wait up.' She went back upstairs to her own room and Harry left.

There was a thin covering of frosted snow on his windscreen, but a few minutes of the heater shifted it. He drove over Ravelston heading down Craigleith Road. He was playing out a dilemma in his head: what to get Jessica for Christmas. Something that would show his appreciation for all she had done in looking after Grace but still keep within the boundary of her being his sister-in-law.

He parked in the small multi-storey car park and found Miller in the Anne Ferguson Building on a head trauma ward. It was relatively quiet with a few nurses floating about.

Andy Watt was sitting with Maggie, both of them drinking vending-machine coffee from plastic cups.

'Hey, Frank,' Harry said, patting his friend on the arm.

'Harry. Thanks for coming.'

Watt stood up. 'Good to see you again, sir.'

'You too, Andy.' Harry stepped forward to speak to Maggie. 'Hi, Maggie. How's he doing?'

'Hello, sir. They're running all sorts of tests on him now. CT scan and whatever else they think he needs.'

'Did the doctor tell you anything?'

'He thinks Paddy has had bleeding on the brain. He hasn't regained consciousness.'

'Has Paddy been unsteady on his feet lately?'

Maggie shook her head. 'No. He likes a few whiskies at night. Even when he's going out for a drink he'll knock back a few drams before going out.

You know him – he's an Irishman who likes a wee drink to himself.'

'He does. Don't we all?'

Harry stepped away from Maggie and walked back to Miller. 'Frank, you mentioned something about a person you met tonight.'

Miller took him by the arm and walked away from the sitting area. Watt was back sitting with Maggie as Harry and Miller turned a corner into the main corridor.

'The minister from the church next to Maggie's place heard her screaming and went running over. Maggie had been at the knitting club and this guy was locking the front doors when he heard her. We spoke to him and he was a right stroppy bastard.'

'What's his name?'

'Reverend Tom Michaels. That's all we know about him, but I'm going to run his name at the station tomorrow.'

'That church is an independent place, isn't it?' Harry said.

'Yes. It's the New Life Fellowship Church. Open to all denominations. Paddy was talking about it one night in the pub. "Bunch of hippies" was how he described them, but I think he was exaggerating as usual. Michaels told Andy to fuck off.'

Harry raised his eyebrows. 'Did he indeed. You sure he really was the minister and not somebody there for a fancy dress party?'

'Your guess is as good as mine.'

'Harry!' They both heard the voice at the same time and turned to look at the young female approaching them.

Kelly Gibb, Paddy's daughter.

'Frank!' she said, not quite shouting but announcing her presence in a shrill, panicky voice.

She threw her arms around Miller when she reached them and started sobbing. He held on to her while Harry put a hand on her shoulder and they let her ride it out until she couldn't sob any more. Then she pulled away and Miller gave her a paper hanky to dry her eyes.

'What happened to my dad?' she asked eventually.

'It looks like he was going up the outside steps at the flat and he fell and hit his head.'

'Oh, God. Is he going to be okay?'

'They're running tests on him now,' Harry said with an enthusiasm in his voice that he didn't feel inside.

'Where is he now?' she asked.

'He's with the doctors.'

'Oh, Kelly,' Maggie said, coming over to her. Kelly hugged her and started sobbing again.

'I can't believe it,' Kelly said.

'They'll put him in intensive care after the scans. He's in the best place,' Maggie said.

They all sat down and Watt helped get refills of coffee and they waited for the consultant to come back. When he did, his face was grim.

'Ms Parks? I'd like a word in private,' he said, standing in front of the seated group.

'This is Kelly, Paddy's daughter,' Maggie said. 'And the others are like family. You can tell me in front of us all.'

'Very well,' he replied, but Harry could tell he wasn't happy about it, like it was his round in the pub and his pal had invited some of his other mates along.

'I'm sorry to tell you that there has been massive bleeding on Mr Gibb's brain. We will be doing further tests, but initial indications are that he won't be regaining consciousness. If, by a miracle, he does survive, then he will be in a vegetative state for the rest of his life.'

Maggie and Kelly were crying as the others sat in numb shock.

'Mr Gibb will be in intensive care for the time being. You can see him in a little while.'

With that, he turned away and disappeared round a corner.

'I'm sorry, Maggie, Kelly,' Miller said.

They all sat around like the last survivors in a lifeboat, nobody saying a word, wondering who they were going to eat first. Then Kelly stood up.

'I need to get some fresh air,' she said. Then she looked at Harry. 'Can you come with me?'

'Of course.'

He escorted her off the ward and downstairs into the cold night. It was quieter. Like the whole world had stopped.

'My dad was drinking heavily again,' Kelly said as their breath plumed into the chill.

'He always was a bit of a drinker, to be fair.'

She lowered her voice a bit even though she hadn't been talking loudly to begin with. 'It wasn't just the drinking; he had something on his mind. Something he wanted to talk to me about.'

'Did he say what?'

'No. I was supposed to be having lunch with him tomorrow. There's something going on. Regarding an old case. That's all he would say. He called me and he'd been drinking, but not enough that he didn't know what he was talking about. He sounded scared.'

'Shouldn't you mention this to Frank? He was part of Paddy's team.'

'Dad said to talk to you if anything happened to him.' Her eyes were wide as she spoke and her breathing was getting faster. 'He said that because you were Standards you'd know what to do.'

'You have absolutely no idea what he was talking about?' Harry asked.

Kelly shook her head. 'No. But he was worried and you know that isn't like him. You worked with him years ago, didn't you?'

'I did. And I agree, Paddy wasn't the sort of man to panic or worry.'

'Something was bothering him, Harry.'

'Do you think this wasn't an accident?'

'I'm not sure.'

Harry looked around them. Nobody appeared to be listening. 'I trust Frank Miller with my life. If you think there was something going on, I'd like to run it by him.'

'Fine. Dad trusted Frank and Andy. I just wish he'd told me what was on his mind.'

Harry put a hand on her shoulder. 'Are you still married?'

'I'm still with Billy, but we're not married. My dad wasn't happy about that, but he loves Gillian, my daughter.'

They walked back inside and up to the ward. Maggie was gone.

'They've taken her in to see Paddy,' Watt said. 'She's waiting for you, Kelly.' He led her towards a room.

'Poor bastard,' Miller said.

'I know.' Harry looked at his friend. 'We have to talk, Frank. But not here. I'll meet you tomorrow at your station.'

Miller looked concerned. 'Anything wrong?'

'Could be. I'll bring Kelly along. We need to have a talk, but don't say anything to anybody. It has to be just the three of us for now, maybe Andy later.'

'Okay. Give me a call tomorrow.'

Harry watched as Kelly disappeared into the room, then he walked away.

NINE

Jessica made sure Grace was up in the morning and ready to be taken to the nursery. Harry had inherited the nursery at Murrayfield, and Jessica was now the manager. She had opened a section for babies that had proved popular and had hired new assistants to take care of them. It was a profitable business.

'Will you be home for dinner?' she asked Harry as he finished his coffee and put the empty mug in the dishwasher.

'I'll let you know. There are some things I have to do today.'

'Okay. If not, Flora will leave us something and I can heat it up for you when you get in.'

'Thanks, Jess. You're an angel.'

'I know I am.' She smiled at him as she pushed Grace out of the door in her pushchair. Harry joined her outside and helped her down the steps with the pushchair. He stopped by his own car and Jessica waved as she walked along towards her car. Harry had thought about giving her Alex's little red Audi, but the car held too many memories, so he had sold it and bought Jessica her own brand-new car.

The day was sharp and cold, with a light covering of frost on the cars. Harry put the pushchair in the boot of the car and waited until Jessica had Grace strapped into her car seat before putting his head into the car and kissing his daughter. 'Daddy loves you, sweetheart.'

He gently closed the door as Jessica made her way around to the driver's seat. 'See you tonight, Harry.'

'Call me if you need anything.' He said the same thing to her every day.

'I will. Go get 'em, Harry,' she said, her daily response to him. She got in the car and drove away while Harry walked over to his pool car.

He cut over Ravelston, heading down to the station in Leith, joining the long lines of cars whose drivers were sticking it up the climate change brigade. He hit the VR button on the steering wheel and told the car to call Maggie Parks. There was no answer and it went to voicemail, so he disconnected. Then he called Kelly Gibb.

'*Hello?*' she said.

'Kelly, it's Harry McNeil. I tried calling Maggie, but there was no answer. I was wondering if you'd heard any more about your dad.'

'*Nothing this morning. I'm going into the hospital soon.*'

'I'd still like to have a coffee with you later on. Me and Frank.'

'*I'd like that, Harry. I'll call you after we've seen the consultant.*'

'Great. Then we can arrange a time to meet up.'

'*I look forward to it.*' There was a pause for a moment. '*Thanks for caring, Harry.*'

'Of course. I've known your dad for a long time.'

She cut the call and Harry followed the route of the Water of Leith for a bit until he drove down Broughton. A light snow shower fell onto his windscreen, no match for the wiper blades.

He thought about Paddy Gibb, pictured him falling down the stone steps. How many had he fallen down? Was he that blootered that he couldn't steady himself going up? And what about the reverend Tom Michaels? Harry hadn't had the pleasure but already he didn't like the man.

He parked outside the station and walked up the stairs to his office, giving thought to requesting a chair lift be installed. The things were slow, but he could get another quick coffee in while he was moving up.

DI Ray Walker was in the incident room, his face looking like a constipated Pug. He ignored Harry as he walked in.

'Morning, sir,' DS Lillian O'Shea said as Harry took his overcoat off.

'Morning, Lillian.'

Harry saw Colin Presley sitting over by a computer. 'Where's Pierce this morning?' he asked him.

Walker turned round to look at Harry. 'He was in a car accident last night. Him and Ricky Dawson.'

'Jesus. What happened?'

'They were on their way to interview somebody and they got hit.'

'Are they okay?'

'A bit bashed-up, but they'll live. They'll be off for a few days. Dawson got a broken nose and Pierce smacked his face off the dash.'

'I thought he was working undercover?'

Walker looked at him with a face that was almost a snarl. 'He meets with Pierce to pass on information. You should know that, sir. You used to be one of us.'

Harry looked at him. 'Remember the wee conversation we had about respect?'

Walker ignored him.

'Leaves us a bit short-staffed,' Lillian said.

'We can draft in from Gayfield Square and the West End,' Walker said.

Colin Presley looked over at Harry. He said nothing, but a look passed between them.

'I have to go out shortly, but you can hold the fort, yes?' Harry said to Walker.

'Of course I can.' Again with the sneer.

Harry walked into his office and sat at his computer. It was already on, although he was convinced he had shut it down last night.

He opened the intranet and started doing a search. He typed in 'Ian Pierce' and looked at the man's service record. One thing jumped out at him right away: he'd been disciplined for being heavy-handed with members of the public. He'd had a warning. He looked at Pierce's commanding officer at the time: DCI Roger Barton. Barton was now a DSup.

Next he looked up Ricky Dawson. Same deal. Accusations of assaulting prisoners but nothing corroborated. Barton was his boss as well at the time. This was before Harry was with Professional Standards, and he wondered how he would have handled the situation. He'd reprimanded officers for less and had recommended giving some others their marching orders.

Harry had known Barton by reputation but hadn't worked directly with the man. He ran his name through the system and found a clean record. There had been a few complaints against Barton, but nothing had stuck.

He played around on the computer for a little while, then Frank Miller called.

'Hi, pal. What's up?'

'I just got a call from Kelly Gibb. She asked if we could have that coffee now. She's just left the Western.'

'Just tell me where.'

'I suggested the Tattie Scone on Comely Bank Road. Near the flat.'

The flat. Meaning the flat where Miller and his first wife had lived before she died. The flat that Harry had rented from him and then bought with

Alex. The flat where Alex had collapsed with her ruptured brain aneurysm.

'Sounds good.'

'She told me she's scared, Harry.'

'Scared of what?'

'She wouldn't say on the phone.'

'I'm leaving right now. I'm going to blues-and-twos it up there. I think there's more to Paddy falling than meets the eye.'

'Agreed. I'll see you down there.'

Miller disconnected the call and Harry got up from behind his desk and grabbed his coat. In the incident room nobody was talking, like they'd had a falling-out and they were all waiting for the other one to speak first.

'Colin, you're with me,' Harry said. Presley looked up from his desk as if to make sure he'd heard correctly. He poked himself in the chest.

'You're the only Colin here, aren't you?'

'Where are you going?' Walker asked.

'I told you earlier I'd be going out. Now I'm going out and I'm taking Colin with me.'

'Suit yourself, neighbour.'

Harry gritted his teeth, but all he could see was the back of Walker's head as the DI spun in his office chair.

Presley got up and walked over to the coat stand and pulled his coat on.

'Lillian, I'll catch up with you later.'

'Okay, boss.'

Harry walked out to the car with Presley. 'You comfortable driving with lights and siren?'

'I was born in the back of an ambulance. A siren is like music to my ears.'

Harry tossed the DC his keys and they got in. 'Stockbridge. A wee café called the Tattie Scone.'

'Oh, I know that place.'

Presley got the siren going as he pulled away from the station and headed up towards Great Junction Street and Bonnington Road.

'Were you really born in an ambulance?' Harry asked.

Presley looked at him for a moment. 'No, sir. I thought you'd feel more comfortable if I said that.'

'How the bloody hell would that make me feel more comfortable? It's not like you popped out of your mother's birth canal and started driving.'

'I meant psychologically. Like when you play music to a pregnant woman's belly and the bairn comes out and can play the piano like Beethoven.'

'Just make sure you don't get us under a bloody bin lorry.'

'I've been on many a shout, sir, and I've never put a patrol car through a hedge.'

'First time for everything, and today better not be your first time.'

When they made it to the end of Henderson Row, Harry turned off the sirens and lights.

'This is my part of town,' Presley said.

'You live round here?'

'Henderson Place.'

'I'm impressed, but Standards might be crawling over you.'

'Well, when I say *I* live here, I mean my girl-friend lives down there but I spend most of my time there. I have a flat in Claremont Court, up the top of Broughton Street. Standards wouldn't look twice at me for living there.'

'I've heard of it.'

'It was my grandad's flat. He bought it from the council years ago. I was brought up by him. As he got older, I just stayed with him.'

'Good for you. Is he still around?'

'No. He passed a couple of years ago and left the flat to me.'

'Sorry to hear that.'

Presley nodded.

Tattie Scones was literally round the corner from Harry's flat and Presley managed to park outside it.

'I'm meeting somebody here. Wait in the car and tell me if you see anybody hanging about outside acting suspiciously.'

'Wearing a raincoat and sunglasses. Check.'

'Don't be a smartarse. And keep your eyes peeled.'

'Yes, sir. And if you feel in a charitable mood when you get out, I only take milk in my coffee and no butter on the bacon roll.'

'I'll bear that in mind.'

'You won't really, will you?'

'You're a quick learner.'

Harry got out and looked over at the hotel across the road where he and Alex had spent many a good night. Then he turned and walked into the café, a little bell above the door announcing his arrival.

Frank Miller was seated at a table with Kelly Gibb and waved him over. Harry sat down and a young woman came over with a small pad.

'Just coffee, thanks,' he said.

She scuttled away and he looked at Kelly. 'How's your dad?'

She tried talking to him, but her lips trembled and she had to take a sip of her tea to calm herself down before she could speak. 'He hasn't regained consciousness. The consultant said he won't unless a miracle happens.'

'Jesus, I'm sorry, Kelly.' He reached out a hand and placed it on one of hers. He squeezed, and then the woman appeared with his coffee and he took his hand back.

'Who's that in the car?' Miller asked.

'One of the DCs from my station. Colin Presley, but everybody calls him Elvis.'

Miller nodded. There was only one other person in the café, an old man sitting at a table by the window and reading a paper.

'As I said on the phone, Kelly's upset in more ways than one,' Miller said.

'You said last night you wanted to chat today,' Harry said to Kelly. 'You can trust Frank and me. We've known your dad for a long time.'

'I know.' She looked into the mug of tea as if doing a reading before looking Harry in the eye. 'I think somebody wanted to hurt my dad.'

'What makes you say that?'

'He was being elusive, but he wanted us to have lunch today. He wanted to talk to me about an old case. That's all he said. But he warned me not to talk to anybody about this. Not even Billy, my boyfriend.'

'Where's Billy now?' Miller asked.

'He's between jobs, so he's at home with Gillian.'

'How old is the wee yin now?' Harry asked.

'She'll be four in January. She's the light of my dad's eyes. He loves her so much. He told me that he was giving me a heads-up and to take extra care of the bairn. He also told me to watch my back and to make sure nobody was following me. I'm assuming that was related to what he wanted to talk to me about.'

Harry looked at Miller. 'He didn't mention anything in passing about an old case?'

'Not to me. I'll ask Andy if he heard anything, but it seemed to be business as usual.'

Harry looked at Kelly again. 'Maggie said Paddy had been drinking a lot more at home. Did he mention this to you?'

She shook her head. 'He always has been a bit of a drinker, you both know that. I know he likes a wee dram in the house too.' She made eye contact with Harry. 'Do you think somebody harmed my dad?'

'It's a possibility. He was on his own while Maggie was at the church next door. Maybe somebody watched her leave and either waited for him or somehow got him to leave the flat.'

Harry didn't want to voice his opinion that somebody could have dragged Paddy out of the house and shoved him down to the stone pathway at the foot of the steps and slammed his head into it.

'You don't know what old case he was talking about?' Miller asked.

'No,' said Kelly. 'He said we would talk today and he would explain.'

'Where do you live?' Harry asked.

'Longstone. Near the bus garage.'

'Did you drive down to the hospital?'

'No, I got a bus.'

'I'll drive you home,' Miller said.

'No, Frank, honest, it's fine. I want to go back to the hospital. You know, just to be with Dad.'

'I understand. I'll drive you round there.'

Harry drank some of his coffee. 'Is Maggie still at the hospital?'

'Yes, she's there.'

'I'd like to come round and see your dad.'

'He'd like that. Even if he doesn't know you're there.' Kelly stood up and looked at them. 'We can go now, if you don't mind.'

'No problem,' Harry said.

'Right then.' She started to walk out, then stopped. 'There is one thing. It might be nothing, but I found it strange. I thought at first that it wasn't my dad texting me and that somebody had got hold of his phone, but I'm not sure.'

'What is it?' Miller said.

'I'll show you.' She took her phone out and opened up the text messages and showed them the text her father had sent her a couple of nights ago. 'He started off by saying he'd see me today, but we'd already established that. I said I loved him, and he wrote back, *"Me too M8."* He's never called me "mate" before. But I'm thinking it might have been intended for Andy Watt.'

'Maybe he'd had a few,' Harry said.

'That would be the most likely explanation,' Miller agreed. 'Maybe he thought he was talking to Andy.'

'That's probably it. I'll just nip to the ladies' before we go.'

She walked away and Harry looked at Miller. He told him what had happened the night before in the flat in Dumbiedykes.

'Jesus, Harry, that could have gone badly.'

'The thing is, when we got there, Elvis there said, why don't we just check it out without waiting for the uniformed patrol. Then he tells me they tossed him outside and locked him out, and then the three of them came after me.'

'Then you said he kicked the door in and came in and helped you. Even fought them off.'

'What if that was an act? What if he was in on it and it was meant to look like he was helping me?'

'You were in Standards, Harry. What does your gut tell you?'

'Honestly? I don't think he was part of it. But I'm going to keep an open mind.'

Kelly came back. 'Ready?'

'Let's go,' Miller said. 'We'll see you round there, Harry.'

Miller and Kelly walked out into the cold morning air while Harry paid for his coffee.

'Don't tell me they ran out of bacon?' Presley said when Harry got back into the car.

Harry ignored him as the DC started the engine. 'Before you go, I want to say something. If I ever find out you were involved with those attackers last night, I don't give a fuck how good a boxer you are, I will put my boot so far up your arse, your nose will bleed.'

Presley looked at him. 'I'm not part of whoever is responsible, and you know why? Because if I was, you'd have been taken out of there on a stretcher. Sir.'

Harry could see the man was indignant and in

that moment he decided to give him the benefit of the doubt. But he'd still watch his back.

'Right then, we're going round to the Western. A DCI I know fell down his outside steps last night and he's in a coma.'

'Jesus. Sorry to hear that.'

'Me too, son.'

TEN

The hospital was busier than it had been the night before. More visitors, more nurses and doctors, like a curfew had been lifted.

Kelly held on to Frank Miller's arm as they stepped out of the lift.

For Harry, a hospital was one step up from the mortuary, a place he hated with a passion. He never once failed to get the boak when he was in there. Last night he'd felt the sleeping lion start to awaken, but he had managed to keep it at bay. Today, though, the sleeping lion was rearing its ugly head.

'You okay, sir?' Presley asked.

'Of course I am. Why do you ask?'

'You look as white as a sheet. Just like when I

said you would have been taken out on a stretcher. Your face went pale and I could see you shaking.'

'I'll shake you down that lift shaft in a minute.'

'Try a rubber band. I hate the smell in the mortuary, and when I go there, I slip a rubber band on my wrist and snap it when I feel my guts going.'

'The mortuary doesn't bother me.'

'That's fine. You could pass that little nugget on to anybody you know who it does bother.'

They came to Paddy's ward. Presley took a seat in the waiting area. In his room, Paddy was hooked up to monitors and had a tube in his mouth. A nurse appeared.

'Has there been any improvement?' Miller asked her.

'No. He's the same.'

'Is he in pain?' Kelly asked, her voice cracking.

'No, he's not. He's on a morphine pump.'

'Where's Maggie?' she asked.

'His wife? She left for a bit.'

'She's his girlfriend,' Kelly said. 'My mum lives down south now.'

'Oh, I'm sorry.'

Just then, the consultant came into the room. 'I'm glad you're here,' he said to Kelly. 'We ran some tests earlier, and there doesn't seem to be any activity in Mr Gibb's brain. There's some bleeding in there, but the surgeon doesn't want to go in just now as there's no swelling of the brain. If that happens then we'll have to operate. Meantime, we're making him comfortable.'

Miller stood looking at his boss. They'd been through so much together and he found it hard to believe the Irishman was now lying in a bed, hooked up to machines.

Then Miller's phone rang. He stepped outside the room to take the call. Harry stepped forward and put an arm around Kelly's shoulders as she started to sob.

A few minutes later, Miller came back in.

Then Harry's phone rang. It was Detective Superintendent Percy Purcell, head of CID. Harry answered the call as he left the room.

'Sir?'

'Harry, I need you to take the lead. We have an unidentified off Parliament Square, and since Paddy Gibb is in hospital, you need to lead the MIT.'

'I'm in the hospital with Paddy now, sir. DI Miller is here too.'

'Tell him you need to get up to the High Street. You'll be transferring there from Leith for the time being.'

'I have one of my DCs with me. I can take him. I'd also like DS Lillian O'Shea.'

'Whoever you need.'

'We'll leave right now, sir.'

Harry put the phone back in his pocket and walked back into the room. 'That was DSup Purcell. He wants me to take the lead on a case with your MIT, Frank, since Paddy is in here.'

'That's fine, sir. Where's the shout?'

'Parliament Square.'

'We don't have a case just now, but we were preparing to draft in CID because Julie Stott's off sick and Steffi Walker is on a course at Tulliallan.'

'That's not a problem. We can take Presley there, and I'll call for my DS Lillian O'Shea.'

Miller nodded, then looked at Kelly. 'You'll be alright here. Call me when you want to leave and I'll have a patrol car take you home.'

'Thank you.'

The three men left, Harry explaining to Presley where they were going. Outside, Miller told Harry about the call he'd received. 'That was forensics. They combed every inch of the steps outside Paddy's house and there are minute amounts of blood on one of the steps halfway up. That would fit in with the cut on the back of his head. They reckon he fell backwards, hit his head and slammed his head at the bottom.'

'Jesus.' Harry shook his head, picturing it in his mind, then he made a call to Lillian on the way to the car.

'*I'll be right up, sir.*'

'Quick as you can. I'll see you up there.'

'*I'm on my way, sir.*'

ELEVEN

The High Street was blocked off from George IV Bridge to the High Street station, where Miller was based. A uniform waved both cars through when he saw the flashing blue lights behind the grille on each car.

They pulled in at the side of the station beside the Mercat Cross. Harry got out of the car with Presley.

'Walker isn't going to like this one bit,' Presley said for the umpteenth time, a big grin on his face.

Harry ignored him as he pulled up the collar on his overcoat. A biting wind was running down from the castle. He looked over to the corner of the square where he knew there were steps – Barrie's Close, an alleyway connecting the square with the close behind the station's car park.

DS Lillian O'Shea was standing next to DS Andy Watt.

'You got here quickly,' Harry said to her.

'Heavy boots and a siren,' she explained. He looked down at her feet, expecting to see Dr Martens, but she was wearing some cheap knock-off that barely resembled the original.

'What do we have?' he asked as Miller came up beside him.

'It's a bad one,' Watt jumped in, screwing up his face. 'I mean, you see this kind of thing on TV, but by God, I haven't seen anything like this for a long time.'

'What's going on?' Miller asked, impatience creeping into his voice.

'Female. Found on the steps round the corner down there. Mutilated. And I mean –'

'We'll see for ourselves, Andy,' Harry said.

'DCI McNeil is the lead on this one,' Miller explained. 'Since Paddy is incapacitated.'

'Couldn't ask for a better replacement, albeit a temporary one, I hope. No offence,' Watt said.

'None taken.'

Harry could see the forensics crew working down at the bottom of the steps, and he had a flash-back to where Paddy lived. Stone steps, lurking in the dark, ready to catch the unwary off-guard.

They started making their way down, and stopped as a tech fired off some more shots from a camera. When they got to the bottom, they continued along the pathway, flanked by the police station on one side and a tall stone wall on the other. A man wearing a white forensic suit stepped into view: Jake Dagger, one of the city's pathologists.

'Ah, it's the formidable detectives,' he said. 'And Andy Watt.' There was an old, friendly rivalry between the two men.

'They did say they were calling out the best pathologist the city had,' Watt countered, 'but since she isn't available, you'll have to do.'

'And the dance begins,' Dagger said, grinning.

'How you doing, Jake?' Harry asked. He liked the man but didn't enjoy seeing him in his place of work. Outside in the fresh air was fine, though.

'Keeping busy, Harry. Come and have a look for yourself.'

They turned the corner, where another pathway led to a flight of steps that exited down into Old Fishmarket Close next to the police car park.

A forensics tent had been placed in the narrow passageway. Harry and Miller stepped forward and followed Dagger into the tent itself, where the deceased lay, while the others stayed outside.

'The forensics team have finished photographing the victim, but they're still taking photos of the area.' Dagger looked at both of the senior officers in turn. 'I haven't seen this level of violence in a very long time.'

The woman was dressed casually in a skirt and white blouse with a flower pattern on it. Her throat had been slashed. Her arms and legs hadn't escaped unscathed. But it was the bright colours of her hair that caught Harry's attention: pink, yellow and green. Three colours, each on a third of the woman's hair, give or take.

'Christ, this is on a whole new level,' Harry said. 'And clearly not done here.'

'Exactly. There's literally no blood. She has stab wounds in her chest, done postmortem. There's no blood on her clothes, so she was murdered and dressed. She's been dead for about four days, I would say. All the blood has been drained out of her and she was discarded here like a piece of rubbish. And as you can see, the killer removed three fingers and a thumb from her right hand.'

'Any sign of them around here?' Miller asked.

'No. But on the other side of the tent, behind

your station, there are large industrial bins, so forensics are going through them now. Just in case.'

'I don't think we'll find them there,' Harry said. 'It doesn't make sense for him to have cut them off somewhere else just to bring them here and dump them in a bin.'

'Agreed,' Miller said.

'Has anybody taken her fingerprints yet?' Harry asked.

'One of the forensics team,' Dagger said.

'Who's leading in Maggie's absence?'

'Craig Thompson. He'll have the fingerprints into the system by now.'

'The wonders of modern technology,' Miller said.

'You're too young to be thinking like that,' Harry said. He was at least ten years older than Miller, who was in his early thirties. 'But can you get one of the others to call the station and see if there are any hits yet?'

'There's nobody up there. We'll be going up there shortly, so we can do it then.'

'Right then.' Harry looked at the woman's features. They were pale after the exsanguination. 'It doesn't look like she's a street worker or homeless.'

'Agreed,' Dagger said. 'She doesn't have malnutrition. You can tell from her face, and her teeth are in good shape.'

'Sexually assaulted?' Harry asked.

'Not immediately apparent.'

'I wonder why he cut off those fingers?' Miller said. 'If he didn't want her identified, why didn't he cut them all off?'

Harry frowned. 'Who knows what goes through the mind of a psycho?'

'I'll get her down to the mortuary and see what else I can find out,' said Dagger. 'I'm hoping for her sake that one of the stab wounds to her neck killed her before she was stabbed over and over.'

'We'll get round to the station and get an incident room set up,' Harry said.

'Right. I'll send over the report as soon as.'

'Thanks, Jake.'

Both detectives left the tent and they made their way back up to Parliament Square, where they got into their cars and moved them round to the back car park.

TWELVE

The building was old but with that came old, solid radiators. Harry took his coat and jacket off and took Miller aside.

'I don't want to use Paddy's office. It wouldn't seem right, so I'll use a desk out here.'

'You could use my office, Harry.'

'No, you're okay. I'll sit out here with the other members of my CID team.'

'I'll take a desk too, then.'

Harry patted him on the arm and sat down at a desk.

Presley and Lillian had settled at a desk each and Andy Watt was organising coffee at the table that had the kettle.

'Lillian?' Harry said, calling her over. She got up

and crossed over to his desk. 'How was Walker when you told him you were coming here? And it's not talking out of turn. I just want to know what mood he was in.'

'He wasn't happy at all. He was accusing you of undermining him by taking the remainder of the team away.'

Harry nodded. 'That's okay. He can run it by Percy Purcell if he has a complaint. I told him I was bringing you on board, and if the head of CID is okay with it, then so am I.'

'He was still rattling on when I left.'

'Good. If he gives you any hassle, then tell me.'

'I will.' She went back over to her desk.

'Kettle's off,' Watt announced. 'Senior officers first, then if the kettle needs more water, Elvis there can fill it.'

Presley looked over at Watt but said nothing.

Harry and Miller got a mug, then Watt and Lillian.

'I only wanted half a mug anyway,' Presley said as the water dribbled out of the kettle into a mug that had seen better days and was practically begging to be thrown against a wall in a temper.

'I think we got a hit on our victim,' Lillian said after a few minutes.

'Her prints are on file then?' Watt said.

'Yes. Prints were put into the central system earlier today, but they were from a bunch of fingers found at a scene in Glasgow. They match a woman from here in Edinburgh.'

'What's her name?' Harry asked.

'Tess Grogan. She's a solicitor, but she works with an outreach here in the city. She also represents a group called the Scottish Action Group,' Lillian said.

'What do they do?' Harry asked.

'They're behind the protests about the statues in Scotland. The ones that are basically honouring slave owners. There are a lot of people who think they should be pulled down, including the Scottish Action Group.' Lillian looked at them, not expressing an opinion but they could read between the lines. As police officers, they had to remain neutral, but Harry felt that this was the right time for people to know that some rich men had got their money from human misery hundreds of years ago.

'There's a demonstration organised for tonight,' Presley said. 'At the Duke of Wellington statue at the east end of Princes Street.'

'Thinking of going, were you?' Harry asked.

'I have a previous engagement, so I'm going to have to sit this one out.'

'I heard on the radio this morning that the street outside the Gallery of Modern Art in Glasgow had to be closed off after somebody threw a bucket of blood over it. It's technically a job for a hazmat team to clear up, so they were there for ages,' Lillian said.

Harry and Miller exchanged a look. Bucket of blood; a victim exsanguinated.

'I'm going to give Jimmy Dunbar a call and see if he knows anything about this,' said Harry.

He walked into Miller's office, closed the door and sat down at the desk. He took his phone out and dialled a number.

'Jimmy? It's Harry.'

'Harry! Nice timing. I was about to call you.'

'You were?'

'I was indeed. Seems we have a victim in common.'

'Don't tell me: the missing fingers.'

'Correct. We had the prints put into the system and got a hit. Then I saw the victim they belonged to was already in the system. DSup Lynn McKenzie called Percy Purcell and he filled her in. Now me and the boy are through in your fair city.'

'When will you be here?'

'We're here now, pal. We would've been here earlier if Heid-the-Baw hadn't been driving the car like it was a streamroller. But we'll be at the High Street in a few.'

'I'll get the kettle on.' Harry went back into the incident room. 'Guess what?'

'What?' Presley said.

'That's not how *guess* works,' Watt said. 'He asks you to guess and you throw out some thoughts, and if one sticks, you guessed right.'

'Somebody found the fingers of our victim,' Presley said.

'Don't talk pish,' Watt said.

'He's right,' Harry said.

Presley lifted his eyebrows in an *I told you so* kind of way.

'Whereabouts?' Miller said, jumping in.

'Jimmy Dunbar and Robbie Evans are almost here.' Harry looked at Presley. 'They're the colleagues from Glasgow I was talking about.'

Presley nodded.

'Did they say where?' Watt asked.

'They'll explain when they get here in a few minutes. How about getting the kettle on?'

Watt indicated with his head that it was Presley's

turn, and the DC got up from his chair without a word and refilled the kettle.

Just then, the incident room door opened and the Glasgow boys were back in town.

Harry made the introductions for Presley. Lillian had met them before.

'Kettle's just gone off,' Presley said.

'Thanks, son,' Dunbar said. His face looked like a well-skelpt arse, his cheeks red and his nose doing a fair impression of Rudolph.

'I'll make the coffees,' Evans said. 'I know how the boss likes it.'

'I'm just a DC, sir,' Presley said. 'I should be doing it.'

'Pish. You can help carry the mugs.' Evans followed Presley across to the table and they mucked in.

'Right then, Jimmy, you said your victim was ours too. What name do you have?' He wanted to make sure the victim was the same.

Harry sat at a desk and the others followed suit.

'Tess Grogan. Solicitor through here in Edin-burgh,' Dunbar said. 'A couple of scallies threw buckets of blood over the grand old Duke of York, or rather the Duke of Wellington, but there were four fingers in it. Forensics searched for finger number five, but it was nowhere to be seen.'

'That's our victim alright,' Miller confirmed. 'She was dumped round the corner in Barrie's Close. Eviscerated and drained of all her blood.'

'Did you find out who threw the blood?' Watt asked.

Dunbar shook his head. 'No. With it being cold, the bastards had balaclavas on. We saw them on CCTV, but there was nothing to identify them. We're following up on that. Clifford Dunn was on his soapbox about how we're a shower of bastards for keeping statues in the city centre that honour the old Establishment who were slave owners.'

'Aye, that's certainly getting attention these days,' Miller said. 'I mean, people are sickened by those rich boys having slaves, and I agree with them. To be honest, I never looked twice at the statues before the demonstrators started pointing them out. But I don't think we should be looking at those statues, reminding us of a bloody past.'

'I agree,' Harry said. 'It's sticking it up the ordinary working class. I think the council should pull all the bloody things down and be done with it. We can't erase the past, but we don't have to shove it down the throats of the ordinary citizens.'

'It's the same in Glasgow,' Dunbar said. 'And you boys – and girl – have the same kind of statue here in Edinburgh. The Duke of Wellington sitting on his horse at the east end of Princes Street.'

'We don't have a traffic cone sitting on top of our man's head, though,' Lillian said with a grin.

'Trust me, the council wanted to raise the height of the plinth, but the people caused a ruckus,' Evans said, coming over with two mugs and handing one to Dunbar and one to Harry.

'Elvis was telling us about a demonstration going on there tonight,' Watt said.

'Interesting,' Dunbar said. 'We should have a team watching the event in case somebody tries to throw blood on that one too.'

'Have you spoken to this Clifford Dunn?' Harry asked.

'No. He isn't at his usual haunts. Nobody knows where he is. But we'll keep checking.'

'You might wonder why I'm here with Frank's team as well as my own,' Harry said.

'It had crossed my mind,' Dunbar replied.

Harry told him about Paddy Gibb.

'Oh, boy, that's bad news. I hope he's going to pull through.'

'We all do, Jimmy. It would be a miracle, though.'

'Miracles happen.'

Harry looked over at Lillian. 'Did you get a next of kin for Tess Grogan yet?'

'There isn't any information about one. On her arrest record, there's no one listed. It was just for public disorder. But I did find a news article about her where she mentions being in a relationship with none other than Tom Michaels, the reverend at the church next door to where Paddy lives.'

'New Life Fellowship Church,' Miller explained to Dunbar. 'They're a multi-denominational church.'

Lillian carried on. 'It also says the outreach group she worked with is based in a little shop on Broughton Street.'

Harry turned to Miller. 'Can you take Andy to the outreach and ask them about Tess? I'll go with Jimmy and Robbie to talk to the reverend. You might ruffle his feathers again.'

'Bit feisty is he?' Dunbar asked. 'All fire and brimstone.'

'He told Andy to fuck off.'

'Did he now? I hope he tells me to fuck off.'

'I'm sure if you rub him the wrong way, you'll get your wish, sir,' Miller said.

Dunbar put his mug down and rubbed his hands together. 'I can't wait to meet this joker. It's been a long time since I skelped a man of the cloth.'

Miller just looked at him.

'Long story, son,' Dunbar said. 'Right then, Harry, let's get round there and have a wee word.'

'We'll take my pool car.'

'Nae bother.'

THIRTEEN

They all filed out of the station and out the back door to their cars.

'What kind of church is this, sir?' Evans asked once he and Dunbar were in Harry's car.

'Not affiliated with the Church of Scotland, that's for sure.' Harry drove up the High Street, turned down Bank Street and headed down The Mound.

'Are you heading back to Glasgow tonight?' Harry asked.

'How's that for a welcome?' Dunbar said, turning to look at Evans sitting in the back seat. 'Here's your hat. What's the hurry?'

Harry laughed. 'I was just wondering if there was a wee sesh in our immediate future.'

'Of course there is. I've left DI Tom Barclay with Lisa McDonald. They're under the watchful eye of DSup Lynn McKenzie. She told us to come through here and liaise with you. Whoever killed Tess has a connection to both Glasgow and Edinburgh. We're here for the duration.'

'You staying at the hotel in Stockbridge?'

'Aye. Pity you don't live down there now.'

'I can still come and have a pint. It's not that far in a fast black.'

'Good. I spoke to Chance yesterday.'

Chance McNeil was Harry's son, a uniformed officer based in Dunbar's station. Still on probation.

'I hope he had nothing but good things to say about his old man,' Harry said.

'You wish. He said he's going to be a better detective than any of us.'

'He probably will be. He called the other night to say he might pop through next weekend.'

'He's still seeing Katie,' Evans said. She was also a probationary police officer.

'I haven't seen her in a wee while,' said Harry. 'She keeps in touch, though, and when Chance is through, we go for a meal.'

'He's a good lad,' Dunbar said. 'He'll go far. I'll

make sure Calvin Stewart knows to let on to Lynn McKenzie so she can keep an eye on him.'

'I want him to get up the ladder on his own merit, Jimmy.'

They crossed over George Street and headed down Dundas Street.

'Relax. He'll get on just fine, but it doesn't do any harm to have a mentor.'

'You're mental, did you say?' Evans said.

'Hear that sound from the peanut gallery?' Dunbar said. 'Just you sit and look out at the cars going by. And we'll see who the mental one is when it's time to buy a round.'

'I might not be able to join you gentlemen in a light refreshment tonight,' Evans said.

'Stop talking like fucking Danny La Rue.'

'I'm otherwise engaged.'

'Did you hear the news, Harry?' Dunbar said. 'Young Robbie's thinking of having an ankle-biter with Vern.'

Harry looked in the rear-view mirror. 'Is that right? Good for you, Robbie.'

'That's not exactly what I said. I'm talking about the future,' Evans said.

'He wants to know if getting a punch in the balls

is more painful than a woman trying to pass a melon through a hosepipe,' Dunbar told Harry.

'Well, there goes my dinner,' Evans said, screwing his face up.

'If that puts you off, I can't imagine how you would feel seeing a live bairn come sliding out.'

'God Almighty,' Evans said. 'I wish I'd never brought the subject up now.'

'It's a natural thing, Robbie,' Harry said as he drove along Great King Street. 'It will be a terrific thing for you to see.'

'They have a wee while to go,' Dunbar said. 'He wants to move in with her first. Try before you buy. They want to move into a neutral place in case Vern gets turned off by Robbie cleaning his skids with a box of matches.'

'It's not like I haven't stayed over at her place before,' Evans said.

'It's different when you're wenching and you stay over when you're blootered after a night out. Just wait till you have to stay in and watch a rerun of the *Antiques Roadshow*.'

'I'll be happy just watching TV with her,' Evans countered.

Harry and Dunbar looked at each other.

'Poor lad,' Harry said.

A few minutes later, they were in Bellevue Crescent, parking outside the church.

'Big place for this hippy church crowd,' Dunbar said, looking up at the tall pillars.

'I think it used to belong to the Church of Scotland,' Harry said. 'They've sold a lot of churches over the years.'

'You said Paddy Gibb lives around here?'

Harry pointed across the pathway that ran alongside the church. 'That basement flat right down there.'

Dunbar walked over and looked down the stone steps to the garden flat below. 'Jesus. That must have hurt.'

'He hasn't regained consciousness. He's in a bad way.'

'You think he's going to make it?'

Harry looked at both men before answering. 'I don't think so.'

They were silent as they turned and walked up the steps to the church doors. They were open, letting in the cold air, but there was a vestibule area before the doors into the church proper.

The church had a balcony above the pews and was semi-circular. The pulpit rose into the air at the end of the room. The pews were arranged more like they were in an arena with the middle reserved for some rock band.

'Bit different from when my old ma used to drag me to church on a Sunday,' Dunbar said. 'How about you, Robbie?'

'I never went to church.'

'That explains a lot. Bloody heathen. You, Harry?'

Harry blew his cheeks out. 'Can't say my parents dragged me either.'

'What are you two like? How come I was the only sap who was dragged along? Sunday best and everything. Had my hair slicked down, the whole nine yards.'

'I suppose you'll be telling us next that if your old man ran out of Brylcreem, he'd gob in your hair to flatten it,' Evans said.

'Manky bastard. My mother ran a comb under the tap. Obviously, you could have done with going to church.'

They walked forward and then heard voices and two men appeared through a door. They both stopped when they saw Harry, Dunbar and Evans.

'Help you?' the taller one said.

'Police,' Harry said. 'And you are?'

'Reverend Tom Michaels. I'm the minister here. This is a friend of mine, Clifford Dunn.'

'Gentlemen,' Dunn said.

'We've been looking for you,' Dunbar said to Dunn. 'Me and Sergeant Evans are from Glasgow Division.'

'Oh, really?' Dunn smiled.

'Yes, really. We heard you gave a rip-roaring speech last night. Gave the old duke a right seeing-to, so you did. In fact, you could say you painted the town red.'

'Ah, yes. Those hooligans. We were there having a peaceful demonstration when they showed up and turned it into something else.'

'What are their names?' Evans asked.

Dunn turned to look at him and the policemen all noticed the slight change in his demeanour. It was obvious he wasn't used to speaking to the lower ranks.

'I don't know who they were. The demonstration was open to anybody who felt like turning up. It is a free country, after all.'

Harry addressed Michaels again. 'We want to ask you some questions about Tess Grogan. Is there somewhere more private we can talk?'

'We can go into my office. This way.' Michaels turned and Dunn followed suit.

The office was large and an imposing desk sat at the far end. Michaels sat behind it while Dunn sat on a two-seater leather couch. There were other chairs in the room but nobody else sat.

A bay window overlooked a garden and Harry could see a conservatory further along, a large addition to the back of the church. There was a group of people in it.

'You have something on today?' he said to Michaels, nodding in the direction of the conservatory.

'Yes, we have a senior citizens' club on a Thursday afternoon. That's the garden room.'

Snow remained against the back wall, hiding in the shadows. Harry imagined the view from the garden room would be quite pleasant in summer, but just now the sky was the colour of a bad day at work.

'You said something about Tess,' Dunn said, cutting to the chase.

'How do you know her?' Dunbar asked him, annoyed by his barging in.

'She's a member of the church,' Michaels answered. 'And my girlfriend. She's also a solicitor for the church. And now you're up to speed on how she fits in around here, can you tell us what trouble she's got herself into now?'

'She's dead,' Harry said.

Michaels looked quickly at Dunn before looking back at Harry. 'Dead? What do you mean, dead?'

'She was found dead earlier today. In Barrie's Close.'

The reverend gripped the edge of the desk and pushed back in the chair but kept a hold, stretching his arms out. Harry thought the man was going to burst into tears, but then he pulled himself back to a sitting position.

'How in God's name did she die?' Michaels' eyes were glistening.

'We can't reveal that at the moment,' Harry said. 'But we were hoping you could give us a rundown of her whereabouts over the past few days.'

'She was with me in Glasgow,' Dunn said. 'She works with an outreach group through there too. Giving homeless people legal advice, sometimes representing them in court if they've got themselves into a bit of bother.' He stared into space for a moment, the shock hitting him.

'When did you last see her?' Dunbar asked.

'A few days ago. We were going over our strategy for the demonstration.'

'Strategy? Like who you were going to get to throw blood over the statue?'

Dunn curled his lip like he wanted to go boxing. 'Exact opposite. We make sure that every protest is peaceful. We tell people that we'll get change through words, not violence.'

'What was her demeanour like?' Harry asked.

'Just her usual self. She was happy with the way things were going. We were all happy with the way the public were getting on board with the thought that these despicable slave owners should no longer be in full view of the public. Scotland has blood on her hands, Inspector, and it's about time that the ordinary man in the street saw this. We have famous authors on board. Even an actor who used to be on a soap opera. Albeit as a dead body, but still. The public aren't going to be fooled anymore.'

'And you two are the very men to point them in the right direction,' Dunbar said.

'Of course we are,' Michaels replied. 'We have the backs of the people. We care about the community we live in.' His voice was hoarse and had little conviction.

'What's in it for you?' Harry asked.

Michaels and Dunn looked at each other like

they were passing a secret, but Dunn managed to make it look like he was passing a kidney stone.

'To see justice served after all this time.'

'Who were the two men who threw the blood?' Harry asked.

Dunn shrugged his shoulders. 'How should I know? In fact, I don't know anybody who turned up last night. Your guess is as good as mine.'

'There's a demonstration tonight, isn't there?' Evans said.

'Yes, there is. At the Duke of Wellington statue at the end of Princes Street.'

'How many people are going?'

'How long is a piece of string?' Dunn stared at Dunbar.

'We'll be having the demonstration well covered,' Harry promised.

'I hope you do,' Michaels said.

'Can you think of anybody who would want Ms Grogan harmed?' Dunbar said, turning away from Dunn.

'No. She was liked by everyone. She helped a lot of people. She had no enemies,' Michaels answered.

'Where did she live?' Harry asked.

'We have a flat at the top of the church here.

This place was refurbished years ago and the owner back then created a flat in the attic.'

'What about you, Mr Dunn?'

'I live in Albany Street Lane. First house as you go in from Broughton Street.'

'Do you have CCTV?' Evans asked the reverend.

'No. People come here to find peace. They don't need to be spied on,' Michaels said.

'We'll need a formal identification done on Ms Grogan,' Harry said. 'I'll have one of my officers attend with you. He'll give you a call when the mortuary is ready.'

Michaels nodded.

'If you think of anything else, please give us a call. And if you could give me your number for my officer to call you...'

Michaels took the proffered business card and rattled off his own phone number and Harry put it into his contacts list.

Outside, the temperature had dropped a couple of degrees and the sky was now the colour of *I'll give you something to cry about*.

'What do you think of those two?' Harry asked, turning the engine on in the car and waiting for it to share some heat.

'Pair of wankers,' Dunbar said. '"We do this in peace." Give me a break. They've got some kind of money-making scam going on. I can smell it.'

'DSup McKenzie is having a team do a background check on Dunn,' Evans said.

'I wonder how Frank's getting on?' Harry said, then he took his phone out. 'I have to make a call.'

'You need us to step out?' Dunbar said.

'No, no, you're fine.' Harry told them about how he and Presley had been attacked in the flat.

Then he called the Royal Infirmary.

FOURTEEN

'Hello, I'm Detective Chief Inspector Harry McNeil. Two of my officers were involved in a car crash yesterday. Ian Pierce and Ricky Dawson.'

The lady at the hospital told him to hold on and she came back a few minutes later.

'Two detectives were in A and E yesterday, but they weren't in a car crash. They told us they were injured in an operational incident. They couldn't disclose any more than that.'

'You're sure the names were Pierce and Dawson?'

'Yes I'm sure.'

Harry thanked her and hung up.

'What did they say, mucker?' Dunbar asked.

Harry looked at him. 'They told the hospital they

were hurt in an operational incident. Why not just say they were in a car accident?'

'Because they weren't in an accident. I'm not saying they were part of that gang, but we know what coincidences are like.'

'Aye, we do that.'

They were about to drive away from the church when Harry spotted Maggie Parks pulling her car into the side of the road and getting out.

'There's Maggie, Paddy Gibb's girlfriend,' he told the other two, switching the engine back off. 'Come on, I'll introduce you.'

They got out of the car and Maggie jumped as they approached.

'Sorry, I didn't mean to startle you,' Harry said.

'Oh, it's okay, Harry. I was miles away.' She looked at the other two.

Harry introduced them. 'We're working a case.'

'Pleased to meet you both. Would you like to come in for a cup of tea?' she asked.

'That would be good,' Harry said, and she led the way down the stairs. There was nothing to see now, the blood having been cleaned off the steps. There was no indication that anything had happened to Paddy.

'It's so surreal,' she said as they reached the bottom and she let them in.

'I can imagine,' Dunbar said.

Evans was the last man in and he shut the door behind them.

'What's the latest?' Harry asked as they went into the living room.

'No difference. They're doing more tests, but it's not looking hopeful.' Her eyes were red and it looked like she was all cried out.

'You want me to put the kettle on?' Dunbar said.

'Thank you.'

Dunbar turned to Evans and gave a slight sideways nod of his head.

'Allow me,' Evans said, and they each told him what they wanted in their drink. He then went in search of the kitchen, which was next to the living room.

Harry saw an almost empty bottle of Jameson's on the coffee table, with a finger of whisky still in a crystal tumbler sitting next to it.

'I can't bear to move it,' Maggie said. 'I'm waiting for Paddy to come back through the door and finish it in front of the TV.'

'He drink a lot?' Dunbar asked.

'He's Irish. It goes with the territory,' Maggie replied.

'You think he was half blootered when he went out?'

'He always is. He likes to get a few in before going to the pub. It's cheaper than giving the landlord all the money, he says.' She rubbed her hands together.

'You mind if we have a seat?' Harry said.

'No. That might be a good idea.'

Maggie and Harry sat on chairs and Dunbar sat on the settee, along from where Paddy had sat.

Evans came in with some mugs of coffee and put them down on the coffee table. 'That was easy,' he said. 'Just milk all round. I wish it was like this in the pub.'

'Just hand out the mugs, Sergeant,' Dunbar said, and Evans did so and then sat on another chair, not wanting to sit in Paddy's spot on the couch.

'How's your daughter getting on?' Harry asked Maggie. 'It's Lizzie, isn't it?'

'Yes. She's through at Glasgow University now. Film and television studies. Well, uni has broken up for the holidays, but she's spending time there with her boyfriend. She's bringing him through on Christmas Day.'

'It's a good place to study,' Evans said. Dunbar raised his eyebrows at him in a *How do you know?* look. 'So I've heard.'

'Have you called her to let her know about Paddy?' Harry asked.

'I have, but I'm waiting to hear back from her. She isn't returning my calls. It isn't like her, to be honest.'

'Did you have a falling-out?'

'Oh, no. Her boyfriend is her whole world now. But you know the world we work in; I'll never stop worrying about her. My mind goes a million miles an hour if I don't hear from her every couple of days.'

'If you give me her address, I can have one of my team go and check on her,' Dunbar said. 'Put your mind at ease.'

'Oh, would you? That would be so good of you. I really want her to come through here and see Paddy.'

She found a piece of paper and wrote down Lizzie's address and gave him her mobile phone number.

'I'll make a call,' Dunbar said.

Maggie smiled and put a hand on his arm.

'I'll be down to see Paddy this evening,' Harry told her.

'Thank you, Harry,' she said, and her eyes filled with tears.

He gave her a hug, patting her on the back and telling her to stay strong. He couldn't tell her it would be alright because he knew it wasn't going to be.

FIFTEEN

'I wouldn't mind a wee place here,' DS Andy Watt said as Miller parked the car at a bus stop in Broughton Street and put the police sign on the dash.

'You lived in a big house in Colinton.'

'It wasn't mine, though.'

'And now you live in a modern flat in Holyrood. You're never happy.' Miller opened the driver's door and got out into the cold afternoon. It was windy and the sky was the colour of a grandpa's Y-fronts.

'I'm not complaining,' Watt said. 'I mean, if I was ever on my own again and fancied a wee flat that was within walking distance of the boozers up town...'

'There are plenty of boozers round here,' Miller said.

'That's what I mean. Look at this street; it's

downhill all the way to East London Street. You just keep your balance and stagger in the right direction and you're home in no time.'

'They're a nice price nowadays too.'

'There's always a catch.'

The shop was large, sitting between two smaller ones. Its facade was painted a bright red, a beacon for those in need of its services.

They walked into the heat and both men could smell the incense. Miller thought it smelled like cigarettes rolled from cow dung before being stuck up a sheep's arse. They were in an open area with three desks, each with a plastic chair in front. Nobody was sitting at them.

'Fucking minging,' Watt commented. 'Smells like shite,' he added, backing up Miller's theory.

'I wonder if they get used to it, working in here. I'd have to wear a gas mask.'

'I'd have to turn down the job offer at the interview stage. I couldn't work here.'

'Just as well we're not recruiting then,' a female voice said from behind them. The woman came out of what looked like a broom closet, but the sound of a cistern refilling confirmed she hadn't been hiding from them. Maybe flushing her stash, but not playing hide and seek.

'DI Miller, DS Watt. We'd like to talk to whoever is in charge here.'

'Then you've found her. I'm April. My mum's name was June and my dad's name was August.' She smiled as if they'd asked her for a condensed version of her ancestry and she'd passed a polygraph.

'Can we talk somewhere private?' Miller asked her.

'Sure. Follow me.' She walked past and led them towards the back of the shop.

'I wonder what they would have named her if her mum and dad had been called Dick and Fanny?' Watt said in a low voice as they followed her.

'I hate to imagine,' Miller said. She looked to be in her mid- to late-twenties and had purple hair. Her jeans had tears in the knees. She'd probably paid a lot of money for them when she could have saved a few notes by taking home a normal pair and having at it with a pair of scissors.

A door faced them, and April opened it and they entered an office. She sat behind the desk and indicated for the two men to sit on the hard plastic chairs before it. Miller did so while Watt stood, keeping an eye on the door. This routine had saved them in the past when somebody had come bursting in.

'How can I help you police officers today?' April asked.

Miller's eyes were drawn to the stud that was poking through the side of her nose. It constantly amazed him how people could suffer through getting a piece of metal stuck through a part of their body that wasn't designed to be poked and prodded.

'Can I ask your last name?' Miller said.

'Donegan,' she replied.

'Not Showers, then?' Watt commented.

'I don't follow.'

Watt could see that the young woman really didn't get what he was saying. 'Nothing,' he said, waving it away.

'I have some bad news, I'm afraid,' Miller said to her. 'Tess Grogan was found dead this morning.'

April's eyebrows rose. Miller noticed they had avoided the bottle of dye that her hair had been tortured with.

'Dead? Tess? What happened?'

'She was murdered.'

April's eyebrows came back down, front and centre. She was trying to form a response, but no words would come at first. 'Who would want to murder her?'

'We thought you could tell us that.' Miller kept

studying the young woman's face, but she didn't look like she was faking the shock.

'Tess was loved by everybody. Nobody had a bad word to say about her.'

'Do you know if she'd been threatened recently? Anybody bothering her?' Miller asked.

April curled her lip and shook her head. 'No, nothing at all. Not that she told me, that is.'

'What did she do here?'

'She's a solicitor – was a solicitor. But she worked in this outreach as well as our sister place in Glasgow. We work with homeless people. Trying to get them off the streets by getting them a job interview, getting them the clothes they need to go to that interview, and trying to help them get accommodation.' Tears sprang to her eyes. 'Where was she murdered?'

'We can't comment on that, but she was found here in Edinburgh.'

'The last thing I knew, she was going through to Glasgow to work in the centre there. She wasn't due back for a couple of days.'

'Do you know Tom Michaels?'

'The reverend from down the road? Yes. He comes here often.'

'What about Clifford Dunn?'

'Him too. He's a real stick of dynamite. Always

championing the small man. He's helped many a homeless person get back on their feet.'

'Do you know where he lives?'

'Just round the corner in Albany Street Lane.'

'Do you know how long Tess had been Tom's girlfriend?' Miller asked.

'I'm not sure. I've worked here for three years and they were together when I started. We were close but not that close.'

'Do you know anybody who would want to harm her?' Miller asked. 'Somebody from the outreach here? Or through in Glasgow?'

'Nothing was ever mentioned to me.'

'And her relationship with Michaels seemed to be fine?'

'Yes, of course. I never saw anything to the contrary.'

Miller nodded. He knew he'd reached the end of the road with April and didn't want to waste his time going round in circles. He stood up.

'Thank you for your time.' He gave her a business card. 'In case you think of anything else. Please call me.'

She took it without standing up. 'I will.'

Miller and Watt left the shop and went back to the car.

Watt looked at Miller as the DI got behind the wheel. 'So far, Tess Grogan had no enemies that we know of and hadn't had an argument with anybody. Everybody loved her. You think this is just a random attack?'

Miller shook his head. 'No, Andy. I think she was targeted. There was too much planning in this, what with cutting off the fingers and draining her blood out.'

They drove away as the sky promised to give them a kicking.

SIXTEEN

They all met up back at the incident room. Presley was sitting there with a cup of tea and breaking ginger snaps over the hot liquid. 'I'll get the kettle on,' he said, about to stand up.

'You stay there, son,' Watt said. 'I'll be Mother.'

Lillian was also drinking tea, sans the ginger snaps.

'We've been busy since you've been away,' Presley said, as if he'd been caught with his hand in the cookie jar.

'Let's have it then,' Harry said as they took their overcoats off.

'There's not a lot on Michaels and Dunn. Neither has a criminal record. Dunn was a solicitor and worked at the same firm as Tess Grogan. He lived here in Edinburgh before relocating to Glasgow, where he jacked in the law stuff to become an activist. Got quite a name for himself, even appearing on daytime TV.'

'No skeletons in his closet?' Dunbar said.

'Not that I can see, sir.'

'There was one thing,' Lillian chipped in. 'He was questioned a few years ago after a woman made an accusation against him. She said he had slipped something in her drink and she woke up the next day without any memory of how she got home. She told police she had been drinking in a bar with Dunn, but Dunn claimed he was talking to her but left before her. He met up with an old friend, who supported his alibi.'

'And nothing was done,' Miller said.

'Dunn's father was a judge. And you know how they all close ranks. So the Crown Office found there was nothing to answer to.'

'Who gave Dunn the alibi?' Evans asked.

Lillian looked at him before answering. 'Tess Grogan.'

'He knows her and she was through in Glasgow with him and now she's dead. Then he was there when the blood with her fingers was thrown over the statue,' Harry said. 'We need to keep an eye on him.'

They drank their tea and batted ideas about until it was time to go. Harry told Dunbar he'd see him in the bar later and invited Miller along too.

He stayed behind as the others left to speak with Presley.

'I called the Royal,' Harry said. 'Pierce and Dawson weren't in a car accident. They said it was an operational incident.'

'What the hell does that mean, sir?'

'It means, why did Ray Walker tell me that they were in a car accident?'

'Do you think they were two out of the three guys who jumped us?'

'I wouldn't bet against it.' Harry pulled his over-coat on.

'What do we do now?'

'We don't do anything but watch our backs. For now.'

SEVENTEEN

Jack Miller wasn't exactly at a loss for something to do; he was just used to having his girlfriend around. Samantha Willis was an American crime writer who had moved into an apartment along from Jack's son, Frank. When Jack and Samantha had first met, they'd hit it off, and now he lived with her. Before that, Jack had lived with Frank after becoming a widower.

Now he'd finished his dinner and was watching some TV. Samantha was off on a research trip back home in New York. She was going to catch up with her sister while she was there.

He had just settled onto the couch with a beer when his doorbell rang. They had a security buzzer at the main entrance on North Bridge, which meant that the person at the door had either circumvented the security system or lived in the building.

If it was a stranger, Jack wasn't worried. Sure, he might be knocking on sixty, but he was six-five and still looked after himself. He got up and went to the door.

'Frank, come in, son,' he said before the door was fully opened. He hadn't checked the peephole.

'How did you know it was me? I didn't see the peephole darken, so you just opened the door without checking. I might have been a loony.'

'You are a fucking loony. You want a beer?'

Miller came in and closed the door behind him. 'I do. But I'm going to the pub and Harry McNeil asked me to invite you along.'

Jack turned as he reached the living room. 'He did?'

'Don't act so surprised. You've met Harry before. You got on well enough.'

'Yes, Harry's a good guy. Shame about his wife.'

'Alex was nice. It brought back a lot of memories for me.'

Jack looked at Miller for a moment. 'Aye, I miss Carol too. At least you can relate to Harry and can offer him some advice on how to get through it.'

'He's coping.'

'He left and went to live in Newton Stewart, didn't he?'

'He was having a hard time of it.'

They went into the living room and sat down.

'I don't blame him, Frank,' said Jack. 'You went loopy after Carol died. You didn't leave, but you were definitely not yourself.'

'I know. It affects us all differently. Harry's a good guy.'

'He is. I'd like to have a pint with him.'

'And two guys from Glasgow will be there. DCI Jimmy Dunbar and DS Robbie Evans.'

'Come on then, let's go. Which pub is it?'

'The St Bernard down in Raeburn Place. Jimmy and Robbie are staying in the Raeburn hotel round from my old flat.'

'Harry's old flat too.'

'Yes, Harry's too,' Miller said.

They got up, Jack fetched his jacket and they left to go and get a taxi.

EIGHTEEN

Colin Presley felt knackered as he walked down the side of Claremont Court towards his flat. Back in the day, these were all council flats, but the rules were, if you lived in a council house for a certain number of years, then you got to buy the flat at a huge discount. He was glad his grandad had had the foresight to buy his. Presley had helped the old man pay off his mortgage when he started working.

His grandad had been his only family, and now the four-bedroom flat seemed way too big for Presley. His girlfriend, Amy, was a nurse and had told him when he felt the time was right he could move in with her. He had planned to tell her at Christmas that the time was right.

He climbed the few steps up to the landing,

which was lit up now that darkness had come down like a madman. All the flats were main door and faced a car park.

He walked past all the doors until he came to his own. He was about to put his key in the lock when the door along from him opened.

'Hello, Colin.'

He turned to face his neighbour. 'Mrs Kennedy.' The woman was in her late seventies and walked with a stick, but apparently there was nothing wrong with her eyesight.

'I hope you don't mind, but I gave your uncle the key to your house. He said he was desperate for the toilet.'

Presley's heart kicked up a gear. 'My uncle?'

'Yes. Him and your cousin.'

'Which uncle of mine is it?' he asked, playing along.

'Oh, now, he did tell me. Billy? Bobby? I can't remember now.'

'When did they get here?'

'Oh, about an hour or so ago. Or was it longer? I can't remember now, Colin. Sorry.'

'Oh no, please don't apologise. You know what? They like a few beers and I don't have any in the house. I'll nip back out and get some. Thank you for letting them in.'

'No trouble. Enjoy your evening.'

'I will. Now get yourself away in. It's cold.'

She said goodnight and went back into her flat. Presley walked back across the wet car park and got into his car. He turned it on without putting the lights on and moved it so that it was behind a van but if he craned his head forward he could still see his front door.

Then he took out his phone.

He searched through previous calls and found what he was looking for and hit the screen. The phone at the other end rang a few times before it was picked up.

'Colin!' DI Ray Walker said. *'How can I help you?'*

'Call them off.'

'What? What are you talking about?'

'You know what I'm talking about. The two men who are in my flat. Fucking call them off.'

'Here, you can't speak to me like that! Jumped-up fucking DC. I'll make sure you never get above that rank if you talk to me like that again.'

'Call them off. I won't say it again. My next call goes to somebody way above your pay grade.'

'I think you've been drinking, son. Better go and sober up.'

Walker hung up and Presley kept hold of his phone, opening the camera app. If this was something else entirely and the old woman had got confused and there really was nobody in his flat, then he had just kissed his career goodbye. Big fucking deal.

But old Mrs Kennedy hadn't been confused. A couple of minutes later, his front door opened and two men walked out. They were dressed in black, woollen hats on their heads, collars pulled up. He took photos to prove he had made the right call, but he couldn't see their faces.

They got into a car and the lights came on full beam so he still couldn't see their faces, and as they got closer, he had to duck in case they spotted him. Once they had passed him, he sat up, and he took a photo of the licence plate as the car stopped before exiting onto East Claremont Street.

He got out of his car and walked back to his flat. He opened the door, went in and locked the door behind him. *Bastards.* Just the thought of their being in here made his blood boil. But who were they? Some scumbags that Walker knew? The man was a lowlife. For some reason, the DI was targeting him.

Did that mean that Harry McNeil was collateral damage and not him?

He went into the living room and switched a light on before grabbing the TV remote. He didn't see the figure coming into the room, but rather sensed him.

As he spun round, a fist came towards his face, but he was quick to turn and the blow caught him on the side of the head. He staggered a few steps and then corrected himself quickly. Pain shot through his head, but he focused on the figure in front of him. He was all in black and wearing a ski mask again.

Presley stood his ground as the man advanced a couple of steps. Then the other two men came in.

Bastard. He knew in that instant that Mrs Kennedy hadn't seen a third man. Maybe he had come after the first two arrived. Whatever the set-up, there were three now. He himself had told Walker to get the two men out of his flat, so the DI must have realised that Presley thought there were only two and told them to get out, leaving one inside.

Unlike the other day, they didn't say anything to him – they just rushed him. He couldn't tell who they were for the balaclavas, but that was the last thing on his mind as the fists started flying.

When he was knocked to the floor, the boots started flying too.

When they were done, one of them leaned down and whispered to him, 'Tell Harry McNeil he's a dead man. And this will teach you to go fighting by his side. If we ever have to come back, you're a dead man too.'

Then they left.

Blood was pouring from Presley's nose, and as he lay on the floor, he was glad to see one of the men had to be helped out. He wasn't sure how many punches he'd got in; he was concentrating on the pain in his ribs, sure a few were broken.

He reached into his pocket with a swollen hand and took his phone out and managed to search through his contacts until he found the name he wanted.

'Amy? Listen, don't panic. I'm hurt and I need help, but I need you to make a phone call first. I've been attacked. I think I'm going to pass out.'

'God, Colin. What's happened?'

'Never mind that now. I'm going to text you a number. Make the call. Then...hurry.' He hung up and, head swimming, found the number he was looking for. He'd barely sent it to Amy before he passed out.

NINETEEN

'Dad, you know Harry, but I don't believe you've met DCI Jimmy Dunbar and DS Robbie Evans.'

They stood up as Jack Miller held out his hand to shake. 'Former DCI Jack Miller. Pleased to meet you both.'

'Pleasure, sir,' Dunbar said.

'It's Jack.'

Evans shook his hand. 'A pleasure, sir.'

'Didn't you just hear me, lad? I'm no' polis anymore.'

'Fair enough, Jack. I'll get them in.'

Evans took the orders and went to the bar with Miller.

'My son was filling me in on the case you're working on,' Jack said. 'Poor woman.'

'Aye, it's a nasty one, Jack,' Harry said. 'We got the corpse, but Jimmy and Robbie got the fingers. Mixed in with blood.'

'It was thrown over a statue during a demonstration,' Dunbar said.

'Was it her blood?'

'Samples have been sent to the lab for analysis, so we don't know yet.'

The St Bernard's pub was busy, if not packed to the hilt. It was mostly an older clientele who weren't in there to get boozed up on hooligan juice before going up town for a fight.

Jack looked thoughtful for a moment, then Evans and Miller arrived with the pints and sat at the table.

'I remember being in here when that old DCI of yours was acting like an arse,' Dunbar said to Jack.

'Stan Webster,' Harry said.

'I remember him,' Jack said. 'Being in prison is the best thing for him. He's a disgrace.'

'Good riddance to him,' Miller said.

They all clinked their glasses together.

Jack looked at Harry. 'Frank said that when the woman was found, all the blood had been drained from her. That would narrow down your suspect list. Not many people would know how to do that.'

'Funeral directors,' Harry said.

'Maybe a butcher,' Dunbar said.

'Or somebody who watches YouTube,' Evans said. They all looked at him for a moment. 'Hear me out. You know how many people try to save money by watching YouTube to see how something's done? I'll bet there's a video on there showing you how to drain blood.'

'What? Away,' Dunbar said.

'Hear the boy out, Jimmy,' Jack said.

Evans put his pint glass down on the table. 'For instance, you want to change the light bulbs inside your car for LEDs; there's a video on that.'

'He's got a point,' Miller said. 'There are millions on there, and unless it's one showing somebody getting a vasectomy with a chainsaw, they'll show it.'

They bounced ideas off each other until Miller mentioned Paddy Gibb. 'Poor sod's lying in a bed just along the road and he'd have loved to be here instead. Let's raise a glass to our friend and colleague. To Paddy.'

They all drank, and then Harry's phone rang. He excused himself and took the call.

'Hello?' He was overly cautious after his tussle in the abandoned flat.

'Is this Harry McNeil?'

A female voice. Irish. 'Who wants to know?'

'*I do! My name's Amy Foster. I'm Colin Presley's girlfriend. He's been attacked in his flat and he gave me your number. He said to call you for help. I need you, Harry.*'

'You live off Henderson Row, don't you?'

'*Yes. But we need to be quick. He's hurt. I know this sounds crazy, but he sounds scared.*'

'Give me his exact address.'

She did. '*I'm going over there.*'

'Don't go in the house until we get there, Amy.'

'*We?*'

'I'm bringing the cavalry.' Harry hung up and looked over at Dunbar. 'You remember I told you what happened in that flat with my DC, Colin Presley?'

'Aye. What's happened now?'

'He's been given a going-over in his flat.'

Dunbar and Evans jumped up from the table. 'Lead the way.'

TWENTY

'It's just one little whisky,' Liam McDonald said. 'I'm not going to get blootered.'

Detective Inspector Lisa McDonald looked at her grandfather, who had a whisky glass in one hand and a Barbie doll in the other. 'Maybe Barbie has other ideas.'

Liam grinned. 'I don't think wee Alice would let me fall about.'

Usually, in the evening Lisa would sit down with Alice and play before watching some TV. Her ex-husband was dead and she had no life now beyond her four walls, and that was the way she liked it. Tonight, though, she was doing Jimmy Dunbar a favour by going to talk to a young woman who originally hailed from Edinburgh but was now at

Glasgow Uni. The daughter of the head of forensics in Edinburgh. Lisa was to swing by Helen Street station, where she was based, and pick up DI Tom Barclay. She liked the other DI and was glad she had been posted back at Helen Street.

'Hopefully, I won't be long. I just have to do a quick interview,' she said, grabbing her car keys from the coffee table.

'I know. You told me ten times already. I also told you to relax. This isn't my first rodeo. Now go. The kids will be fine.'

Bella, their Lemon Beagle, looked at Liam like she had just been told that it was her birthday and she was going to the park again and there would be cake when she got back. She yawned, and put her front paws down on the floor and stretched her back ones as she slid off the settee.

'Not you, honey,' Lisa said, petting the dog on the head. It was like a fresh battery had been installed as Bella tried to break the world record for wagging a tail.

As Lisa walked away, the dog jumped up at Liam, grabbed the doll and ran away with it.

'Have fun, you lot,' Lisa said as she left.

The drive was quiet. The roads were wet but not quite slick, and the trip to the station didn't take long.

She headed inside and upstairs, expecting to see Tom Barclay beavering away at a computer. Instead, she found DSup Calvin Stewart.

'Lisa! I was about to call somebody to see if they were interested in buying one of my fucking organs, I'm growing that old waiting for you.'

'Liver might be a little shrivelled, sir.'

'Aye, it's had a fair kicking over the years, right enough.'

'I'm expecting to go out with Tom Barclay this evening,' she explained.

'He's a married man, you know.'

'No, I meant –'

'I know what you meant. Don't get your corset in a riot. Barclay was sent on an errand by Lynn McKenzie, so you're stuck with me. Barclay told me what Jimmy Dunbar wants: check on the daughter of the Edinburgh head of forensics and see why she hasn't been answering her phone. She lives with her boyfriend, so maybe she's had other things on her mind. Is that about right?'

'Right. It's basically a welfare check. Her name is Lizzie Parks. His name is Ben Tasker.'

'Tasker? Sounds like tadger. I bet he got a belting in school over that. But anyway, let's get a move on. I'm meeting somebody later on.'

'A woman?' Lisa asked as Stewart held the door open for her.

'Don't sound too surprised. I've still got enough sauce in the bottle to cover a fish supper.'

'Jesus, that makes you sound like a deviant, if you don't mind me saying.'

'I do, actually,' Stewart replied as they made their way downstairs. 'It was my way of saying, there's life in the old dog yet. But without the *old* bit thrown in. Aye, don't you worry, Lisa, this dinosaur knows how to treat a woman, despite what my ex-wife would say to the contrary.'

'I hardly think buying a fish supper counts as treating a woman to a good night out.'

'Don't be so bloody lippy. My earlier reference to a fish supper by no means indicates how a woman would be treated in my company.'

'So, not twice round the dancefloor and outside for a bit of how's-your-father?'

'That would never be on my mind. Too cold this time of year.'

'You amaze me, sir.'

'That's what my ex-wife used to say, but we were on first-name terms.'

Lisa shook her head, patted her hip before she

remembered that she didn't carry a sidearm, and got in behind the wheel.

'You don't mind me driving?' she asked, starting the car up.

'You can't be any worse than Robbie Evans. He drives like he's never been behind the fucking wheel before. The gearbox crunches more than a box of Rice Krispies. If you're ever in a car with him, take a change of underwear with you.' Stewart held on to the *Oh shit* handle above the passenger window.

Lisa set off from the station, remembering the route she'd looked at on Google Maps.

'Looking forward to retirement, sir?' she asked as she saw Stewart yawn.

'I am actually. I'm bored out of my tits right now because they're trying to keep me away from the public, which isn't working. But I'll be working as an investigator with Michael McInsh. Finbar too.'

'You get on with Finbar now, don't you? After what happened?'

'Aye. He's a good lad. I read him completely wrong.'

'And you thought he worked with forensics. Instead, he's a forensic pathologist. Or was, before he resigned.'

'Am I never going to live that down? I interrupted him and jumped to the wrong conclusion. We're fine now, though. Get on like a house on fire.'

'I'm glad, I really am. Finbar's a nice man.'

'His wife's coming down soon. She's a GP and she's transferring to a practice here.' He looked out the windscreen as they passed by tenements and shops that were shuttered, keeping out the night crawlers.

'This is it.' She looked up at the windows of the tenement, trying to guess which one was their target.

'Come on, Lisa. We don't want him having a wee deek out and thinking there's a couple of window-lickers waiting to tan his place.'

'Speak for yourself,' she said, not bothering to lower her voice.

He walked up to the door and was pleased to see that obviously nobody gave a shit about the security of the students who lived here. He turned the handle and opened the heavy front door.

'Right then, which floor?' he asked.

'Second.'

'Of course it is. They couldn't live on the ground floor. That would be too easy.'

They reached the flat shared by Lizzie Parks and Ben Tasker. Stewart stepped up to the brown door, which had seen better days, and knocked hard.

'Who is it?' a voice from the other side said.

'Pizza.'

The door opened and Stewart held out his warrant card.

'I thought you said *pizza?*' the young man said.

'Clean your ears out. I said polis. You mind if we come in?'

'What's it about?'

'Your girlfriend, Lizzie Parks.'

'Oh, God. Has something happened?'

'We need to come in, Ben,' Lisa said. Tasker moved aside.

They walked up to the living room, and to nobody's surprise, it was a shithole. Papers left lying around, empty fast-food containers that might once have held food but should now carry a government health warning, and some laundry hanging on a clothes dryer.

'What are you studying at uni?' Stewart asked. 'Home economics?'

'Film and TV. I want to become a TV producer.'

'We're here because Lizzie's mum is worried about her, Ben,' Lisa said, taking the more softly-softly approach with him. 'Do you know where she is?'

Tasker ran a hand through his hair before

answering. 'She left me. That's the only thing I can think of. She just upped and left.'

'When was this?'

'A few days ago. Monday, I think. We had an argument about Christmas. Lizzie wanted to go through to spend Christmas Day with her mother, but I suggested we spend it here.'

'Drinking and shagging?' Stewart said. 'Beats having the future mother-in-law's Christmas pudding.'

Tasker looked at him with disdain. 'I just wanted a quiet day, that's all.'

'Did she say where she was going?' Lisa asked.

Tasker shook his head. 'No. I went out to spend the day with my friend and we ended up getting drunk and got invited to a party. I tried calling Lizzie to tell her I'd just crash at my pal's house, but she didn't answer. It went to voicemail.'

'Weren't you worried about her?' Stewart asked, trying not to breathe in through his nose.

'Of course I was. But I thought she was pissed off at me and was teaching me a lesson.'

'Why didn't you call her mother?' Lisa said.

'I don't have her number. I've never talked to her before.'

'You didn't know her but you were going to spend Christmas with her?'

'That's right. Lizzie wanted me to go through and meet her mother and the mother's boyfriend. I wasn't keen, and she was hacked off at me. But I didn't think it was serious enough for her to walk out.'

'Do you know if her bank account's been touched?' Lisa asked. 'Like if she withdrew money?'

'I don't know. We don't share a bank account. But she has a little lock box in one of her drawers. I never thought to look. She keeps emergency money in there. Lizzie's one of those people who think society is going to crash one day and she doesn't want all of her money in the bank.'

'Can you go and look?' Stewart said.

'Yep.' Tasker left the living room.

'Do you think he's capable of harming her?' Lisa whispered.

'No, he looks like he couldn't fight his way through wet toilet paper,' Stewart answered in a normal voice, making Lisa cringe.

'I heard that!' Tasker shouted through.

'I wasn't hiding it,' Stewart answered. 'Earwigging bastard,' he whispered.

Tasker came back through holding the lock box. He'd obviously unlocked it, as he flipped the lid and showed them money in a money clip. 'She told me she kept a thousand pounds in here, in case the zombie apocalypse started. And she told me not to touch it, which I never would, and you can check it's all there.'

'If she was going to run off, then she might have taken this money,' Lisa said. 'Does she work?'

'No. She got an inheritance from her father after he passed away a few years ago. She uses that because she wants to spend as much time studying as possible.'

'Can you give us a list of her friends?'

'I can, but I don't have their numbers.'

'Give us the list anyway,' Stewart said.

Tasker scribbled down some names before handing the list to Lisa. 'If you see her, tell her I'm okay about going to her mother's for Christmas. I was just being an arsehole about it. I don't want it to affect our relationship.'

'Hopefully, we'll get the chance,' Lisa said.

Tasker closed the money box and held it to his chest as if Stewart was about to make a grab for it.

'If she comes back, call us right away,' Lisa said, handing over a business card.

'I will. But there's one more thing before you go.'

'What's that?'

'Lizzie's last name isn't Parks; it's Armstrong. Her mother is her stepmother and *her* name is Parks.'

Tasker looked numb as the detectives walked out of the flat.

'What's your opinion?' Stewart asked Lisa when they were back in the car.

'I don't think she just left. Something's happened to her.'

'And Tasker?'

'He's either a very good actor or he doesn't know where the hell she is.'

'My thoughts exactly.'

Lisa drove away from the tenement as the sky opened up and showered the city.

'Drop me off at the Admiral. I'm meeting my female friend for a drink.' He looked at her. 'I know what you're thinking: *do you think I'm a bloody Uber driver?* But let me finish. It's closer than the station and not far from you. Win-win.'

'I wasn't thinking any such thing,' Lisa answered.

'Then why are you pulling a beamer? You're a terrible liar, DI McDonald.'

'I learned from the best.'

'Amen to that, sister.'

TWENTY-ONE

Amy Foster was pacing in the car park when the taxi pulled in. The four detectives bailed out after Harry took care of the fare. Amy froze for a second, thinking it was the attackers come back to finish the job.

'I checked on him. He's hurt, but he'll live.'

'You went in?' Harry said.

'I did. I know you said not to, but I would never forgive myself if I was standing out here and he passed away when I could have been in there helping. I'm a nurse, remember.'

'Okay. Show us the way.'

They followed her up the steps and along the landing towards Presley's flat. Inside, he was still on the floor.

'I tidied him up. His nose is burst but not broken. His ribs are bruised, but again, not broken. He'll be stiff and sore in the morning, but it's nothing major, thank God,' Amy said.

'Well, look, my friends have popped in unannounced and I have no beer in the fridge,' Presley said, then he grunted and held on to his side.

'What happened here?' Harry asked.

Presley took a minute to get his breathing in order before answering. 'I was coming home when my elderly neighbour next door said she'd seen my uncle and cousin at my door. She offered them my key, she said, thinking she was helping. We have each other's front-door key in case we get locked out. I knew the men inside weren't my uncle and cousin, so I went back to my car and called DI Walker. I told him to call them off. The two men. That's all I said. Then two men came out of my flat. But unbeknownst to me or old Mrs Kennedy, there were three of them. When I came back in, thinking the flat was clear, the third was waiting, and then the other two came back in and we had a bit of a pagger.'

'And you lost, son,' Dunbar said to him.

'Don't be so hasty, sir,' Presley answered, and held up a hand while he coughed up a lung and tried not to die on his living room floor. 'I kicked one of them hard on the front of his right knee. He screamed, and while they were distracted, I belted another one of them in the mouth. But then two of them got the better of me and started kicking the shit out of me.'

'I think this was some kind of a message,' Miller said. 'If they'd wanted to put him out of commission, they'd have broken a few bones.'

'You're right, sir,' Presley said, then held his breath as though this would miraculously rebuild him. He looked at Harry. 'Before they left, one of them told me to give you a message. He said you're a dead man.'

'Did he now?' Harry said. 'I'd like to meet him face to face.'

'That won't happen. I think it was the three from the flat in Dumbiedykes. Except there might only be two now. One of them will have had to go to A&E if I kicked his knee hard enough. Hopefully he'll be out of commission for a while.'

Dunbar looked at Evans, who nodded in understanding: call the Royal. The DS stepped out of the room and made the call.

'Sounds like these guys aren't going to stop until they get what they want, mucker,' Dunbar said to Harry.

'That's just the problem, Jimmy; I don't know exactly what they want. Unless it's just to give me a kicking.'

'From your days in Professional Standards,' Miller said.

Harry looked at him. 'There are a lot of bastards who'd want to see me dead.'

'Why give the lad a belting too?' Dunbar said.

'This DI Walker he was talking about has a few cronies. They're their own wee team. Colin doesn't fit in. Neither does my DS Lillian O'Shea for that matter.'

Presley looked at Harry. 'Maybe give her a call, sir? Make sure she's alright?'

'I will.' Harry walked out of the room and looked up his contacts. Hit Lillian's number. There was no answer. He tried again with the same result. He hung up, trying not to let thoughts run riot. Then he called Jessica.

'Are you and Grace okay?'

'We're fine, Harry. What's up?'

'I don't want to alarm you, but somebody's targeting me and one of my team members. Elvis got a hiding tonight. The guys gave him a message for me. I just want you to take extra precautions.'

'I will.'

'Call me immediately if you think something's not right. If you can't get hold of me, treble-nine it.'

He cut the call and then looked up another number. 'Tony? It's Harry McNeil.'

'Harry! How's things, m'man?'

DCI Tony Burns was an old friend of Harry's and now an officer with Professional Standards.

'I've got a bit of a problem. Nothing that I can officially put in a complaint for, but I thought I could run it by you. Maybe tomorrow?'

'In my office?'

'I was thinking maybe Starbucks. The one down from the High Street.'

'Fine by me.'

'I don't know if you've heard, but I was seconded to Alpha MIT after Paddy Gibb's fall. I'm working with Frank Miller and I brought a couple of my team from Leith CID.'

'I'd heard about Paddy Gibb, but I didn't know you were in the High Street. That's handy, then. Give me a call when you're in and I can meet you down there between interviews.'

'Thanks, Tony. See you tomorrow.'

Harry joined the others. 'You can't stay here tonight,' he said to Presley. 'In fact, you should be in the Royal.'

'I don't want to go there. I'm not slagging off security at the hospital, but my attackers could come for me there. Though I think you're more in danger than I am now. I'm just the messenger.'

'Colin's coming home with me,' Amy said. 'They don't know where I live.'

'Are you going to bring this Walker joker in for a wee chat?' Dunbar said. Harry didn't know if the other man meant a wee chat or taking Walker outside for a kick in the bollocks.

'I'll have a talk with him. First, though, I'm going to meet with an old friend of mine.' Harry told them about Tony Burns.

'Maybe give Jessica a heads-up,' Dunbar said.

'I already did, Jimmy. She's fine.'

'Right, I want to get Colin back to my place,' Amy said.

'We'll come back with you,' Harry said, and looked to the others for confirmation. They all agreed.

'There's only one problem,' Amy told them. 'I just have a small car. We won't all get in.'

'Harry, you and Frank go. Me and Robbie will get a Joe Baxi. Just give us your address, hen,' Dunbar said to Amy.

She told him and they managed to manhandle

the young DC to a standing position, which made him yelp in pain.

'At least I didn't get a punch in the goolies,' he told Harry.

TWENTY-TWO

Watt got off the bus and walked round to the entrance to the Anne Ferguson Building at the Western General. Upstairs, he found Maggie Parks sitting in the room with Paddy.

'Hello, Maggie,' Watt said.

'Hi, Andy.' Her eyes were red and shiny. She was sitting next to the bed holding Paddy's hand.

'I had grapes, but I ate them all on the bus,' he said, giving her a weak smile.

'He wouldn't have expected any less from you,' she said, smiling back at him. She let go of Paddy's hand and stood up. 'I'll get another chair.'

'Don't be daft. I'll stand.' Watt looked at the board behind Gibb's bed and saw a child's drawing pinned to it. 'The grandbairn's fairly coming along,' he said. 'Unless Paddy just can't master a box of crayons.'

Maggie gave a little chuckle. 'You always were daft as a brush, Andy. But you know what? Paddy wouldn't have you any other way. He told me that once. He thought the world of you.'

'Thinks,' Watt said.

'What?'

'You said he *thought* the world of me. He thinks the world of me. He's still here. I can't think of him in the past tense.'

'You're right. I'm sorry.'

'No need to apologise. Seeing him lying there makes me think that this isn't the real Paddy Gibb. He's hiding somewhere and he's about to walk in the room and tell us this is all a big joke.'

'I wish it was. I don't know what I'm going to do...' She caught herself again.

He nodded slowly and gently lowered himself down onto the edge of the bed. They chatted and reminisced for a while before Watt felt his right leg going numb. He didn't want to make an arse of himself by falling on top of Gibb, so he stood up.

'I'll get going up the road, Maggie.'

'Of course. Thanks for coming in, Andy.' She got

up and came round the bed and gave him a hug. 'Best to Kate.'

She sat back down as he left the ward.

Outside, the cold night air was starting to cover the cars in frost. He shivered in the bus shelter until the bus came and he was lost in his own world until he got off on the North Bridge in the city centre.

He walked up to the High Street, and then it was all downhill. That was the thing about Edinburgh: it was built on hills. Up and down; you never knew if you were coming or going.

He had started walking down towards the Canongate, where he would cut through a close to the flat he shared with Kate Murphy, when he felt his phone buzz. He took it out and looked at the screen. It was a text. From Maggie's daughter, Lizzie.

Andy, I need ur help. I think somebody hurt my dad. He's trying to hurt me. I think I'm being followed. Please help! I'm near your flat. I'm safe for now, but I need to see you.

He felt his pulse quicken now. First Paddy and now Lizzie. He had thought there was more to this accident than met the eye.

He looked across to the Radisson Blu hotel and the taxis that sat in the rank. He ran over to the first one in line and showed the driver his badge before taking out his wallet. 'Here's a twenty. I'm just going down to the foot of Holyrood Road.'

'Cheers, squire.'

The driver booted the cab round in a tight circle and floored it down the High Street, then turned right into St Mary's Street before hitting Holyrood Road. It reminded Watt of being on the waltzer at the Burntisland fair. He wondered if the driver was having flashbacks to some traumatic event in his life as he floored it round the corner, throwing Watt sideways onto the back seat. He sat upright again, hoping the driver was still conscious.

'Where exactly?' the driver asked.

'The flats at the bottom,' Watt told him. 'On the main road is fine.'

Watt got out of the taxi and walked into the lane where the main door to the building was. He looked around for Lizzie. He hadn't seen her for a while, but he would recognise her anywhere.

She wasn't near the main door and the underground garage doors were closed. It wasn't the best-lit street, but there were outside lights on the side of the hotel next door; their reflections glistened on the wet road.

'Hey!' he heard a voice shout from further up the street. He saw a face appear from around the end of the building, then move back. He couldn't make her out but presumed it was a frightened Lizzie.

'Lizzie!' Watt shouted. He stood and waited for her to reappear. Instead, headlight beams cut through the gloomy cold air as a car came round the corner, moving slowly towards him.

He thought she was being cautious and was glad she was safe in her own car. Then the beams came on full and the car engine revved harder as the car shot forward.

Watt thought the young woman was panicking. Did she recognise him? He waved at her, blinded by the lights, and expected her to see who it was and stop.

But the car didn't stop.

It shot forward, going faster, and too late Watt realised it wasn't going to stop. He moved as fast as he could for an unfit bloke in his fifties, but it wasn't quick enough.

The passenger-side front wing hit his left leg and he was thrown into the air, towards the entry door of the building.

He lay on the ground, pain coursing through him like fire, and heard the distinct *thunk* of a car gearbox being thrown into reverse.

Then the car came back into view, the white

reverse lights mixing with the red taillight reflections on the wet road. The driver stopped and was obviously deciding what to do. Then the driver pulled forward, angling the car.

Watt tried to crawl, but he didn't have the strength. He couldn't feel his left leg. He knew in that instant that the car was about to reverse over him and finish the job.

Just as it started to reverse, more headlights appeared from around the back of the building and headed slowly towards them.

The first car's lights suddenly went out as it shot forward, leaving the scene. The second car appeared slowly, then stopped. A man and woman got out and the man ran over to him.

'Andy! Can you hear me? It's Brian, your neighbour.'

Watt couldn't speak.

Brian turned to his wife. 'Call for an ambulance!'

Then the sounds got fainter until all Watt could hear was his own heart beating. And then darkness claimed him.

TWENTY-THREE

DS Lillian O'Shea was used to doing surveillance work, although it wasn't her favourite pastime. But this was on her own time now. She was skulking about down in East Scotland Street Lane, next to the church in Bellevue. She'd parked her car in Scotland Street and walked through the lane on foot as it had now been closed to traffic and was pedestrian only.

She walked past the front of the church and reached Paddy Gibb's flat. She looked through the railings and saw the flat was in darkness. Her nerves were going now. As a police officer, she was used to being thrown into the deep end, going up against lowlifes who would think nothing of taking a swing at her, but this was different.

This was on her own time.

It was cold, the temperature dropping fast. Her breath fogged as she stood looking at the building in front of her, her mind going over and over the text she'd received last night:

'I need to talk to you, Lillian. This is important. You can't tell anybody you're meeting me. It's a matter of life and death.'

Cryptic, yes. But she had worked with Paddy Gibb years ago, when he had been seconded to work on an undercover operation. He trusted everybody on his team, he had told her, but they had grown close. Lillian had lost her own father years ago, himself a detective who had worked with Paddy in their younger days, and Paddy had taken her under his wing. He had known her before she had become polis and had mentored her. They had a mutual respect and trust for one another.

Paddy had obviously trusted her last night. She had agreed to meet him in the Cask and Barrel on Broughton Street. She had taken a taxi from her flat in Comely Bank and had waited for him, but he hadn't turned up.

Now she knew why.

Paddy had fallen down the steps, and she would have been gutted at finding that out, but knowing he had wanted to meet her on the quiet before he fell devastated her even more.

Now she stood in the dark and cold, looking down the stone steps where Paddy had fallen, picturing in her mind her friend falling backwards, banging his head on the way down and landing with a thud. Had he banged his head again as he clattered to the stone floor before, or had the bang on the step been enough to do the damage?

She wondered what he had wanted to tell her and kept running the conversation through her mind. Paddy's tone seemed not only secretive but scared, and Paddy wasn't a man who scared easily.

She had one hand in her pocket and felt the key there. The key that Paddy had given her in case of emergency, even though it was Maggie's flat. Still, it was his home, and if he had told her she could go in it, then that was that.

She took the first step down, then the next, tentative at first. But then she hurried down the rest, the need for stealth propelling her, and maybe a little bit of fear thrown into the mix.

She reached the front door and wondered what she would say if Maggie appeared. There were no lights on, but maybe she had gone to bed early.

She couldn't stand out here all night, speculating. It was now or never.

She had deliberately worn a short winter jacket. Easier to run in. She took the balaclava out of her pocket and slipped it on, before quickly taking the key out of her other pocket and inserting it into the lock. She turned it and the door opened easily. She stepped into the warmth, gently closing the door behind her. If Maggie appeared now, Lillian could either reveal her identity and try to talk her way out of the situation, or pretend she was a burglar and run. After shoving Maggie to the floor, which she didn't relish doing.

She took a small torch out of her pocket and shone it around. Nobody came out of any of the rooms to confront her.

She remembered how when she was a little girl she would sometimes go with her dad to meet Paddy and the Irishman always made her laugh. She tried to focus on those good times now as she walked along his hallway.

He had stood by her side at her dad's funeral, putting a comforting arm around her shoulders. 'If you ever need me for anything, you just shout,' he had said.

She had looked him in the eyes then. 'You too. I

mean it, Paddy. If you ever need me for anything, don't hesitate.'

They'd had a bond from that moment on. So it had come as no surprise when Paddy had called her one night recently.

'Listen,' he had told her, *'I'm not saying this to be dramatic, but if anything ever happens to me, then I want you to use the spare key I gave you to go into my flat. There's a box file...'*

And now here she was. Paddy wasn't dead, but he had told her 'if anything happens to me', not 'wait until I'm dead'. She prayed that he was going to come out of this alive, but Lillian had been a realist ever since her father had died. You never knew what was around the corner.

That was why she was creeping about in Paddy's flat right now, because she was the only one in the world he could share his theories with. Sometimes they would chat on the phone, sometimes they would have a beer in the police club, and they would each talk over the case they were working on. Paddy would run ideas past her, ideas that he couldn't talk to anybody else about. No matter how outlandish they seemed, she would listen. And he the same.

She hadn't been here before. Paddy felt comfortable here, but it was always at the back of his mind that the place wasn't actually his. Maggie made people feel welcome, but Paddy was aware that if their relationship went south, then he would be the one leaving. Lillian thought Paddy felt uncomfortable having friends round for a drink, so that was why he very rarely invited people over and Lillian had never set foot in the place.

She didn't know where Paddy's bedroom was, but she found it easily enough. He had told her about Maggie having a built-in wardrobe constructed years before he moved in and she moved towards it, the torchlight bouncing off the white paint.

She opened the door and saw clothes hanging. Male and female. Paddy had told her about the shelves on the top. There were two, each one divided into three compartments. He said the one of the far left was the hardest to reach so he had put junk up there.

And the box file was there.

There were a few light boxes that she pulled down. She couldn't see the box file at first, which, she supposed, was the whole point. She put a hand up and felt it sitting at the back on its side. She had to stretch up and reach right in. Nobody would find it with a casual look.

She got her fingers on the edge and managed to

grab hold of it and bring it forward. It sat on the edge of the shelf and she carefully pulled it down and laid it on the bed before putting the boxes back up.

She closed the wardrobe door and made her way back out of the flat, remembering to lock the door behind her. She felt bad that she had gone into Maggie's home without her knowing, but how could she have explained this away? Maggie wasn't a police officer like Lillian was, and only a detective would understand the thought process.

That was how she justified herself being in the flat like a housebreaker.

Back in her car, she kept the light off but opened the box file to have a quick look inside.

And her blood froze.

There were newspaper clippings, or rather printed-out copies of newspaper clippings. One headline blazed across the front of a newspaper read: *M8 killer strikes again!*

Why would Paddy be keeping this stuff? Was it a case he'd worked on? She looked at the date on the top corner of the paper: the tenth of August 1986. Thirty-five years ago.

She took her phone out and called control to ask for a phone number. When she got it, she dialled it and waited for the call to be answered.

'*Hello?*'

'Detective Superintendent Stewart?'

'*Who's asking?*' Stewart answered.

'DS Lillian O'Shea,' she answered. 'We worked together on a case in Edinburgh.'

'*I remember. What can I do for you, Sergeant?*'

'Sir, I don't know who else to ask about this, and it's going to sound strange, but I have a box file full of newspaper clippings and stories relating to the M8 killer. There are police reports in here too. I was wondering if you knew anything about this case? It's old, but there are police reports in here from a Glasgow division.'

'*Interesting. Can I ask where you got the box file?*'

'I'd rather not say just now, sir. It's...how can I put it? Delicate.'

'*Okay, but I still want to know.*'

'I promise I'll tell you. Meantime, could you do some research on your end? Please just trust me.'

'*Okay, Lillian. I'll get somebody onto it and get back to you.*'

'Thank you, sir.'

She closed the box file and drove away.

TWENTY-FOUR

'The cold isn't keeping them away, I'm glad to see,' Tom Michaels said.

Clifford Dunn smiled. He stood on the small platform they'd erected, which consisted of a couple of wooden boxes with a wooden board placed on top. Some of the church members had hastily put it together when the crowd had started getting bigger.

They were in St Andrew Square, a garden square at the end of George Street. Christmas lights were everywhere, bathing the square in a festive glow. But there was no festive message from Clifford Dunn as he stood on the board with his megaphone.

'Thank you, ladies and gentlemen, boys and girls! By coming here tonight, I know that you are as concerned as we are about the audacity of this city.

Look around you! We all love the glitz and glamour of Christmas. Time to spend with the family. To eat, drink and be merry. That's what we love. But while we're sitting round the table this Christmas, remember the families who weren't so fortunate hundreds of years ago! Families who were here not through their own choice but the choice of rich men who were only getting richer through the blood of those people. And what happened afterwards? Huge monuments to the rich men were erected, so they could stand high and lord it over you, the people, long after they were dead! So let's do the right thing and bring these monuments to greed and degradation down to the ground.'

The crowd erupted and the uniforms kept an eye on them, but nothing went out of control.

Dunn gave the megaphone to Michaels, who was just as good at revving the public up. While it wasn't quite fire and brimstone, it still got the crowd cheering. Michaels believed in that moment that he could have told them to go and burn the castle down and they'd have formed an orderly queue and marched up to it and thrown flaming torches at the old fortress.

After his spiel, Michaels stepped down and members of the church began handing out flyers illustrating that evening's speech and directing them to the website, where they could donate funds to help fight the good cause. The flyers also suggested people to bombard with complaints, including politicians, who might read them after having a few gins with the elite who had put them in power.

Michaels had liked that about Dunn right from the off: he hated politicians even more than Michaels did.

'That was a resounding success,' he said as Dunn clapped him on the shoulder.

'Indeed it was. And I made sure to get a photo of the uniformed sergeant's badge number. Plus plenty of photos of you and I being here. And look, nobody threw a bucket of blood over the monument.'

'That was a stroke of genius,' Michaels said, 'changing the venue at the last minute. Then having people down there directing the protesters round here instead. Genius, Clifford.'

'Thank you. I think being at Wellington's statue would have focused more on the fingers found at the Glaswegian version of the duke's statue, and that's not what we want. Our aim is to make the public aware of the blood that seeped into Scottish soil at the hands of these egomaniacs.'

Michaels looked at his friend, the hairs on the

back of his neck standing up. There was just a touch of insanity behind the man's eyes, enough to keep his engine running without it backfiring. He was certainly passionate about his work. Something that Tess loved about him. Her death hadn't sunk in yet, not fully. Michaels had brought the mental curtains down on the show, knowing he would have to raise them again, but not now. If he didn't think about it too much, it almost felt like a dream.

'Reverend Michaels,' a young woman said to him, breaking his reverie. He smiled at her.

'Yes,' he answered, not sure if she was wanting him to confirm that was his name or if she was just trying to get his attention.

'I have to say, that rebel-rousing is just the kick in the backside this city needs.'

'Thank you. I agree. It's been a long time coming.'

She held out a hand. 'I'm April Donegan. I worked with Tess.'

Michaels smiled. 'Yes, she mentioned you. She thought very highly of you.'

'I can't believe she's gone.' Suddenly, her face was sombre, as if she was replaying memories in her head.

'None of us can. But she wouldn't have wanted us to stop our work.'

'That's true. And I'm glad to see there's been a big turnout tonight. I want to see this whole city changed. It's about time the city was about its people and not the ancestors who made money from the misery of others.'

'I highly agree,' Dunn said. 'It's an ongoing cause, but now we've woken up the sleeping bear, hopefully the powers-that-be will listen.'

She nodded and shivered in the cold, her breath coming out in a plume. 'I hope to see you again,' she said.

'I'm sure you will.' Michaels smiled at her and watched her walk away, heading across the square. 'What say we wrap this up?'

'Sounds good to me,' Dunn said.

April Donegan had always liked Christmas. It had been a special time for her when she was a little girl and it was still special. Even more so this year. The love of her life was meeting her.

She had agreed to go to the demonstration just so she could see him in action and had played it cool afterwards. She felt a shiver as she walked down Broughton Street towards the shop and it wasn't from the icy cold air.

She reached the red shop. Looked up at the facade and felt a sudden hatred for it. Yes, it gave her employment, but the longer she worked here, the more she realised that she wasn't fully on board with what they stood for. Sure, helping the homeless get a home or a job was great, but it was all the other nonsense that went with it. Constantly thinking up ways of sticking it to the Establishment.

Yes, she agreed that the rich bastards of old shouldn't be put on a pedestal for all to see, but how many of the half-dead Edinburgh workers really noticed when they were sitting on a cold bus in the morning going to work? How many of them walking across St Andrew Square garden looked up to the top of the monument and thought, *Look at that rich guy who made his money from slavery?*

None of them.

It had taken Tom Michaels and Clifford Dunn to bring it to everybody's attention. Did they have an ulterior motive? At the end of the day, more people knew about Michaels' church now. He got grants from the government that helped pay the bills.

April unlocked the front door and stepped

inside, keeping the lights off. She didn't want anybody trying to come in at this time of night. The lights from outside filtering through the windows were just enough to see by, and she walked through and settled down in her office.

She only just heard the front door opening, the noise was so quiet. Tom Michaels had promised to meet her here. They'd arranged to meet before he'd learned of his girlfriend's death. Though he was cut up about it, theirs was an open relationship, April knew. He was no longer excited by Tess, and her death had probably come as something of a relief to Tom. And now April was here to fill the void.

She heard the footsteps on the carpet approaching her office. Just the faint pressure of feet shuffling along, trying to be quiet, although there was no need for stealth in here just now. Nobody knew they were here. She certainly hadn't told anybody, and Tom wouldn't.

She swung round in the leather chair, hiding herself from view. Turning round would be her big reveal, his chance to see her in all her glory.

She heard the footfalls stop at the door momentarily before entering her office.

She smiled. 'Glad you could make it,' she said, swinging the chair round.

Then she saw the knife and sucked in a lungful of air to scream, but the knife was in her before she could let out a sound.

And then her mouth was being prised open, but she couldn't do anything about it.

TWENTY-FIVE

Harry made sure Jessica was okay before he left home the next morning. The patrol car he'd organised was sitting outside, and the officers had explicit instructions not to take orders from anybody but Harry or his team members. If DI Walker turned up, then Harry was to know immediately. When Jessica left for the nursery, she was to be followed.

Harry wasn't sure if his new home in Murray-field was listed in the system yet. They might have the address of his old flat in Comely Bank, but it was empty save for a few bits of furniture. He called Mia, his former next-door neighbour, and warned her to be on the lookout and to call him if she needed him.

Then he drove down to Stockbridge to see Colin Presley.

Amy Foster was cautious at first, making sure it really was Harry at her door. She was relieved when she saw it wasn't three masked men there to finish the job.

'How's he doing?' Harry said, stepping into the warmth of the flat.

'Like all men – being a big baby.' She smiled as she spoke, leading him through to the living room.

'I heard that,' Presley said.

'I'm not saying anything that isn't true.'

'Ever seen that Stephen King movie *Misery?*' Presley asked Harry.

'I've read the book. Don't worry, I'm here to save you.'

'No, sir. Get out while you can. Save yourself.'

'You're a couple of jokers,' Amy said. 'Coffee, Harry?'

'I'm fine, thanks. My bladder isn't exactly at the wearing-a-nappy stage, but it is cold outside.' Harry looked at Presley. 'How are you feeling today?'

'Stiff as a board, blinding headache, I think my ribs have been snapped in two, but apart from that, I'm fine and thanks for asking.'

'He wouldn't let me take him to the Royal last night after we got home,' Amy said. 'I tried again, but he's stubborn.'

'You know the hospital isn't safe,' Presley countered. 'Those nutters could walk in and have another go.'

'We both need to be on the alert now, Colin,' said Harry. 'And I'll be talking to Walker sometime today. I don't want you talking to him.'

'Listen, sir, if I talked to him, it would only be to rip him a new arsehole.'

'Try and avoid that. I have a meeting with a friend of mine this morning who'll look into it.'

'I don't expect a bunch of grapes from Walker anytime soon. But I'd like to come to work this morning. If Amy will let me.'

'You know my feelings on this, Colin,' Amy said. 'I have to go to work, but you should stay here. If you came into Casualty like this, the doctor would tell you to take time off work.'

'I'm just a bit stiff, love. I'll get even stiffer sitting around all day. DCI McNeil will see to it that I don't break my back.'

'Glad you think so,' Harry said. 'No slackers on my team.'

'See? Told you.' Presley got up off the couch and oohed and aahed and then made his way past Harry, saying he would be back in five.

'I'm worried about him, Harry,' Amy said. 'That's twice he's been attacked.'

'I feel bad. It's me they're after and Colin got dragged into it.'

'It's not your fault,' she said.

'I wish they'd come after me again instead.'

'Don't you have a baby, though? You don't want any harm coming to your family. It wouldn't do to have them come to your house.'

'That's true.'

'Right, sir. We ready for the off?' Presley said, walking back into the room like an old man.

'You sure you're up for this?' Harry asked.

'No. But I'm going in anyway.'

'Right. Let's go.'

Amy put a hand on Harry's arm before they left. 'Call me if he faints or something.'

'I'm made of sterner stuff than that,' Presley complained as he opened the front door.

'Sure you are,' Amy agreed. 'That's why you get me to take the lid off a jar.'

Presley grinned at her. 'Have a good day at work,' he told her.

'You too.' She gave him a kiss.

'Right, Rocky, let's get you up to the station,' he said.

Harry and Presley took the lift down to the car.

'Are you really up for this, son?' Harry said.

'I am. I'm not going to let the bastards get to me.'

Harry nodded and they drove away.

TWENTY-SIX

'Andy, it's me, Frank. You slept in again?' Frank Miller left a voicemail then hung up, holding his phone in case Andy Watt had heard the phone and was about to call him back.

'No answer?' Jimmy Dunbar said.

'Nothing, sir.'

'Is this a habit of his?'

Miller disconnected the call. 'Not really. Once or twice, but he usually manages to make it to work.'

'Maybe he was out having a social few beers and got carried away,' Robbie Evans said. 'Happens to the best of us.'

Dunbar looked at him. 'Us older blokes can hold our drink.'

'Maybe I'll go down and give him a knock,' Miller said.

'That might be a good idea, son,' Dunbar said. 'But is there a possibility that he had a lie-in with his missus this morning? Or does he live alone?'

'No, he lives with one of our pathologists, Kate Murphy. She's away doing lectures right now. Maybe he got wired into a few tinnies and overslept.'

'Go down and check on him now,' Dunbar said.

'I will.'

Harry and Presley walked in, the latter walking like he was eighty.

'Morning, sir,' Miller said.

'Morning, people.' Harry looked around the incident room. 'Has anybody seen Lillian?'

'Christ, not another one missing,' Dunbar said.

'What do you mean?' Harry said.

Dunbar told him about Watt being MIA.

'Have you tried calling Kate Murphy?' Harry asked Miller.

'She's away doing some lectures.'

'That might explain it. He's probably overslept,' Harry said.

'I'm leaving right now to check on him.' Miller left.

The door to the incident room opened and Lillian O'Shea walked in. 'Sorry I'm late.'

'At least you're here now,' Harry said, feeling more relief than anger. 'Let's start digging into Tess Grogan's life. And that other pair from the church, Michaels and Dunn – I want a full background done on them.'

They sat down at their desks while Harry went into his office with Dunbar. 'I'm going to call a friend of mine, Tony Burns in Standards. I want to meet him outside of the station. And get onto uniform. I want to know if there was anything amiss at that demonstration with Clifford Dunn.'

Dunbar looked at him. 'Good. Calvin Stewart went over to Maggie Parks' daughter's flat last night. Her boyfriend, Ben Tasker, said she's been gone for days since they had an argument. There's been no sign of her. I think we should talk to Maggie later and let her know.'

'That's a good idea. Do you think Lizzie got upset about Paddy?' Harry asked.

'Not sure. But why wouldn't she just come through to see her mother?' Dunbar said.

'We can talk to her later. Maybe at the hospital,' Harry said, then he made the call to his friend.

TWENTY-SEVEN

'You wanted to see me, sir?' Lisa McDonald knocked on the open door to Calvin Stewart's office.

'I want to talk to you about something.'

'Is it about last night, sir?' Lisa asked.

'Don't be talking like that. Barclay, the deviant, will think we're seeing each other if he overhears you.'

'I don't think anybody would think such a thing.'

'No need to say it like that. A lot of younger women like an older bloke like me.'

'Really?'

Stewart shook his head. 'Where did I go wrong? Took you under my wing, and now all I get is bloody lip. Come in and sit down, but shut the door behind you.'

She did as she was asked. 'How did your date go? If you don't mind me asking.'

'Well, as a matter of fact I *do* mind. Nosy wee nebber.' Then he looked at her. 'Quite good, actually. I was on my best behaviour and we're seeing each other again at the weekend.'

'You're taking it slow, then?'

'I'm a gentleman, Lisa. Despite what you and your cronies think.'

'I'm not thinking anything.'

'Good. And I'll update you on next week's episode on Monday. Will Calvin Stewart make an impression on the new woman in his life? Or will he blow it by opening his mouth and watch it all come crashing down? You'll have to tune in to find out.'

'I'll mark it on my calendar.'

'Right, this is what I've been thinking about: the M8 killer.'

'I've never heard of him, sir.'

'It was a long time ago. I had a phone call from a source. It got me thinking about the M8 killer.'

'This isn't a recent case. Not in my time, anyway.'

'Indeed it's not. This happened about forty years ago. It went on for about five years. I was in uniform at the time. It was all over the papers. You know, back in the day when they reported the real news, not drivel about finding Lord Lucan in an old bomber on the moon.'

'Those were the days.'

'I'd like you to do some research on it. See what old files you can find and get back to me.'

'I can do that.'

'And Lisa?'

'Sir?'

'Keep this between us. For now.'

'Yes, sir.'

Lisa left the office and went back to her computer. Got the machine up and running.

She found articles on the internet pertaining to the killings. Five women brutally murdered over a five-year period in the early- to mid-eighties. Nobody was ever caught. One unique thing about the killer was that he cut off five fingers and left four behind in a bucket of blood. The fifth one was found shoved down the throat of the next victim. It had been frozen before being used in this way.

Lisa sat up straight. Tess Grogan was the first victim. But if history was repeating itself, there would be more.

TWENTY-EIGHT

Harry walked down the wet pavement towards the Starbucks that was on the corner of Hunter Square.

DCI Tony Burns was sitting at a table as far away from the door as possible, a coffee in front of him. He waved Harry over. There was another coffee on the table in front of a vacant chair.

'Black,' Burns said, nodding to the cup.

'Cheers.' Harry took it and added milk before sitting down. 'Thanks for seeing me, Tony.'

'No problem. I haven't seen you in a while.'

'Since the funeral.'

'I'm sorry. I meant to –'

'No need to apologise,' Harry interrupted. 'We all have our lives to live.'

'Aye. But that was a shocker, let me tell you.'

Burns shook his head and sipped his coffee. 'How's the bairn?'

'Grace is doing well. I have a housekeeper come in to help and Alex's sister lives in the house with me.' Harry looked at Burns. 'Just as family, nothing else.'

'I wouldn't have thought anything otherwise, my friend.' Burns put his cup down. 'You explained on the phone you wanted to know about some of your CID team.'

'I did. I'm working with Frank Miller, as I told you, and a couple of my CID team came with me.'

'You trust them?'

'I've known Lillian O'Shea for a while. I trust her. There's a new guy I'm not too sure of. Colin Presley. He seems genuine, and when we went to the flat in Dumbiedykes we both got attacked.'

'Could have been a smokescreen on his part,' Burns observed.

More people were coming into the coffee shop, but they seemed to be tourists.

'I did consider that,' Harry said, 'but then last night he got a kicking in his own flat. He thought there were two of them and called Ray Walker to call them off. It turned out there were three of them. Colin gave as good as he got but was overwhelmed by them. He booted one of them in the knee and thought he'd dislocated it, but there's been no admissions at the Royal for that, so maybe he didn't do as much damage as he thought. I did a quick search on Pierce and Dawson but couldn't access the Standards records.'

'I did a search on them. Lillian O'Shea has a clean record. Very capable officer. Colin Presley the same, although he's been in CID for just eighteen months.'

'You being in Standards means you can access the records.'

'I'm getting to him, Harry.' Burns sipped more coffee and shook his head. 'Ian Pierce. How he's still on the force is beyond me. But I wasn't the investigating officer on him, or else there might have been a different outcome.'

'What did he do?'

'He's had complaints for being heavy-handed with prisoners. He also had a complaint against him for fighting with another detective. Sexual misconduct complaints from a young female uniform. He said it was a party that got out of hand. They'd both been drinking.'

'A bit of a bad bastard, then?' Harry knew that

not every complaint would be listed in the ordinary files but that Standards had a lot more.

Burns nodded. 'He'll go no further. DS is pushing his limit. And Ricky Dawson is another one. Skating on thin ice, but his excuse was always that he was working undercover. He had a report of sexual misconduct made against him as well. It came down to "he said, she said". Then the woman dropped the allegation. She didn't want to pursue it, but we still gave the little bastard a roasting. He's been flying under the radar ever since.'

'Ray Walker?' Harry asked.

'He's clean.'

'Probably slipped under the radar like Dawson. Keeping his nose clean so he doesn't draw attention to himself.'

'You asked me on the phone about Stan Webster,' Burns said, 'the DCI you worked with in the cold case unit.'

'Yes. He murdered his friend's daughter twenty-odd years ago. And now he's serving life in Shotts.'

'He is, but there's a connection between him and the officers in CID.'

'He was their commanding officer at one point?'

'Nope. But his brother-in-law was – Detective Superintendent Roger Barton.'

'I read that he'd worked with them. Can you talk to Barton?'

Burns drank more coffee. Then shook his head. 'Not now. I did a year or so ago. We investigated him and recommended his termination. They gave him the opportunity to resign, and he did.'

'That would certainly give him a motive.'

'You mean he'd want to get back at you because you were in Standards and now you're the boss of his team? I would think so.'

'And he's friends with Ray Walker too, so he'd have his inside man to organise things,' Harry said.

'This is all circumstantial. Unless you catch one of them in the act.'

'Presley called Walker and told him to call his men off when he knew they were in his flat, and a couple of minutes later the two guys came out. Walker's up to his neck in it.'

'I wonder why he would risk his own career?' Burns said. 'It's not like you personally investigated him.'

'Maybe he's just pissed off at Standards in general and when I moved into his little world in Leith, I unbalanced him.' Harry drank some of his coffee.

'You really believe that, Harry? These are serious

complaints against them. They can't go about attacking officers and expecting to get away with it. And if Presley is sure he heard right, now there's a death threat thrown in for good measure.'

'It's a stretch right enough, Tony.'

'What about former members of your team?'

'There's Ronnie Vallance and Simon Gregg. Ronnie is built like a brick shithouse and Gregg is six-six. Both of them would stand out, and I can assure you, none of the attackers fit that description.'

'You want me to bring Pierce, Dawson and Walker in for questioning?' Burns asked.

'Not right now.'

'Christ, they sound like they're not going to stop until they kill you, Harry.'

'I think they're just trying to put the frighteners on me.'

'Good God, man, they got physical with you.'

'I know, but if they're going to make a move, I want them to do it to me on neutral ground. I don't want them to go into hiding.'

'You have Grace to think about. I hope they don't come to your home.'

'I don't think they'd be that stupid.' Harry hoped he sounded more convinced than he felt.

His phone rang. The mortuary, requesting his

presence. His stomach did cartwheels at the thought. It wasn't the sights in there, it was the smell, he kept telling people, but nobody listened. He was sure they all thought he was a useless fanny behind his back.

'Got to go,' he told Burns. 'Thanks for your help.' Then he called the station.

TWENTY-NINE

Frank Miller parked in the underground car park at Andy Watt's building and saw the man's Mondeo was still there. He got out of the car, walked to the lift, pressed the button and waited.

He knew Andy Watt liked a good drink. God knows they all liked a drink and were regulars in the pub after work, but Miller made sure he always made it to work the next morning. He couldn't understand why Watt had slept in. Usually the older DS made it to work on time.

The lift arrived and he stepped in, pushing the button for the second floor. He had known Watt for a long time, and the older man had taken him under his wing when he had first joined CID. Miller's girl-friend at the time, Carol Davidson, had joined at the same time and Watt had looked after them both. When Carol had died on duty, the older man had given Miller a shoulder to cry on.

Miller stepped out of the lift and made his way along to the flat. He knocked hard on the door and waited. Knocked again. No reply. He took out the key for the flat. The emergency key.

He unlocked the door and opened it. 'Andy!' he shouted. 'It's Frank! You awake?'

Still no reply. All the doors in the small hallway were closed. He put a light on and knocked on Watt's bedroom door. He knew which room it was because he'd helped Kate put Watt to bed one Christmas night when they were all four sheets to the wind.

No answer.

'I'm coming in, Andy. You'd better not be starkers.' Miller turned the handle and opened the door. He hoped he wasn't about to be blinded by the sight of a naked Watt.

Watt wasn't in the bed and it looked like it hadn't been slept in. Miller left the door open and walked towards the living room. He knew the kitchen and living room were open plan. Maybe the older detective was already up and making a coffee, sobering up.

'Andy, you in there?' Miller shouted. Once again,

no reply. He opened the door and walked in. The room was empty. There was no sign of a kettle being on, or toast having been in the toaster. No sign that anybody lived here.

Then a thought struck Miller, one he tried not to entertain, but it came unbidden into his head: what if Watt had met somebody last night and had spent the night at her place?

No. Watt knew Miller would boot him in the nut sack for cheating on Kate. It had to be something else. He took his phone out and called Watt's number again. Straight to voicemail.

'Andy, give me a call when you get this.' He hung up and checked the other bedroom and bathroom on his way out, finding nothing.

He was locking the front door when a man approached him.

'Hello?' The man stood well back in case Miller was about to pull out an axe and chase him down the hallway with it.

Miller turned to him, sizing him up in his usual way: *what sort of force will I need to use to take this bastard down?*

'Can I help you?' he asked, the answer being, *not much force at all.* The man was smaller, thinner and wore glasses. Which meant absolutely zero when push came to shove, but Miller was already wired up like he'd been drinking hooligan juice for breakfast.

'Are you a friend of Andy's?' the man asked.

'Why are you asking?'

Now the man wasn't sure, and looked like he'd just caught an upscale housebreaker, one who wore a suit as a disguise.

'You're locking his door.'

Miller straightened up and brought out his warrant card. 'DI Miller. I'm a friend and colleague of Andy's.'

There was relief on the man's face as he took a step forward, not quite getting into Miller's personal space but certainly approaching the border.

'Andy was knocked down in a hit-and-run last night. He's in the Royal.'

'Christ, what time was this?'

'Eight thirty, nine, something like that. My wife and I had just got into our car and we were driving round the side of the building when we saw Andy being thrown through the air, and then the car stopped and reversed. Like...like the driver was going to reverse over him. Then he must have seen us coming. He put his lights out, presumably so we couldn't see his number plate, and took off. My wife and I helped Andy as best we could, but he was mostly out of it. We called an ambulance and they came and took him away. A uniformed officer came and took a statement.'

'What kind of car was it?'

'A small red one. Volkswagen. The badge on the back was hard to miss.'

'What's your name, sir?'

'Brian Cannon. I live next door to Andy and Kate. But here, take this.' He brought a phone out of his pocket. 'It's Andy's, I think. It was lying close to him when we went to help.'

'Okay, thanks.' Miller rushed to the stairway door, taking his phone out.

THIRTY

Harry stood in the mortuary with Jimmy Dunbar and Colin Presley at either side. Robbie Evans stood next to Presley. Harry was trying not to gag, but there was nothing he could do about the sweat lining his brow.

'You okay there, mucker?' Dunbar said.

'I'm fine. I don't mind this place, but it's the fucking smell.' Harry had said it a million times and still there was a look of scepticism on his colleagues' faces.

'Gentlemen, I'd like to proceed,' Professor Archibald Baxter said. He'd worked at the mortuary for a few months now, and the others were on the fence as to whether he was likable or a dick. Harry was on the dick side, having taken an instant dislike to the man for some reason, but the others were neutral so far.

The woman lay on one of the three stainless-steel tables, like she was in for a routine operation instead of having experts probe her and weigh her organs.

Baxter had Jake Dagger by his side, along with Gus Weaver, one of the mortuary assistants. Weaver stepped forward and, like a magician's assistant minus the glittery leotard, whipped the cover back.

Harry noticed Tess Grogan's hair had been washed and looked nothing like it had when her body was found. In a while, the two remaining detectives would witness a cut being made on the back of her head and the skin pulled forward, so the assistant could cut the skull open to remove her brain to be weighed. Her face still had the waxy appearance she'd had when she had been found dead.

'She was stabbed,' Baxter said, 'but I'd say her throat being cut was the cause of death. Dr Dagger and I will be performing the PM shortly, but I can see that whoever did this knew what they were doing. She was expertly ensanguined. There's a puncture wound in her neck. I'm assuming whoever killed her let the blood drain out of her neck into a receptacle below. That's my opinion.'

For some reason, Harry thought back to the last

time he and Jessica had shared a bottle of red wine, and he swore to himself there and then that he would only drink white from now on. No, fuck that. Beer only. Jessica didn't drink much at all now because of helping with Grace, but he himself wouldn't be tempted by the grapes ever again.

'I'm assuming the killer wouldn't kill somebody this way in his living room,' Dunbar said.

Baxter looked at him. 'It depends how comfy he would be having a living room with blood spatter as décor.'

'I've had some dodgy wallpaper in my time, but that was all the wife. None of it was red, though.'

'Whoever drained her blood would have done it in a place that was easy to clean up, or at the very least a place that he wouldn't have been bothered about leaving in a mess. I would guess a warehouse, or even a lock-up. A garage even, but it would have to be one that nobody could easily see into.'

'Makes sense,' Harry said. He'd already put the chest rub under his nose, but the damn stuff didn't seem to be working worth a sook.

'Would it have taken any specialist equipment?' Evans asked.

'Not if you know what you're doing. It would be a lot easier if you had a pump but not impossible.'

'Thanks, Doc,' Harry said. 'If you could send over the report when you're done...'

'Absolutely.'

Harry's phone buzzed in his pocket. He took it out and looked at the screen. Frank Miller.

He walked out of the PM suite.

'Frank. How's things with Andy?'

'Christ, Harry, it's bad news. I think somebody tried to murder him last night.'

'Where are you right now?'

'I'm going to the Royal.'

'Swing by the mortuary. You can pick me and Jimmy up.'

'On my way.'

THIRTY-ONE

Lisa McDonald rubbed her eyes as she popped some coins into the coffee machine in the corridor. Then she yawned and covered her mouth with her hand.

'Too many late nights?' Lynn McKenzie said, coming up behind her. Lisa jumped a little.

'Oh, sorry, ma'am. Didn't see you there. And sort of. Henry is going through a bad spell again, with the nightmares.'

'I was there when we got him back. I fully understand. I can't imagine what he must have felt like, being away from his family for a year, and with him being autistic. I hope his therapist is good.'

The coffee cup came out of the machine. 'He is. You want one?' Lisa asked, grabbing the cup.

'No, I'm fine, thanks.'

Lisa drank the hot liquid and burnt her top lip a bit.

'DSup Stewart said he has you looking through an old case. The M8 killer,' Lynn said.

'Yes, I just got started a little while ago, and it's fascinating. Especially since they didn't get him.'

'It was a long time ago. Before my time too, of course, but I've read up on cold cases. That was a particularly brutal one.'

'It was. And there's somebody copying him. I wonder why now?'

'Why don't you think it's the original killer?'

They moved slightly to let a uniform go by.

'Age,' Lisa said. 'It was forty years ago, and they had a witness who put the man in his late thirties to early forties. They weren't a hundred per cent sure it was him, of course, but what if it was? Let's say he was forty at the time; now, forty years later, he'd be eighty. Tess Grogan's injuries were inflicted by a much younger man. Had to be. To overpower her and then kill her and drain her blood.'

'I agree. But what if the witness did in fact see the wrong man? What if the original killer was only twenty? That would make him sixty now. He might be older but still capable.'

'Which still begs the question, why now?' Lisa said.

'There had to be some trigger. Or else we're looking at a copycat. And we have to ask, why did he choose to start now?'

'Who knows with some of these psychos. But I'm reading up on the previous murders, seeing if anything jumps out that might point us in a new direction today.'

'You're doing good work, Lisa. I'm proud to have you on my team.'

'Thank you, ma'am.'

Lynn smiled and walked in the opposite direction from the incident room. Lisa went back to her desk and saw Stewart look at her as she sat down. She knew he would be out later to ask for a progress update and she wanted to tell him that she was wading her way through it.

She read one of the articles. A second body had been found.

The M8 killer strikes again!

A body was found yesterday, dumped behind some bins at the small Harthill Services area. The victim has been identified as twenty-year-old Shona

Lamb from the Muirhouse area of Edinburgh. Her throat had been slashed and there was no blood at the scene. She was found just yards from where the first victim was found. Twenty-three-year-old Denise Drever from the Gorbals area of Glasgow was found partially clothed behind the bins at the services area almost a year ago. Police are speculating that the killer may be a commercial driver who has used the services before and knows his way around them. One witness gave police a description of a man she saw near the bins, but so far nobody else has come forward.

Lamb's family are devastated and say their daughter had set off to hitchhike down to London, further fuelling the idea of the killer being a commercial driver. So far, no leads have panned out, leaving the police clueless.

One thing that stood out for Lisa was that the women's fingers had been cut off on one hand but the papers didn't report that one of Denise Drever's fingers had been found in Shona Lamb's mouth, stuck right down in her throat. Lisa had read that fact in the police report, and they had obviously kept it out of the papers so that if the real killer was caught, only he would know. If there was some nutter with a false confession, they would have to know this fact.

Lisa knew that there was a possibility that

another victim was going to be found, and that victim could have Tess Grogan's missing finger in her mouth.

She stared at the screen, at the black-and-white photo of the Harthill Services with police officers searching the grass area behind it. They were wearing the old-style police uniform, which she preferred.

She sipped more of the hot drink, the taste of which hadn't changed for the better on its journey from the machine to her desk.

'I would have put the kettle on,' Stewart said, hovering over her shoulder. She jumped a little for the second time.

'Didn't see you standing there, sir,' she said.

'I'm hardly a skinny malinky, Lisa. I'm halfway between beanpole and fat bastard.'

'I was busy with this assignment,' she explained. 'It makes for fascinating reading.'

'Aye, especially since we have the real thing going on just now. I have one of the team combing through CCTV to see if we can get a trail on the pair of bastards who threw the blood. If we can get hold of them, we're one step closer to identifying the killer.'

'Don't you believe that Clifford Dunn knows them?' she asked.

'Of course I do,' Stewart said. 'Horrible bastard. Unfortunately, there's nothing on him. Apart from getting arrested at some protest or other. He probably had a bee in his bonnet about the price of doughnuts or something.'

'I don't trust him.'

'Well, keep at it and see if anything jumps out at you.'

'One thing does: the two women who were killed were in their twenties. Tess Grogan was in her late thirties.'

'She was one of those women who dyes her hair different colours. I mean all at the same time. I've seen her photo online in the papers. She was mouthy as well. Not to speak ill of the dead, but alive, she was a thorn in a lot of people's sides. Maybe she had some enemies that her boyfriend didn't know about.'

'She dealt with homeless people, and a lot of them have mental health issues, but her murder was a bit sophisticated for a homeless person. Like, where would they have drained her blood? Maybe it was somebody she worked with?'

'Could be. Keep at it, Lisa. Then send those links

through to Edinburgh. If Jimmy and Evans think they're going to be pissing up against a wall while we're here busting our ging-gangs, they can think again.'

He walked back to his office and Lisa felt a pang of something inside. She hated to admit it, but she was going to miss Stewart.

THIRTY-TWO

The Royal Infirmary at Little France in Edinburgh was buzzing with activity when Miller, Harry and Dunbar walked in.

'I called ahead,' Miller said. 'I ordered a uniform patrol to guard Andy's room. They wouldn't tell me much over the phone.'

'Well, they'll tell us now to our face.' Harry felt a jolt of adrenaline rush through him. Miller had told him what Watt's neighbour had seen: the car deliberately knocking Watt down and then reversing. If it hadn't been for the neighbour, Harry was certain that Watt would be dead.

But who would want to kill him?

They took the lift upstairs to the ward Watt was in and saw the uniform standing outside a room. They approached and showed the uniform their warrant cards. A nurse was in the room with Watt.

'How's he doing?' Harry asked.

They all looked at their colleague lying in the bed with tubes going into him.

'He's sedated for the moment. I'll have the doctor come in and speak to you,' she said, leaving the room.

They stood in silence for a moment.

'What a bastard,' Harry said. 'Using a car to injure somebody instead of being a man and getting up close. Give the man a fighting chance.'

'I know. I didn't think Andy had any enemies,' Miller said.

There was a knock on the door and a woman wearing a white coat walked in. 'I'm Dr Simpson,' she said. She was a short woman with dark hair. Mediterranean roots, Harry figured.

'What's the prognosis?' Miller asked.

'He's sedated just now, so he's not in pain. When he was brought in last night, he was in a bad way, but it could have been a lot worse. He has a broken femur, a broken wrist, two fractured ribs and a dislocated shoulder. If it had hit him square on, he probably would have died. As it is, there was no internal bleeding, and no head injury. From the shoulder dislocation, I would say that's what he landed on. Very lucky.'

'How long will it be before he can speak to us?' Dunbar asked.

'A little while, I'm afraid. We're keeping him sedated for the time being. Maybe tomorrow. We'll see what his pain levels are before we decide.'

'He's going to be okay, though?' Miller asked her.

'He should be. But he won't be back to work for a while. He'll have to get physiotherapy first, of course, but in time he'll get back to as normal as possible after such an accident.'

'He could have long-lasting effects from this?'

'We can't speculate. Everybody is different.' She looked at them. 'Does he have any family who might want to come in?'

'He has two daughters,' Miller answered. 'I'll contact them.'

'You might tell them not to come in at the moment. Give him time to rest.'

'Will do.'

They watched the doctor leave the room and shut the door gently behind her.

'We'll have to contact Kate,' Miller said.

'Do you know where she is just now?' Dunbar said.

'Inverness. It will be a few hours before she can get down here.'

'Can you call her now?'

'Yes.' Miller took his phone out, then remembered the phone the neighbour had given him. 'This is Andy's,' he told Harry. 'The neighbour found it in the dark after Andy had been taken away.'

'Is it locked?'

'It is. Maybe Kate will know what his password is.'

Miller made the call and told Kate what had happened.

'She's a basket case,' he reported back to Harry and Dunbar once he hung up. 'But I asked her what the password is for his phone and she said it's his year of birth.' Miller entered the four digits into Watt's phone and it sprang to life.

'I hope he hasn't been taking pictures of himself to send to Kate while she's away,' Harry said. 'You know, just to tide her over.'

'I don't think there's any danger of that,' Miller said. He opened the messages page and scrolled to the latest texts.

'Jesus Christ,' he said after reading them. 'He got a text from Maggie Parks' daughter, Lizzie. She said she was in trouble and needed to see him. She thought she was being followed and somebody wanted to hurt her.'

'We need to talk to her,' Dunbar said. 'What if she went down there to meet him and somebody ran Andy down?'

'I wonder if she saw it?' Miller said.

'We need to find out where she is now.' Harry nodded to the phone. 'Call her.'

Miller hit Lizzie's number and it rang but then went to voicemail. 'Nothing,' he said, hanging up.

'Calvin Stewart went with Lisa McDonald to speak to Lizzie, but she wasn't there. Her boyfriend said she left a few days ago. Now we know where she came to. But we need to find out who she's afraid of,' Dunbar said.

'I'm starting to wonder if there's somebody after not just her but Paddy as well. Why would somebody target them both?'

THIRTY-THREE

By the time the call came in, Harry and the others were finished at the infirmary. The traffic was crawling down Broughton Street, impeded by the police vehicles sitting outside of the outreach centre.

Harry had been driving a bit fast, angered by the fact that one of their friends had been attacked.

'Do you think it could have been the same crowd who attacked you and young Presley?' Miller said.

'Not with that text from Lizzie.'

'They're very resourceful, from what we've seen. They knew where Presley lived.'

'I need to go to the flat in Comely Bank,' said Harry. 'For all I know they went there and they don't know I live in Murrayfield now. I didn't update my address in the system.'

'I'll come along with you, Harry,' Miller said. 'I've been looking over my shoulder ever since that laddie was attacked in his flat.'

'And now Andy. If it's two different entities, then we could be well fucked. Don't trust anybody.'

They got out of the car and the chill air grabbed them by the shorts. The sky was the colour of a regrettable morning-after.

There were forensics officers going in and out. Harry spotted the mortuary van further down the hill, lurking about like a bad smell.

They entered the shop, nodding to the uniform standing guard. Inside, the rest of the team were there. And Jake Dagger.

'All hands on deck,' Evans said to Dunbar.

'A bad one?'

'To say the least. One of the outreach workers came in and found the manager dead in her office. And it's connected to Tess Grogan.'

'How can you be so sure?'

'Come and have a look,' Dagger said, jumping in.

Presley and Lillian O'Shea were talking to other members of staff who had appeared for work and were in a state of shock. Miller stayed with them.

Dagger led them through to the back. He stopped at the doorway of the office.

A forensics officer was just finishing up taking photos. 'She's all yours,' he said, leaving.

Miller stood looking in at the victim. 'That's April Donegan,' he said. 'We just interviewed her.'

'Baxter and I hadn't started the PM yet when this call came in,' Dagger explained.

Harry looked at the young woman. There were stab wounds in her chest and her throat had been cut. Similar to Tess Grogan's injuries.

'You said this is connected,' Harry reminded Dunbar.

'Come over here, Harry,' Dagger said, moving forward. He gently prised open April's mouth and Harry could clearly see the finger inside.

'Pound to a penny it's Tess Grogan's,' Harry said.

'I'll have forensics print it after I remove it,' Dagger said.

'Do you have a rough time of death?'

'I'd say no more than twelve hours.'

'Sometime yesterday evening.' Harry nodded his head. 'Thanks, Jake,' he said and they turned away from the room.

'I wonder why this MO was different?' Harry said to Dunbar.

'It's strange. Maybe he was disturbed?'

'Could be.'

They walked back to the main shop area.

'I need to go and find Maggie with Frank,' Harry said.

'I'll look after the shop,' Dunbar replied. 'If you'll pardon the pun.'

'I want to track down Tom Michaels. See if he's in the church. This is the second death connected to this outreach place.'

'After she's been taken to the mortuary, I'll get the team back to the station.'

'See you in a wee while.'

Harry left with Miller and they drove the short distance to the church at Bellevue.

Harry called Maggie's number.

'Hello?'

'Maggie, it's Harry. Are you at home?'

'No, I'm at the hospital. Is everything okay?'

'No, I have some bad news. Andy was knocked down last night. He survived, but he's in a bad way. A witness thinks it was deliberate.'

'Oh my God. Why would anybody want to do that?'

'Sometimes it's because of the job. But listen, a couple of my colleagues from Glasgow visited

Lizzie's flat and there's no sign of her. Ben said she left days ago.'

'*What? I don't believe it. Why would she leave and not tell me?*'

'I was hoping you could tell me. You see, Maggie, it seems that Lizzie was through here last night. She sent a text to Andy asking to meet him at his flat. She said she was in danger, and then when he got home, he was run over.'

'*Oh God, Harry, you think somebody's trying to hurt my Lizzie?*'

'I'm not saying that, but if she was in danger from somebody, maybe he followed her there and hit Andy. I really don't know what's going on.'

'*Do you think...somebody could have hurt Paddy? Like, they pushed him down the steps?*'

'I'm not ruling anything out at this point, Maggie. So be very careful when you come home. Make sure you're not being followed.'

'*I will, but I'm spending most of my time here. I only go home for a short time to freshen up. Have a shower and change. Then I come back here. I sleep in the chair all night in Paddy's room. I don't want to leave his side, Harry.*'

She started crying and Harry waited until she had finished before speaking again.

'If you see or hear from Lizzie, I need to talk to her. Please get her to give me a call.'

'I will. Thanks, Harry.'

She disconnected the call, and then Harry and Miller went into the church.

THIRTY-FOUR

'She's pretty cut up,' Harry said as they walked into the main part of the church.

Miller nodded. 'I remember when all they did was slag each other off, but then they found a connection, with Maggie being a widow and Paddy being a divorcé. They were right for each other, and one of the cases we worked on threw them together. I just hope to Christ he pulls through.'

Tom Michaels came out of his office and was about to turn away when he spotted the two detectives skulking about like they were there to pinch the silverware.

'Inspector McNeil,' he said, his face like a pound of tripe. 'I wish I could say it's good to see you again, but I'd be lying. You seem to be the harbinger of bad news, and I doubt you're here to tell me you've caught the man who killed Tess. So what's happened now?'

'I might have been here to escort you down to the mortuary to identify Ms Grogan.' *Smartarse.*

'And are you?'

'No.'

'And there we go.'

'We're here to ask you about April Donegan,' Miller said.

'Who?'

'The manager of the outreach centre. You know, the one up the hill where Ms Grogan worked?' Miller said it in a tone that conveyed he was beyond pissing about now.

'What about her?' Michaels answered.

'She's dead,' Harry answered. 'She was murdered in the shop last night.'

'April? Murdered? Jesus Christ.' Michaels looked around him for a moment as if he'd just realised where he was. 'When did this happen?'

'Where were you yesterday evening?' Miller asked, ignoring the question.

'I was at the demonstration in St Andrew Square.'

'Can you prove that?'

'Just take a look at our website. I asked our followers to post photos. There are dozens of them. Plus I had a selfie taken with one of your uniformed officers. Very nice man. I was with Clifford, and afterwards we went back to his house for a couple of drinks so we could plan our next strategy. Tess wouldn't have expected anything less, so we have to keep the momentum going. Otherwise it's all been for nothing. We have to keep her legacy going.'

'Somebody is targeting people who work for the outreach centre. Can you think of anybody who sticks out?' Harry asked. 'Somebody who's been violent in the past?'

Michaels smiled a sad smile. 'In this day and age, people try to convey the image that they care about those less fortunate than themselves, but the stark reality is, they turn a blind eye. Most people do, but not the church. We have programmes where we raise money to help those less fortunate, whether it be homeless people or the elderly. Those people who find themselves in hard times, like somebody who has lost the sole breadwinner in the family and they're struggling. We have our kitchen open every day for those who need a hot meal and somewhere warm to spend their days. So they can save on their own heating bills. We do a lot for the community,

Inspector, despite people thinking we're some kind of cult.'

'That's very admirable,' Miller said, 'but you must come across people who aren't too happy.'

'Absolutely. There are some homeless people who complain about the food, or the service. We get a lot of food donated by stores. It's out of date by a day or two, but we know the maker of the food adds a good few days or even weeks before the food spoils, so it's safe to eat. And most of the recipients are grateful for what they get.'

'Just angry homeless, then?' Harry said after Michaels had finished his spiel.

'Pretty much.' Michaels took his phone out and opened the photos to show the policemen the events of the night before, including the selfie taken with a uniform. He kept his finger on the photo until the details slid up from the bottom. It showed the date and time for the previous evening.

Harry nodded. 'What about afterwards? You said you were at Dunn's house? How long were you there for?'

'I can't be sure, but it was late. We had a few drinks, as I said, then we were batting some ideas about. It had to be after midnight when I got home.'

'Anybody vouch for that?' Miller asked.

'No. My girlfriend's dead, remember?'

The three men stood around in silence for a moment, before Harry spoke. 'Thank you for your time, Mr Michaels.'

'Reverend Michaels.'

Harry looked at him for a second but refused to be corrected.

They walked out of the church.

'Let's go and see what Clifford Dunn has to say for himself,' said Harry.

They drove back up the road. There was still an abundance of police vehicles by the outreach centre. Harry turned into the lane opposite the shop. Albany Street Lane, Clifford Dunn's address.

'Working as a uni professor really paid off,' Harry said. 'I wonder how long he's had this place? They go for a fortune nowadays.'

'Probably had it for a while. I don't think a teacher could afford this place,' Miller said.

'I don't know much about him, Frank. Maybe he had family money.'

Harry walked towards the door of the detached house, a former carriage house for the buildings on Albany Street. He knocked hard on the door. No answer.

There was a little car park next door, with a

barrier blocking the entrance. Nobody was around. Same on the other side. There were no windows on either end looking into the car parks. The house was completed isolated, like it was an island, affording perfect privacy.

Harry took out a business card and wrote on the back, *Call me*. Then shoved it through the letter box.

Then he and Miller got back into the car and drove round the corner to head back to Broughton Street.

THIRTY-FIVE

The detectives were in the incident room in the High Street, with Lillian putting up photos on the whiteboard.

Harry stood at the front and looked at his watch. Mid-afternoon already. April Donegan's body had been taken away to the mortuary where a post-mortem would be performed after Tess Grogan's.

'If I can have your attention...' Harry called, and all heads turned to him. 'First of all, DS Andy Watt was hurt last night in a hit-and-run, as you all know by now. He's comfortable in the Royal, where he'll be for the foreseeable future. He'd received a text from Lizzie saying she was in trouble and wanted to meet him. But there's no sign of her. Did she witness him being knocked

down and then run off? We don't know. We can't
contact her and a trace on her phone shows that it's
switched off.

'Now we have a second murder, of April Donegan, who worked with Tess Grogan. Were they both
targeted for some reason that we don't know about
yet? Let's dig into their pasts. Find a next of kin for
April. Let's get to it.'

Harry walked over to Presley's desk. 'How are
you feeling?'

'Like a hungry horse went for breakfast, couldn't
find anything to eat, then decided to kick the crap
out of me.'

'You haven't heard anything from anybody?'

'No, sir. I called Amy and she's at work,
surrounded by a lot of people.'

'What hospital does she work in?'

'The Western.'

'What part?'

'The head injuries unit where Paddy Gibb is.'

'Right. Let me know if somebody calls you and
makes threats.'

'Should I be expecting anybody in particular?'
Presley asked.

'I was thinking Ray Walker. But a friend of mine
is going to have a talk with him.'

'I'd like to have a talk with him, if you know what I mean.'

'I used to be in Standards, remember. My friend is in Standards,' Harry said. He saw Presley's face was turning red. 'But yes, I know what you mean. I'd like a private chat with him too.'

'However, I value my job more than I fancy skelping Walker,' Presley said. 'Not that I'm in a physical position to skelp him, you understand, sir.'

'I know.'

Harry went into his office. He needed to talk to Jessica, just to hear her voice, to know that she and Grace were safe. He couldn't take it if anything happened to them after losing Alex.

'Jess? It's me, Harry.'

'If it weren't for the fact I know your voice and your name came up on the caller ID, I wouldn't have known it was you,' she said, laughing.

'That was a wee bit unnecessary,' he conceded.

'What's up?' she asked, concern showing in her voice now.

'It's been a hell of a day. I just wanted to check in and see that you're alright.'

'We're fine. Everybody at the nursery is fine. Don't worry.'

'Okay. I was thinking of having dinner with Jimmy and Robbie if you fancy coming along.'

'And leave the wee one? I mean, not by herself, obviously, but with a babysitter? No, thanks, Harry. We're going to snuggle on the couch before her bathtime, then I'm going to watch a chick flick in my room. We'll be settled by the time you get in.'

'Thanks, Jess. And I meant it when I said when you want to go out or have a break or a night off, just shout and I'll be able to look after Grace.'

'I know you did. I'll be sure to let you know.'

They said their goodbyes, and Harry sat back, feeling the start of a headache coming on. He felt guilty about Jess not going out. She was a young woman, about to celebrate her thirtieth birthday, and didn't have a boyfriend. She'd been in a long-term relationship, but had found out that her fiancé had cheated on her by sleeping with one of the bridesmaids. Then she'd found out her fiancé had married the other woman instead.

Harry would have to be ready when Jessica felt like going out again. Meantime, they shared a roof and Harry kept the Comely Bank flat empty, in case Jessica ever wanted her own space. So far, she had shown no sign of wanting to move out. Maybe it was something to do with the fact he had pissed off to the southernmost point of Scotland, bought a house and lived in it for three months. Jessica wasn't going to leave him alone with his daughter for a while yet.

Especially since Police Scotland were still making him go to the force therapist once a week. Just to make sure he wasn't going to crack and could still lead a team.

He felt bad about going south for a while. His team had gone on to different things, at the insistence of the high heid yins, but he'd made contact with each of them when he'd got back and had a talk, telling them they should get anything they wanted off their chest, to let him have it and he'd take it on the chin. But every one of his old team had told him they missed him and it had been a pleasure working with him.

The only one he'd had the pleasure of working with since was Lillian O'Shea. He had got on well with her and had welcomed her aboard his new team. Lillian had worked with Alex, and despite a rocky start, they had warmed to each other.

Being here at the High Street station, working with Frank Miller, felt like being home. The younger DI had been at Harry's side when he had buried Alex and had supported him at every step.

Harry hadn't liked Leith CID. If somebody had

asked him to describe them, the word he would have used was *feral*. Walker was lazy, Pierce was incompetent and Dawson was...well, he had only seen Dawson a couple of times. But Harry didn't like him and the feeling had been mutual.

THIRTY-SIX

DCI Tony Burns was what his wife liked to call a nervous old fanny when he was being driven around.

'Watch that lassie waiting to cross the road,' he pointed out to DS Craig Benini, or Banana as the others referred to him. The young sergeant had told him his father was Italian but Burns thought this was just a line he spun to the women in the dodgy hovels he frequented, places that were called nightclubs but were only one step above brothels.

'That lassie standing at the pedestrian crossing?' Benini said.

'No need to be pedantic,' Burns said.

'Just being observant, sir.'

'Stop using words you don't know the meaning of.'

'I know what a lassie is.'

'And there you go, compounding it by being a smartarse.' Burns looked at the younger sergeant. 'I'm surprised you've stuck this out.'

'Being in Standards?'

'No, renting yourself out as a part-time clown at the weekend. Of course Standards. Being a young guy, then knowing one day you'll be back amongst the men and women you had to investigate. That takes balls.'

'I was a military policeman. I investigated soldiers. I didn't choose that regiment because I wanted to make friends.'

'You're certainly going to have fuck-all friends by the time this stint is over.'

'I want to go as high as I can in the police,' Benini replied.

'I'm heading for retirement in a few years. I'll work out my time in this department, then shuffle off to live in Spain or something.'

'I can't see you wearing a sombrero, boss.'

'Me neither, but I can see myself sitting by my pool drinking lager. Besides, the wife suggested it.'

'Then you should do it.'

Benini turned into Albert Street, off Easter Road, and swung a right into Dickson Street. He pulled into a disabled bay and they both got out into an air that would shave the curlies off a badger.

'Fucking Spain can't come quick enough,' Burns said.

'You would miss this December cold,' Benini said, shivering as they walked to the tenement's front door.

'Aye, so I fucking would. My wife thinks it's a heatwave if she doesn't have to wear fur-lined knickers.'

An old woman came out of the stairway and looked at them as if they were bogus gasmen, before scurrying away.

'He's on the first floor,' Benini said, walking ahead of Burns.

'I know he is. I'm the one who told *you* that.'

'Did you? I thought it was Kelso.'

'Kelso couldn't pass on a cold never mind information.'

'I always thought he was a good lad.'

'*Lad* is pushing it a bit. He's older than me.'

'Aye, that's ancient right enough,' Benini said, starting up the stairs.

'Cheeky bastard. You might have spoken like that in the army, son, but this is the real polis now.'

'If I wasn't so thick-skinned, I might have taken offence at that.'

'You can take anything you bloody well want,' Burns said to Benini's back as the younger man moved quickly up the stairs. He was waiting by the time Burns got up. The older detective was starting to get out of breath.

'What kept you?' Benini asked. 'I was about to call in a search party. Did you stop at base camp before coming up?'

'Again with being a lippy bastard. It's this heavy overcoat. I'm carrying too much weight.'

'Well, at least you're here now.'

'Shut up and get the bloody door chapped.'

Benini stepped forward to the red door and banged on it with his fist. 'Ray? It's DS Benini and DCI Burns. We need to have a talk with you.'

'You said you left a message on his voicemail?' Burns said.

'I did. The station said there's nobody in at CID. Sickness, secondment, you name it.'

'What the hell is going on down there in that bloody station? I'll need to have a talk with the super down there and see what's happening. It's like he's running a bloody circus.' Burns tutted and stepped forward, kicking the bottom of the door a few times. 'Walker! Get the door open! We need to talk.'

'Is everything alright?' a woman said from behind them. Burns jumped a bit while Benini merely turned.

'We're police. We need to speak with Mr Walker,' Burns said, irritated now.

'I have a spare key.'

'Okay, can you get it? We want to make sure he's okay.'

'Hold on.' The neighbour left her front door ajar as she retreated inside. Clearly, *she* didn't think they were bogus gasmen. She came back, holding out the key on its keychain like it was some sort of prize.

'Thank you,' Burns said, grabbing it before Benini's outstretched hand could snag it.

The woman went back into her flat and closed the door.

'Senior officer on scene here, son,' Burns said, stepping forward with the key and inserting it into the lock.

'I'll remember that if he's gone off his heid and rushes at you with an axe.'

'No need to get your boxers tangled there. I was just unlocking the door for you. Now get your arse inside.' Burns pushed open the door and stepped back.

'Dearie me. What's it come to when a younger officer has to lead the way?'

'It's called cannon fodder. Now less whining and more walking.' Burns stuck behind Benini as the younger officer turned left into the lobby, which was short.

'Walker! It's DCI Burns! You in here? If so, make yourself known.' Burns shoved Benini further along the lobby.

'Sake, boss. Give me a chance to search the rooms.'

There was a door on each side and one straight ahead. The one ahead opened into a linen closet. The left-hand door was slightly ajar and they both recognised the smell coming from it.

'Ray? You in there, son? It's Tony Burns. We're here to check you're okay.' Which was stretching the truth just a little bit – after they checked he was okay, they had planned to haul his arse up to the station. Burns stepped to one side, indicating with a sideways nod of his head for Benini to go in.

'What if he's killed somebody and he's waiting with a hammer behind the door?' Benini whispered.

'What are you whispering for? When I shouted

his name, that pretty much threw stealth out the fucking window.' Burns pushed hard on the living room door and shoved the younger man into the room under the guise of guiding him.

Now that Benini had been committed to charging in, he moved fast. A figure was sitting on the settee, head flopped to one side. Benini ignored it for a second, checking behind the door and in the little kitchen area that was part of the living room.

When Burns didn't hear any yelling or screaming, he entered the room and looked down at Ray Walker sitting dead on the settee. His eyes were drawn to the bottle of whisky and two not-quite-empty glasses on the coffee table in front of him.

The smell was rank and both officers took out their tubs of chest rub and put some of the gel under their noses.

'Right, I'll call it in,' Burns said. 'Make sure the rest of the flat is clear.'

THIRTY-SEVEN

Dan Foley and Mike Black stood at the kitchen doors at the back of the hotel, the smells of the cooking wafting past them. They were both smoking a cigarette and stepped aside as a driver pulled boxes from his truck in the lane and nodded to them as he walked past.

'What are you going to be doing for Christmas?' Black asked, flicking ash off his cigarette. He dug his free hand deeper into his uniform trouser pocket.

'Why? You asking me round to spend time with you and your ma?'

'First of all, I don't live with my ma anymore.'

Foley took a drag on his own cigarette and tilted his head back to blow the smoke upwards. 'Don't even fucking tell me you moved back in with that hoor?'

'She's not a hoor.'

Foley looked at his friend. 'You told me you met her in a singles' club. You slept with her on the first night. Did you think you were the chosen one?'

'She told me she didn't do that with every guy she met.'

'Good God, Mike, just how naive are you?' Foley shook his head. 'Are you really interested in what I'm doing for Christmas, or was that just a segue into telling me that you have a dose of chlamydia in your future?'

'Don't be like that. Women are hardly beating a path to my door.'

'You shouldn't just settle, though, mate. There's somebody out there for everybody. Even a fat bastard like me.' Foley took another drag and leaned out of the doorway into the cold air. He saw two uniformed police officers walking up the lane towards them, their hi-vis jackets like beacons.

'Fuck. I wonder what they want?' Foley said.

'Funny you should ask that,' said a voice from behind them.

They both turned round.

'I'm polis,' said Calvin Stewart. 'Now, I know

what you're thinking, boys: there's only one of him and two of us. He's older and would probably go down quickly if we rushed him. But let me quell that little scenario. You're outnumbered. I might be old, but I can assure you, I'll kick the shite out of both of you, and in the process, one of you will be having a transgender operation the quick way. If you want to call my bluff, please do. I'll take great pleasure in smacking the fucking shite out of both of you.'

Foley took a step forward, getting right up to Stewart, just as Lisa McDonald entered into the hallway from the lane. She reached behind Mike Black and took hold of his arm as Stewart snatched the cigarette from Foley, rammed him against the wall with his free hand and pinned him there, holding the cigarette millimetres from his eyeball.

'Well, that was a fucking mistake, son. I'll write in my report that you tried to assault me, and in the melee that followed, somehow the cigarette got stubbed out on your fucking eyeball. Who do you think they're going to believe, a highly decorated officer like me or a fat bastard with a criminal record like you?'

Foley didn't answer as he saw Black on his knees and struggling with a woman.

'It wasn't a fucking rhetorical question, chubby. Who will they believe? You or me?'

'You,' Foley said in a soft voice.

'Correct. Especially since there are two uniforms there who witnessed the altercation. Isn't that right, son?' Stewart was looking at the uniforms.

'I saw everything, sir,' confirmed the first one, an older guy. Stewart looked at the younger officer.

'Everything,' the uniform agreed.

Stewart looked back at Foley. 'There you go. Now, fag into the eyeball, or are you going to be a good boy and stand still while these nice gentlemen handcuff you?'

'Handcuff me for what?'

'First of all, you just attempted to assault a police officer. Is your fucking attention span that small? Secondly, we're arresting you on suspicion of murder.'

'What? Murder? What do you fucking mean, murder?'

'Those buckets of blood you pair of bastards threw over the old duke? They had a murder victim's fingers in them. Now, I'm going to let you go, and if you do anything stupid, I promise you one thing: you'll be in fucking rehab learning to walk again for a very long time.'

Stewart tossed the cigarette away.

DI Tom Barclay appeared, coming down the steps from the hotel.

'You take the fucking scenic route, Tom?'

'Sorry, sir. I was getting some grief from the duty manager.'

'Really? I just told him to fuck off.'

'The privilege of the upper rank, I think, sir.'

Stewart took a breath and let it out. 'Anyhoo, cuff the bastard and get him to the station,' he said to the uniforms. 'We're going to be having a chat.'

He looked over at Lisa, who had overbalanced and was on top of Black's body sprawled on the ground. The porter writhed about, trying to fight her, until Stewart stepped over and kicked the man between the legs.

'Oh, God, watch yourselves. Ground's slippery. I just slipped there.'

Black was squealing as Lisa got up and hand-cuffed him. The uniforms stepped in and hauled the still-squealing man to his feet.

Barclay took hold of Foley.

'Your friend obviously thought it would be a wise thing to have a go. He's certainly a candidate for the Christmas carol choir now.' Stewart nodded to Barclay. 'Take him away.'

THIRTY-EIGHT

Harry had left Lillian in the incident room with Presley. They were checking out the M8 killer, comparing that case with what they had today.

DI Ray Walker's flat was a hive of activity with forensics in attendance. It was too small for everybody to be in there at one time, so Harry, Dunbar and Evans were hanging around in the stairway. Frank Miller had been about to come down with them as well, but then he got a phone call from Maggie Parks and left to go to the hospital.

'Pay attention here, son,' Dunbar said. 'There are some officers here who we haven't met before, and they're with Standards.'

'It's not like it's my first day,' Evans complained.

'Just watch your Ps and Qs, that's all I'm saying.'

'Aye, I know.'

Tony Burns and Craig Benini came out of the flat as Harry & Co. stood around like union conspirators. Harry made the introductions.

'How's it looking?' he asked.

'Come in and see for yourself. You too, Jimmy. Sorry, lads, it's a bit crowded in there.'

Evans just nodded and stayed outside with Benini.

The three detectives went into the small flat.

'Pathologist is on his way, but the duty doctor attended and confirmed life extinct.' Burns looked down at the still form of Ray Walker. 'I wonder what the hell he was up to. We're still trying to track down the other two, Pierce and Dawson, and maybe they'll tell us who the third one was who attacked you and that laddie.'

'I have an idea of who's behind it,' Harry said.

'Go on then, I'm listening.'

'Stan Webster. Frank Miller and I worked on a joint case and we ended up putting him away for murdering his teenage girlfriend years ago. He'd got away with it for so long, but he was Roger Barton's boss a long time ago, and Barton worked with Pierce and Dawson.'

'I know you can't accuse Barton of anything,

Harry, but I can certainly have a word with him, you know that.' Burns looked at Dunbar. 'I'm teaching that to the young lad out there: that even though he's a sergeant, he can order an officer in for questioning, even one with a higher rank.'

'It's some power your department has,' Dunbar admitted.

'I'll have Barton in, don't you worry. But where's Webster being held?'

'Shotts,' Harry answered.

'I heard a little bit about him. He was a bit of a bad bastard right enough. Don't worry, if we can prove he was behind this, then we can have some extra years tacked on.'

'Isn't he doing life?' Dunbar said.

'He didn't get a whole life sentence. But there's always room for more charges to be added. Hopefully, they'll throw away the key.'

'What does the doc think happened to Walker?' The smell of death was starting to get to Harry, but he fought it.

'Ah, you know the old doc,' said Burns. 'Old bastard won't commit himself. He told me that wasn't in his remit, or his pay grade. So far as we can see now, there's no obvious sign of death.'

'There are two glasses on the table,' Harry said. 'Looks like he had company round.'

'Maybe his guest left and wasn't here when he died.'

'Was a phone found?'

'It's been bagged by forensics. It's over there on the kitchen counter.'

'You mind, Tony?' Harry asked.

'Go right ahead.'

Harry walked over to the open-plan kitchen, pulling gloves on as he went. He took the iPhone out of the polythene bag. It might be submitted as evidence, depending on what the pathologist found. If the death was attributed to natural causes, the phone would be passed to the next of kin.

Harry took the phone over to where Walker was sitting and tapped the screen. It was set up for facial recognition and he held it in front of Walker's face. The phone opened up and Harry took it over to where the others were standing and they scrolled through the recent activity, looking at texts and phone calls.

'Look at this one,' Harry said. The others read the text exchange with him.

I need to see you, Ray. Can I come over? I'm scared. There's somebody following me.

Do you want me to come and get you, Lizzie?

No, I can get a taxi there. I won't be long.

I'll look out for you.

'I wonder who Lizzie is?' Burns asked.

'I think we might know,' Harry informed him.

'The same Lizzie who sent Andy Watt a text,' Dunbar said.

'That's her number,' Harry confirmed.

'Christ, aye, Watt,' Burns said. 'I heard about that. Somebody called Lizzie sent him a text?'

'She's Maggie Parks' daughter.' Harry looked at Burns. 'Lizzie's known Andy for years, but how did she know Walker?'

'We'll need to have a word with her,' Dunbar said. 'If we can find her.'

'I'll get forensics to print the glasses,' Burns said. 'Do you know if she has a record?'

'Unfortunately, yes, she does. Some demonstration thing she was at. She resisted arrest. Got a fine.'

'She'll be in the system then. I'll get the lab to rush it. They won't take long. We'll know by day's end.'

'I'll get back to the station. We're working a murder investigation. Both victims were linked and it's a bloody headache,' Harry said.

'Benini and I will go and talk to Pierce and Dawson. Grill their arses a wee bit.'

'Just take care of yourself, Tony,' Harry said. 'If those are the two bastards who jumped us along with a third person, then they're not above slapping a copper.'

Burns smiled. 'The laddie was a military policeman. I'll take my chances.'

'Catch you later,' Harry said. 'Let me know the result of your chat, if you don't mind.'

'Nae bother, pal. Good seeing you, Jimmy.'

'You too, my friend. Take care.'

Evans and Benini were having a laugh outside the flat, comparing clubs in Edinburgh and Glasgow.

'If you get through, give's a shout and we'll hit a few clubs,' Evans said.

'You're on, pal.'

Harry, Dunbar and Evans made their way out, while Benini stayed at the scene with Burns.

In the car, Dunbar turned to Evans. 'Bloody clubbing? What will Vern say to that?'

'It's just a laugh. It's not as if I'd mess her about or anything.'

'You'd better bloody well no'. Muckle McInsh will pull your bawbag through your arsehole. I've seen him handle himsel'. He doesn't mess about.'

'I meant we would go out, the four of us.'

'I'm no' going out with you and Vern and the big laddie there.'

'No' you; he'd bring his girlfriend through. Listen to yoursel', clubbing at your age. They don't have bingo nowadays.'

'Harry,' said Dunbar, 'have you ever heard a young man scream after getting a boot in the bollocks?'

'I have.'

'Good. So it won't come as a surprise when Heid-the-Baw gets one.'

THIRTY-NINE

Miller parked his car and looked up at the building in the Western General. It brought back memories of his first wife, Carol. She had been admitted here and a woman had dressed as a nurse and come in to kill her, but at the last minute the nurse had had a change of heart.

He had thought he and Carol would grow old together, but it wasn't meant to be. Carol had died on duty when a ransom drop went sideways and she was pushed by somebody and hit her head on the kerb. She had died later that night in hospital. Along with their unborn baby.

He shivered, as if her ghost had just walked through him. He locked his car and walked over to the hospital, knowing that Paddy Gibb was lying in there. He still couldn't believe it. When he had started in CID, Paddy and Andy Watt had looked after Miller and Carol as they found their feet. Now both of them were in a hospital bed.

Miller started to think about Maggie's daughter, Lizzie, as he walked through the welcome heat towards the lift. She had left her flat in Glasgow and hadn't called her boyfriend or her mother, and she had come through here and made contact with Watt. Telling him she was scared of somebody. Who? Who was Lizzie scared of, and why? A stalker? Somebody she had fallen out with?

He hoped Maggie might have some answers.

He got out of the lift and walked along to Paddy's room. Maggie was inside, holding Paddy's hand in hers, holding it close to her face. Tears were running down her cheeks. The machines weren't on anymore and Miller knew before Maggie spoke.

'He died ten minutes ago.' She struggled to get the words out.

Miller looked at the pallid colour of his friend's face. He looked peaceful, but it wasn't the Paddy he knew and loved.

He walked round to the other side of the bed and put an arm around Maggie's shoulders, and she gently laid Paddy's hand back down and leaned into Miller. And cried like a baby.

They were like that for what seemed like an eon before she pulled away from Miller.

'At least I was with him when he passed,' she said. 'He didn't die alone.'

'I'm sure he knew you were here.'

She nodded and took a paper hanky out of her bag and wiped her eyes.

'Maggie, I want to ask you if you've heard from Lizzie?'

She looked at him for a second. 'No. I'm worried about her. Has she contacted you?'

Miller shook his head. 'No. But she contacted Andy and seemed to be in trouble.'

'Oh my God, I hope she hasn't been hurt. I couldn't take it if she was hurt.'

Then Miller's phone dinged with an incoming text. He looked at it. Harry. 'Maggie, this is work. I have to answer it. I'll be right outside.'

'I understand.'

He walked out of the room into the main hallway and read the text again:

DI Ray Walker had been contacted by Lizzie. She might have been at his flat. Two whisky glasses. Just to give you a heads-up.

Miller read it again. Lizzie had been trying to meet Andy Watt and he'd been run down. Now she'd been with Ray Walker and he'd been found dead. A chill ran through him. What if she was responsible?

Christ, no, don't think like that, he chided himself. Then he replied to Harry.

Sorry, pal, but Paddy just died.

Harry replied: *God rest his soul.*

Miller: *I'll talk to you later.*

Harry sent a thumbs-up emoji.

Miller went back into the room.

FORTY

Dan Foley was sitting back in his chair in the interview room and looking across at Lisa McDonald when Calvin Stewart walked in. He sat up a bit straighter when the big man closed the door.

'Right, DI McDonald, get the tapes going,' Stewart said as he sat down.

As Lisa prepared the tape machine, a camera looked down on the proceedings.

After they went through the usual rigmarole of naming who was in the room, they started.

'I want to ask you about the night you threw blood over the Duke of Wellington statue outside the art gallery,' Stewart began.

'It wasn't us.'

'I never used the word *us*. I said *you*.'

'It wasn't me,' Foley amended.

'Now, this is where we have a little problem. Or should I say, *you* have a little problem. You see, this city is full of CCTV cameras. They're everywhere. I got one of my detectives to track your movements after you both threw the blood. You and your friend. He managed to track you right back to the hotel. Where you both pulled off your masks and can clearly be seen on the camera footage. He skipped back through the timeframe and saw you both leaving the hotel carrying the small backpacks, which we know had the buckets of blood in them because we watched you take them out. And, as it turned out, they also contained the fingers of a murder victim. So let me ask you this: where did you kill her?'

Foley's eyes went wide. 'I told you in the car that I didn't kill her. I can't speak for my friend, but I had heehaw to do with it. He picked up the blood from a friend of his.'

'You do know that if you threw animal blood, or even water dyed to make it look like blood, then that wouldn't have been so bad. But because human blood is regarded as hazardous waste, the fire service had to deal with it. That's going to cost you,' Lisa said.

'The rain would have washed it away.'

'When?' Stewart said. 'Next summer?'

'Look, we just bought the blood. We didn't pay for it, but we were given the money.'

'Who gave you the money?'

Foley looked uncertain for a moment.

'Look, son, you have to understand something here. Two of my officers are through in the room next door talking to your pal, and he's kicking back, drinking a coffee, smoking a cigarette –'

'You said I couldn't smoke,' Foley reminded him.

'I said *you* couldn't smoke, but he can. Is it allowed? Technically no, but sometimes we turn a blind eye for those people who are telling their story. Make them more comfortable. And believe me, he's comfortable, because he's singing like a canary. He's admitted to taking part and to buying the blood, but he says you were with him.'

Foley gritted his teeth for a moment. 'Bastard.'

'That's right. If the Crown Office are going to cut a deal with either of you, then Mike Black is the front runner. Who knows, they might give him immunity if he gives us the name.' Stewart made a show of looking at his watch. 'Which, by my reckoning, should be any time soon. Unless he's onto his second cigarette by now, which means he's already secured a deal.'

'You're bluffing.'

'Am I? Okay then. I'll end the interview now, and then we'll have you formally charged with murder.'

'You can't do that.'

'Can't I, Dan? You admitted you had a murder victim's blood, in buckets that her fingers were in, and we saw you on CCTV throwing said blood onto a public statue. When we show the footage to a jury, they're going to go back into the deliberation room and probably break out a deck of cards or something because their decision will already be made but they'll have to make it look like they gave it some real thought. We know that you'll be going down. And now they have a second victim through in Edinburgh murdered in exactly the same way, they'll be looking to pin that on you too.'

'I was never in Edinburgh,' Foley said, not quite sure of himself now.

'You live alone. You have to spend time on your own in your bed. I'll bet they can work their magic through there and narrow down a time of death that will have you in the timeframe.'

Foley sat silently for a moment, weighing up his

options. 'Okay. We bought the blood for Clifford Dunn. We put the money in an envelope through a slot in the metal shutter door, and the two white buckets were waiting behind a couple of bins. A butcher supplied the blood or something. Maybe somebody in an abattoir. Something like that. Black got them and took them and hid them in the hotel kitchen until it was time to splash the duke.'

'How do you know Dunn?'

'Tess Grogan stayed at the hotel when she was through in Glasgow. I knew her before that. I was on the streets and I found the outreach centre one day and she started talking to me. She helped me get on my feet. Got me the job in the kitchen of the hotel and got me set up in a wee flat that's cheap to rent. Then when she came through to work in the outreach shop, she would stay at the hotel. She would come down to see how I was doing, and one day she had Dunn with her. We got talking, and he told me he was an environmentalist, amongst other things.'

'What kind of other things?'

'He came up with the idea of sticking it up the Establishment by rousing the people to make them think that the statues should come down. He said they were monuments to men who'd washed their hands in blood, and I agreed with him. Scotland doesn't belong to the rich, it belongs to the ordinary working man. Why shouldn't we have a statue in *our* honour? Or let's honour the people who were forced into labour all those years ago. It's disgusting the way those people were treated. Naw, it's time those things were put somewhere else so we don't have to look at them. Better still, melt them down.'

'You get on well with Dunn, then?' Lisa asked.

'Aye. He's a good guy. I like him better than that Michaels bloke. I know he was her boyfriend too.'

'What do you mean, *too?*'

'I mean, Dunn was Tess's boyfriend and so was Michaels. She wasn't monogamous by any stretch of the imagination. She said life was too short not to share your love.'

'Were you...' Stewart thought about his words. '... sleeping with her?'

'What? No, of course not.'

'You just said she would sleep with anybody.'

'I never said that, cloth ears. I said she had more than one partner. She believed in an open relationship. Marriage wasn't for her and she wanted to experience having a relationship with more than one man.'

Stewart gritted his teeth but said nothing.

'Do you know if Dunn had a place through here?' he asked instead of punching the fat man in the face.

'He did at one time, but Tess said he sold up and moved through to Edinburgh. When he was through here, he stayed in the hotel. That was why it was easy for him to communicate with us. He would call for Mike and Mike would go to his or Tess's room to speak about the plans for the demonstrations.'

'Tess and Dunn had separate rooms?' Lisa asked.

Foley looked at her. 'Oh, yes. She didn't mind having more than one boyfriend, but she didn't want to spend the night with them. Michaels was her main boyfriend; the others were bits on the side.'

'How many boyfriends did she have?' Stewart asked.

'Again, I wasn't privy to that. She talked to me because she liked me.' Foley looked Stewart in the eyes. 'Aye, hard to believe, eh? You wouldn't think she was a lawyer the way she dressed and dyed her hair different colours, and this might sound like a cliché, but she had a heart of gold. And I don't know one person who would want to hurt her.'

'Where did you get the blood, did you say?'

'From a butcher. I'll give you his address. We had the envelope with money in it and put it through the slot in the shutter. Dunn did the business we just picked up the buckets.'

'We'll have to check him out. Meantime, I'm going to have you stay here in the station. Until we look into things further.'

'Okay, anything. But don't let Black make up shite about me. I can't speak for him, but I didn't touch anybody.'

Stewart terminated the interview and stepped out with Lisa. 'I'm going through to Edinburgh with the reports on the M8 killer. First, I need to call somebody. You and Barclay take over here. I trust you both to deal with things.'

'Thank you, sir.'

FORTY-ONE

'Sir? Can I have a word?' Lillian approached Harry in the incident room.

'Of course. What's up?'

'Can we talk in your office?'

He nodded and they walked over and closed the door. Harry indicated for her to take a seat.

'I have something to tell you, and it's not going to be easy.'

'Okay, I'll listen and then we can go from there.'

Lillian nodded. Then looked at Harry before starting. 'It's about Paddy Gibb.'

Harry perked up at that. 'Go on.'

Lillian took in a breath and blew it out slowly. 'A long time ago, Paddy and my dad worked together, before my dad died. When he passed, Paddy took me under his wing. He encouraged me to join the force and gave me encouragement at every turn. We trusted each other.'

'He spoke highly of you, I remember that.'

'And I of him. The other night, the night when he fell, he'd sent me a text telling me that he was meeting DI Miller and Andy Watt for a drink but asking me to meet him in the pub at the foot of Broughton Street. It was just for a few minutes, he said. I agreed, but he didn't turn up. Now we know he'd fallen down the steps. As soon as I heard, I knew what I had to do. He'd called me recently and said that if anything happened to him, I should use the spare key he'd given me and go look in the wardrobe in his room. There was a box file in there, he said. So I got it, and when I looked inside I found articles from a case from forty years ago. The M8 killer. Have you heard of it?'

Harry shook his head. 'I'm forty-two. That was a bit before my time.'

'Please don't take this the wrong way, but I called Calvin Stewart in Glasgow. The box file was full of newspaper clippings and old police reports from Glasgow, so I figured they belonged to a police officer through there. I don't know how Paddy got hold of them, but when I started reading about the murders, I realised they bear a striking resemblance to our murders. Almost exactly like ours. One victim has her fingers cut off, and one of the fingers is missing but then turns up in the mouth of the next victim.'

Harry took on board what she was saying. 'Just like there was a finger in April Donegan's mouth.'

Lillian nodded. 'Just like that. Calvin Stewart called me a little while ago and he's coming through to talk to you and DCI Dunbar about the case. I hope you don't think I was going behind your back, but we've worked with him before and –'

Harry held up a hand. 'It's fine. You did well. But let me ask you, what was the police officer's name on the police reports?'

'Charlie Armstrong.'

'Charlie Armstrong? That name sounds familiar.' He tapped his fingers on his desk before giving up. 'Nope. If he's a cop, then he'll be in the system. Can you see if you can track him down?'

'Of course.'

Then Harry looked up as Calvin Stewart walked into the incident room.

'Naw, naw, no need to get up on my account. Except you,' he said, pointing to Presley. 'You can make me a coffee if you like.'

Presley made a face and looked around, silently asking who this man was.

'Well? The fucking kettle won't boil itself and I'm freezing my bollocks off.'

'Detective Superintendent Calvin Stewart, this is DC Colin Presley,' Robbie Evans said.

'Oh,' Presley said. 'Pleased to meet you, sir.'

'Right, now we've got the pleasantries out of the way, is that fucking kettle on yet?'

Presley got up quickly from his desk and grunted, holding his side. 'Shite,' he said through clenched teeth.

'Usually, they just switch the kettle on and call me a wanker behind my back, so this is a new one for me. You alright, son?'

'He got a kicking in his flat,' Harry said from the doorway of his office.

Stewart turned to look at him. 'Harry! Good seeing you.' Then he looked at Evans. 'Don't stand there like a spare prick at a wedding – go and help the fucking lad make the coffee.'

Stewart patted Dunbar's back. 'Let's have a wee conference, Jimmy. It seems like the inside of a bovine's rectal passage has hit the air distribution facilitator.'

They went into Harry's office, Stewart stopping

at the threshold to look at Evans. 'If I see bubbles on that and think you've gobbed in it, well, you should be well aware of what I'll do to you.'

Then he stepped in and saw Lillian. 'DS O'Shea, good to see you again.'

'You too, sir. Here, you can have my seat,' she said, standing up.

'Nonsense. Harry will have it. I'll have his.' Stewart looked at Harry. 'You don't mind, do you? Old bastard like me, bad back, knees not what they used to be. You don't mind if I take the comfy chair, do you?'

'Not since you put it like that. We wouldn't want an old bastard to suffer.'

'Less of the fucking old, if you don't mind,' Stewart said as Harry vacated his chair. 'Christ, my arse was expecting to be coddled a little bit more. Obviously no expense was spared by Police Scotland when they became unified. I bet the top brass were all playing musical chairs to see who got the best one, and the poor bastard whose office this was lost.'

Harry, Dunbar and Lillian waited for Stewart to get as comfy as he was going to get before they spoke.

'Lillian told me about the M8 killer,' Harry said, sitting in the other chair while the remaining two just stood.

'Aye. She told me about the box file containing clippings and the like regarding the M8 killer. And police reports by one of our crowd by the name of Charlie Armstrong.'

'I haven't had a chance to look him up yet,' Lillian said.

'Don't worry,' Stewart said, 'I had Lisa McDonald look him up. Charlie was a DI in Glasgow until he transferred through to Edinburgh. This was about ten years ago. He died a year later.'

'Was he married?' Dunbar asked.

'Widower. There's not much information on him now.'

'I wonder what made him start to collect clippings about the M8 killer?' Harry asked.

'They're not originals,' Lillian said. 'They're printed off the internet.'

'Aye, he was forty-two when he died, so he wasn't the M8 killer. He'd only have been about two when the killings took place,' Stewart said. 'But as you know, some coppers can't help but take the job home, so maybe he was looking into it since it's technically a cold case.'

'How did Paddy get hold of the file?' Lillian said.

'Maybe he was friends with Armstrong?' Harry said.

'Maybe. It was strange that he told me if anything happened to him I should go to his house and take the box file.'

'Does Maggie know you have a key?' Dunbar asked.

'I don't know. I assume so. Paddy never said.'

'I wouldn't mention it to her just yet.'

'I was waiting until we were all here before I said anything. I have some bad news.' Harry looked at Lillian. 'I'm sorry, but Paddy died a wee while ago.'

Lillian sucked in some air and her eyes went wide, then she let out a shriek and buried her head in her hands and started sobbing. Harry put his arms around her while the others looked on.

'Lillian knew Paddy before she joined the force. He was her mentor as well as a friend.'

'I'm sorry, hen,' Stewart said.

'Aye, I'm so sorry for your loss,' Dunbar said. 'Both of you. This is a hell of a time.'

Stewart got up from the chair. 'We'll leave you two alone,' he said, coming round the desk. 'You want me to tell the others about Paddy?'

Harry nodded. 'That's fine, sir.'

Stewart and Dunbar left the office and closed the door behind them. Evans came across with the coffee.

'Cheers, son. It's no' true what they say about you.' Stewart took a sip of the hot liquid after checking for signs of it having been gobbed in.

'I have some bad news,' Dunbar said to everyone in the room. 'One of our own just passed away. Not known to me personally, but he was an all-round good guy, from what I hear. Paddy Gibb died not so long ago.'

There was some murmuring.

'I don't want anybody to assume anything at the moment. Young Presley there was with Harry McNeil when they were both attacked. Paddy Gibb supposedly fell down a flight of stone steps. Andy Watt was intentionally run over and left for dead. There's somebody out to get us, so each and every one of you needs to be extra vigilant. You hear me?'

'Yes, sir,' was the chorus reply.

Stewart turned to Dunbar. 'I want to go through everything we know about that M8 murder case. Somebody's copying him for some reason. Why now? And why did Charlie Armstrong pick that case to study? Let's get on it, people.'

The officers turned away to their computers, and Stewart sat down at one with Dunbar.

One of the phones rang. Presley picked it up. He

listened for a few moments before thanking the caller and hanging up. 'Sir?'

Both Stewart and Dunbar turned round.

'That was the lab on the phone. They got prints off the knife that was used on April Donegan and off one of the glasses in Ray Walker's flat and they have a match: both sets belong to Lizzie Parks.'

'Maggie's daughter?' Dunbar said.

'Yes.'

'Armstrong,' Stewart said.

'What about him?' Dunbar asked.

'Not him. Lizzie. Her boyfriend corrected me when I was talking to him. Lizzie's last name isn't Parks, he said. It's Armstrong.'

Dunbar looked at him. 'Let's see now, there's a box file with stuff about the M8 killer in the flat she lived in with her mother and Paddy before she moved to Glasgow. Her prints are on a murder weapon. She was in a flat having a drink with a detective who was found dead. And now we find out she has the same name as a detective who was keeping the clippings. There has to be a connection there.'

'You think she's good for the murders?' Evans asked.

'We don't know her, but it's the best lead we have.'

'Nobody knows where the hell she is, seems like,' Stewart said.

'We'll have to talk to Maggie. She might be in danger,' Dunbar said.

'Paddy told Lillian that if anything happened to him, she was to get the box file, so he knew what was inside it,' Stewart said. 'What if Lizzie knew that Paddy knew? What if she wanted to get rid of him? It would be easy to wait and push him down those steps. If he looked like he was hurt but not in dire straits, she could have run down and finished him off.'

'Then sent a text to Watt, asking if she could meet him. It's not such a stretch that she could have been waiting for him and then run him down.'

'If she's our killer,' Presley said, 'then maybe she was getting inspiration from the original killer and she kept those articles to read them again and again. She couldn't get rid of them because she's using them to commit her own murders.'

'Maybe Paddy was going to drop her in it. He seemed to realise that he was in danger, given that he told Lillian where to find the file,' Stewart said.

'We need to keep a lid on Ray Walker's death just now until we see what his cause of death was.'

'Find out if Lizzie is related to Charlie Armstrong,' Stewart said to Presley. 'If he transferred here, there should be a record of him somewhere, even if it was Lothian and Borders at the time.'

'I'll get on it,' Presley said.

'You sure you're awright there, son?' Stewart asked. 'You're looking awfy peaky.'

'I'm fine, sir, thanks.'

'If you pass out, don't think I'm putting my fucking back out trying to lift you. We'll be sure to step over you, though. Make sure you don't get a boot in the bollocks in the passing.'

'That's very considerate, sir. I think my bollocks have had enough contact with steel toe caps in the past few days.'

'Right, get checking on Armstrong,' Stewart said. 'Meantime, Maggie Parks is grieving, but we can't stand by and let her be in danger. Miller is with her now, but we need more people around her. For some reason, her daughter has gone off her heid and is killing people. That's the theory we're working on.'

Presley got his keyboard clacking and within a few minutes found what he was looking for. 'Here it is, sir. Armstrong was a widower, as you said, but he had a young daughter, Lizzie.'

Stewart nodded. 'Now we have to assume that he and Maggie Parks got together, since Maggie considers Lizzie to be her daughter. We need to find out.'

Harry came out of his office with Lillian. The young DS was wiping her eyes.

'You okay, hen?' Stewart asked.

'Yes, sir, thanks. It was just a shock.'

'Let me ask you: Paddy lived with Maggie Parks. Is it her flat or his, or did they buy it together?'

'It's hers. She and her husband bought it together. Lizzie was his daughter. Maggie always looked at the young girl as her daughter.'

'Right. We have a former cop looking into the M8 killer and keeping a file on the case hidden in his flat. Somehow Paddy found it, because we know he told Lillian about it, but what we don't know is: did Lizzie find it? Or had she been told about it by her father?' Stewart looked at the others. 'Harry? You're senior lead on this. We need to find Lizzie. Maybe her mother will know more.'

'Maggie hasn't heard from her in days. But she might be able to give us some insight into Lizzie's frame of mind,' Harry replied.

'Let's give her a little time to sort out Paddy, like calling the undertaker, which shouldn't take too long, then make sure we talk to her. Call Miller and give him a heads-up.' Stewart said to Harry, then drank more of his coffee.

'We should look into Ray Walker in more depth,' Dunbar said. 'See where he fits in with Lizzie.'

'We'll get right on it,' Harry said, then indicated for Dunbar to join him in the office. 'I have to go to the Royal Edinburgh after work. It's all part of this policy where they have to make sure I'm fit to lead a team. That I'm not going to go off my head and come to work with a shotgun one day.'

'I could have told them you're mental,' Dunbar said, smiling, and he slapped Harry on the arm. 'Don't worry, I'll make sure Miller gets Maggie to safety. We can have a patrol car sit outside the house.'

'Good. Is Calvin staying over, do you think?'

Dunbar looked at the older detective out in the incident room. 'He doesn't have a life and he likes a good drink. What do you think, Harry?'

'Yeah. Silly question. If you can call Frank and make sure Maggie isn't left alone, I'll catch up with you later.'

'Leave it with me, pal.'

FORTY-TWO

It was a bar where you could be the life and soul of the party or be anonymous in a corner all by yourself. As much as he hated to admit it, Harry favoured the latter. Peace and a quiet pint.

'Somehow, I didn't see this place as being your local,' a voice behind him said. Sitting at the end of the bar hadn't made him as anonymous as he'd thought.

He turned to see the smiling face of Dr Morgan Allan. Her smile lit up her face, but not quite as much as her green eyes, which were making contact with his right now. He knew he was going to blink first.

'Drink, Doc?' he asked.

'I will if you call me Morgan. Doc, or Doctor,

would have worked an hour or so ago if you'd bumped into me in the hospital when you were due to have your wee chat with Dr Burke.'

He looked at his watch. 'Is that the time? Sorry, it slipped right by me. What's your poison?'

She sat down on the bar stool next to him. She'd already taken her coat off and hung it up somewhere, he presumed, since it was December and cold outside and yet she was wearing just a cardigan over her blouse.

'Pint of Guinness, please,' she said.

He looked at her for a moment before she laughed. Her smile was wide and her short blonde hair moved slightly as she tilted her head. If he had seen her sitting in a room and had been asked to guess what her profession was, he'd have thought of anything but a psychiatrist. But she was, and he wished she was the one sitting in the office instead of Burke.

'No, wait, I already had a couple of pints today. Make it a Bacardi and Coke,' she said.

He caught the attention of the barman and ordered her drink and another pint of lager. 'One for the road,' he told her. 'For me. You could be in here to get steamboats for all I know.'

'*Steamboats*, Harry? Do I look like the sort of girl who gets *steamboats*?'

That was the thing: he'd been trying to guess her age ever since he'd been coming up to Morningside and he'd met her...what, two, two and a half months ago? If he'd been a betting man, he'd have said late thirties or early forties, much like himself. They had got talking in the corridor one day after his session with Burke, and he had walked her out. Nothing more, just a quick chat. Then he'd seen her in here a couple of times and they'd chatted.

He'd celebrated his birthday by being sent back to therapy. Protocol, he'd been told. A lot of changes had gone on in his life and career before that, and the bosses wanted to make sure that the leader of the new MIT was fit for the job and stayed that way.

He nodded to the barman, like a secret had passed between them silently, as he handed over the money.

'Maybe *steamboats* isn't quite the word to use with you, but you know what I mean. It's a Friday night and this place will be hotting up. You might be in here to meet some friends, have a few drinks before you head into town. Maybe even get a bite to eat here.'

'I like coming to The Merlin, but it's not my

local. Sometimes I pop in and have a quiet drink with a friend of mine, but she's not here tonight. Nothing planned, just a quick "we'll have a drink if you're in" sort of thing. Is this a regular haunt for you?'

'No.'

It was the short answer, but it got to the point.

'You come here just when you're trying to avoid Burke and when it's time for you to be in his office?' She smiled at him again. 'How many sessions is it that you've missed now?'

'One,' he answered.

'I think we're telling porkies, Chief Inspector. Or else I may have to suggest Dr Burke lines up a refresher course in arithmetic for you.'

'One because I chose to. Other times because work got in the way. There's a difference. Besides, why is Burke dropping me in it with you?'

'We were just comparing notes. So what made today so different?' She sipped her Bacardi, watching him over the rim of her glass for a moment.

What *did* make today different? He thought about it for a moment and couldn't put his finger on it. 'I really don't know. I parked my car and was about to walk along to the hospital, but I turned and walked back up the hill to here.'

'Look, I'm not going to give you grief over this, Harry, but I thought you were making good progress.'

'I am. But a friend of mine died today. Paddy Gibb. Another police officer,' he said to her.

'I'm sorry to hear that. Were you really close?'

'I'd worked with him before. He was a good guy. Are we doing my session now, Morgan?'

'No, I'm just talking to you as a friend.' She put a hand on his arm for a second. 'We're just chewing the fat, as it were. Besides, you're not my patient, remember?'

'I'm sorry. I was doing a bit of Christmas shopping last night. Grace will never have the joy of celebrating Christmas with her mum. She has Alex's sister, who's wonderful, but she can't be a mum to Grace. I feel I'm holding Jessica back from having her own life.'

'She's still living in your house? She hasn't left since we last spoke?'

'No, nothing like that. She's great and we get along like a house on fire, but I feel guilty. I know her and Alex's father was a killer, and maybe she feels guilty because their father was in my flat when Alex collapsed. But she shouldn't feel guilty, and I don't want to hold her back.' He made eye contact with Morgan.

'I understand. It must feel overwhelming at times, but it will get easier.'

'I basically ran away from it all, back in the summer. Bought a little house down in the south of Scotland and lived there by myself, leaving Jessica to run my life, to do what I should have been doing. And she didn't have one word of complaint.'

'Because she loves you. Not in a sexual way, but in a family way. Grace is her flesh and blood, so it's obvious she's going to look after her.'

'I know. And I make sure I take Grace at the weekends so Jessica can go and do her own thing.'

'And does she? Do her own thing?'

'She'll go out with friends.'

'I'm glad to hear that.' Morgan finished her drink and caught the barman's attention. 'What are you up for?'

'I'm driving, thanks. Two's my limit. But let me get this.' Harry went to take his wallet out, but she stopped him.

'You wouldn't want to tarnish my impression of you by appearing sexist, would you?'

'Who am I to argue with that?'

Morgan bought herself another Bacardi, and

they clinked glasses after the barman poured. The bar was getting busier as more people finished work for the weekend and came in to get a swift one in before heading home or just to kick it into gear.

'Are you married?' Harry asked Morgan. 'It's never come up in conversation before.'

'It wasn't meant to.'

He smiled. 'This isn't a session, remember? I'm not in your office, I'm not your patient and we're drinking alcohol together in a public bar. I was making conversation. But it's none of my business.'

'You're right; it *isn't* any of your business. But since we're basically two colleagues having a drink in a bar, there's no harm in me telling you. I was married, a long time ago. He died.'

'I'm sorry. I didn't mean to open an old wound.'

'You didn't. James was the love of my life, and he meant everything to me. But that life was very different to the one I have now.' She smiled, but he could see there was a sadness in her eyes now.

'You'll know exactly what I've been going through these past few months,' Harry said.

'I do. We all react to losing a loved one in different ways. You chose to run away, and I don't want that to sound like I'm belittling you, because

I'm not. In your head, you had to get away, so that's exactly what you did. You gave yourself time to heal.'

'How long has it taken you to heal, Morgan? If you don't mind me asking.'

'Ten years on the twenty-fifth.'

'Christmas Day?'

'That date's generally known as Christmas Day, Harry.'

'Yes, sorry. It came as a surprise.'

'People *do* die on Christmas Day.'

'I know, I've just never met anybody who knew somebody who did. I'm sorry to hear that.'

'Ten years seems like a long time, but to me it feels just like yesterday.' She took a sip of the Bacardi. 'Now I feel like we've swapped roles. I'm telling you about my life and you're the one dishing out advice.'

He had felt anxious about his first appointment with Burke weeks ago, and didn't really care for him, but had warmed to Morgan as soon as he'd met her. The first time he had bumped into her in the pub, she had listened when he had told her all about his late wife, and his daughter, and whether the loss of Alex was affecting his job or not. Which it wasn't. Now he felt relaxed around Morgan.

'How's the new team coming along?' she asked him.

'To be honest, I was just back in CID. It was Percy Purcell who sat me down and had a talk. He said that my MIT had been disbanded, some of my team getting promotions and others being transferred, and asked if I'd be interested in heading a new team. They were going to set one up again, he said, and he'd been happy with my performance. I said yes. He understands I still go and see Burke.'

'He must think highly of you.'

'He does, there's no denying it. I thought my leave of absence would go against me.'

'Why would it?'

'I jumped ship, Morgan.'

'You needed help and you got it. There's a difference.' She took a sip of her drink. 'You're going to be okay at the helm again?'

'I will be. They just need to decide who they want on the team that I'm going to lead eventually.'

'Will you be able to go to Paddy Gibb's funeral? I mean, will you be able to cope mentally?'

Harry looked at his second pint, barely touched. 'Yes, I'll be going. I've known Paddy for years.'

They sat drinking in silence for a moment, like

somebody had cracked a bad joke and nobody thought the punchline was funny.

'You never asked,' she said.

Harry looked at her for a moment like he had been about to lean over to try to kiss her. 'I'm sorry?'

'You never asked how my husband died. They usually do. The men who try to chat me up in a bar. When I explain that I'm a widow, the first thing they say is, "You look too young to be a widow." Then they ask how he died, as if I'm making it up.'

'How did he die?' Harry said.

'I asked him to run to the corner store for a bottle of Coke. I wasn't drinking because I wanted to get pregnant. It had been snowing and the roads were slick. He tried to turn a corner, and the car went straight on. He hit a wall and was dead by the time the ambulance got there. I was worried about him, even more so when he didn't answer his phone. The police turned up at the door an hour after he'd left. And my life was changed forever.'

'I'm sorry to hear that,' Harry said. 'What was his name?'

'David.'

'What did he do for a living?'

Morgan looked at him for a moment. 'This is the ironic bit: he was an A&E doctor.'

'What a waste.'

They sat in silence for a bit.

'You can see how that's a conversation killer,' Morgan said. 'A man chats me up and we get talking, then he heads for the hills. Not that I get chatted up very often.'

'You and me both.'

They chatted for a little while longer, then she stood up. 'I'm going to get going now, Harry.'

'Me too. I'm going to meet up with my colleagues again. Our day isn't finished.'

She raised her eyebrows. 'Really? Killers to catch and you're sitting in here with me?'

'I get more benefit chatting with you than I do from talking to Burke. The old boy will probably write a scathing report on me.'

'No, he won't. He doesn't want to rock the boat. He does this part time and he likes playing golf. He doesn't want anybody to tell him not to come back. Just pop in now and again to see him and he can at least write an honest report.' She smiled at him.

'Can I give you a lift?'

'I'm going in the opposite direction, Harry, but thanks.'

He walked her out into the cold.

'I'll cross over and get a bus,' she said.

'Okay. Might see you next week?'

'In the hospital or the bar?'

'Maybe both. We'll see.'

He watched her cross the road before walking away for his car.

FORTY-THREE

Maggie Parks' face looked like a train wreck.

Frank Miller sat beside her on the settee in her flat while Harry and Presley sat opposite.

'I can't believe he's gone,' she said. 'I knew he was hurt, but I always thought he would come home again.'

'It's going to be hard,' Harry said, 'but we're all here for you.'

'We are,' said Miller. He glanced at Harry and then added gently, 'Maggie, there's something we want to talk to you about.'

She dabbed at her eyes. 'What's that?'

'Charlie,' Harry said.

Maggie's eyebrows met in the middle. 'Charlie? What about him?'

'His name came up in our enquiries.'

'How? How did Charlie's name come up, Harry?'

Harry looked at Miller before answering. 'It's about Lizzie. I'm going to be blunt here, Maggie. We think she was involved in the deaths of Tess Grogan and April Donegan.'

'No. You can't be serious.'

'You said yourself you haven't been able to contact her for days. She contacted Andy Watt, telling him she was in danger; then when Andy got home, we think she ran him down. She lured him there to kill him.'

'Oh my God, Harry, I won't listen to this. You're making a mistake. My Lizzie wouldn't do that.'

Miller put a hand on her arm. 'Maggie, her prints are on the knife that was used to kill April.'

Maggie shrugged his hand off. 'I don't believe it. You know how some of those useless arseholes are. It's bloody shoddy work.'

Harry kept his voice even, knowing the woman was in shock. 'Maggie, there's no mistake. We know she was with Ray Walker before he died too.'

Maggie looked at him and her mouth opened but no sound came out right away. 'Ray's dead?'

'Yes. We don't know his cause of death yet, but

there were two glasses in his flat and one of them had Lizzie's prints on it. She was there with him.'

'Did Lizzie know Ray Walker?' Miller asked.

'Of course she did!' Maggie spat. 'Ray was a friend of my Charlie's. She's known him since she was a little girl.'

'She sent him a text telling him she was in danger and asked if she could come over. He obviously agreed and they had a drink, but what happened next is anybody's guess. All we know is that Walker died.'

'That doesn't prove anything. He might have died of a heart attack and Lizzie panicked.'

'What happened in the outreach centre, Maggie?' Harry asked. 'Did she panic there too, and just happen to stab April to death? We need to find her. If you know where she is, then you need to tell us.'

'I don't know where she is.' Maggie started sobbing again.

'We can have a patrol car sitting outside here all night and all day,' Harry said.

'I don't need your protection. My own daughter wouldn't hurt me.'

'I know this is hard, Maggie, but we need to err on the side of caution.'

Maggie sat staring ahead at nothing and stayed that way for a couple of minutes. Then she looked at Miller. 'She was a troubled girl.'

'In what way?'

'I'm her stepmum. I met Charlie, and he introduced me to his eight-year-old daughter. We hit it off and Charlie said he wanted to be with me, so he got a transfer and we got married and bought this flat. I loved Lizzie like she was my own. We'd only been here for a year when he died. I went back to using my maiden name.'

'How did he die, if you don't mind me asking?' Harry said.

'He drowned. He slipped in the shower and went under the water unconscious, they think. There was blood from a head wound where he fell, but the blow wasn't hard enough to kill him.'

Harry exchanged a look with Miller. Maggie saw it.

'You don't think Lizzie had anything to do with that, do you? She was only a wee girl. She was eleven.'

'It's hard to say. Kids have been known to kill,' Harry said.

'Oh my God. Not her own father?'

'Maybe she was jealous of you getting together

with her dad,' Miller said. 'Was he married to Lizzie's mum?'

Maggie nodded. 'Yes. She died of cancer when Lizzie was two.'

'It sometimes happens that a child isn't happy when their single parent gets attention from another adult and they see the dead parent being replaced. It festers inside. Maybe Lizzie did kill her father. We'll never know. But now she's on the rampage.'

'If you have any idea where she is, please tell us,' Harry said.

'I would. Honestly. If only to save her. She needs help. I don't want her being hurt.'

'We won't hurt her,' Miller promised.

'Please don't worry about me,' Maggie said. 'Reverend Michaels has a room where they put up cots in the winter for the homeless. I can sleep on one of those cots. At least I'll be with people and she won't know I'm there.'

'If you're sure.'

'I am.'

FORTY-FOUR

Calvin Stewart, Dunbar and Evans stood outside the mews house. It was cold and the street lamps were doing little to dispel the darkness.

'I didn't know Harry was going to a shrink,' Stewart said.

'It's hardly a shrink,' Evans said. 'More of a therapist, like you go to.'

'Aye, some of us just need a wee chat now and again, right enough,' Stewart said in a lower voice. 'Ian Flucker's a good guy. We just talk about TV and shite like that. Have a wee coffee.' He turned to Evans. 'You'd better no' be giving people the impression I'm some kind of nutter.'

'Me, sir? Not at all.' Evans rolled his eyes behind Stewart's back.

Stewart looked at Clifford Dunn's house. There were no lights on. 'Right, the bastard's either ignoring us or he's out.'

Dunbar went to look in one of the windows. 'Sir, have a look in here.'

Stewart walked forward, his breath smoking in the cold air. He put a gloved hand up to the window to block the light from the street lamp and looked in between the slats of the blinds that weren't turned all the way closed. He saw somebody lying on the floor of what looked like a living room.

Stewart turned to the uniforms who were blocking the lane with their cars, the blue lights flashing in the dark.

'You. Get the ram and get that fucking door in.' He pointed to one of the uniforms, then at the front door of the house, in case the young man hadn't got what he meant when he said 'that door'.

One of the others grabbed the ram from the boot of the BMW and handed it to the first man, as if it was some kind of relay race. And then the uniform was standing in front of the door, positioning himself, wanting to get it right first time.

'Don't just stand there like a used johnny in a brothel,' Stewart barked, 'tan the fucking door.'

The uniform hit the door near the lock and then again. It still didn't break but gave off an alarming thud.

'Pretend you've just caught your best friend shagging your granny. What would you like to do to him?'

The uniform battered the door again and this time it flew open.

'There you go. You'll never look at that ram the same way again. Now get inside and make sure there's no' a fucking axe murderer in there.'

The uniforms rushed in, slapping lights on. Stewart slapped his forehead.

'What if this is a crime scene and somebody had hit the light switch? Fuck me. Come on, you two, let's join the party.'

They heard the sound of boots thudding up the stairs and shouts telling them there was nobody up there with a chainsaw.

The three detectives walked into the room on the right. The living room. The corpse had already started to smell.

They noticed a coffee table in front of the settee that had two glasses on it and an open bottle of whisky.

The body was facing away from them so Stewart walked round and had a look.

'Is it Clifford Dunn?' Dunbar asked.

Stewart straightened up. 'No,' he said simply.

FORTY-FIVE

'How are you feeling now?' Lillian O'Shea asked Presley.

'I was about to ask you the same thing.' He smiled at her. 'Fine. Sore but fine.'

'The boss told you to go home.'

'Which one? There are a ton of them in here today.'

'I like working with Harry. He was great in MIT. The Glasgow boys are good fun too. I'd work with any of them.'

'You met the Glasgow crowd before?'

'I worked a case with them. Somebody had abducted young girls and kept them at his place for years before killing them.'

'Jesus.' Presley looked at Lillian for a moment. 'I

hate CID down in Leith. It's like a wee club where a bit of policing breaks out now and again. I mean, I don't want to speak ill of the dead or anything, but Ray Walker was one of those officers who just skated through life. He was after an easy time.'

'They think Maggie Parks' daughter, Lizzie, somehow killed him, but the PM hasn't been started. They're starting to get backed up, what with Tess Grogan and April Donegan.'

'I still find it hard to believe Lizzie would be capable of something like this. I've known her for years and she's never shown any signs of being violent,' Lillian said.

'That's the thing: sometimes they're good at hiding it, especially if there are mental health issues involved. Lizzie might have been suffering in silence, or it was covered up – the families are embarrassed.'

'I keep going back to Charlie Armstrong and why he would choose that particular cold case to work on in his spare time.'

'He came from Glasgow and maybe the Glasgow angle attracted him to it.'

'I'm sure there are a lot of cold cases in Glasgow too. But one of the victims was from Edinburgh. She was found dead at Harthill a year after the second victim.'

'Here's a thought,' Presley said. 'What if Charlie Armstrong was the killer?'

Lillian shook her head. 'Oh, Colin, just when I thought you had the makings of a detective. You forget that Armstrong was only a small boy when the murders took place.'

'Oh, yeah. I forgot to take that into account.' He grinned. 'Then what if it was a relative? An uncle or something? What if he had a suspicion and kept tabs on him but couldn't prove anything?'

Now Lillian seemed impressed. 'Good thinking. Maybe we should look into Armstrong's family background. See if anything fits the bill.'

'Aye, maybe tomorrow,' said Presley. 'I'm going home. Amy should be on her way home now. I feel like a horse has kicked me.'

Lillian nodded, and then Paddy Gibb's face sprang into her mind. Why would he have kept the box file secret? Why wouldn't he have told Frank Miller or Andy Watt? Or even Harry? He knew them well. If there was something in there that was incriminating, then why wouldn't he have told them?

He'd only told her, Lillian, where to find the file. She was obviously somebody he trusted.

Her head was spinning. She looked at her watch. Wine time.

'Come on, Colin, I'll walk out with you.'

They went downstairs, Presley walking like somebody had used him to play 'pin the tail on the donkey' and it had gone awry.

Outside in the High Street, the Christmas lights shimmered in the cold air, which reminded him to start thinking about Christmas shopping.

'You want a lift?' Lillian offered. 'I live down in Comely Bank. I'm going past Amy's place anyway.'

'Thanks, but I'll get the bus down the road. It's not that far a walk when I get off.'

'Okay. See you Monday.'

Lillian walked down through the vennel to the back car park, while Presley walked up to George IV Bridge, both of them thinking about a murderer from forty years ago.

When Lillian reached her car, she stood with the key out, hunching her shoulders inside her coat. She knew she couldn't go home just now. Paddy was dead. He had told her about the box file and now she had to read through every scrap of paper in there to try to find out if it had caused his death. She had no doubt in her mind that Paddy had been murdered.

She went back into the station through the back door and headed up to the incident room.

FORTY-SIX

Harry and Miller walked into the lane just as the mortuary assistants were loading the body bag into the back of the van.

'What happened?' Harry asked Dunbar.

'DSup Stewart here wanted to have a chat with Clifford Dunn. He interviewed the two guys who threw blood over the statue in Glasgow and they said Dunn paid them to do it, to get publicity. So he wanted to talk to Dunn about it. When we got here, I saw a man lying on the floor and we forced entry. Except the man isn't Dunn.'

'Christ, Jimmy, you make it sound like you're reading it off a postcard,' Stewart said.

'Just covering my own arse, sir, if push ever comes to shove.'

'Well, that's nice. How about us boys sticking together?' Stewart said.

'Us boys are going to be no more in a couple of weeks, sir.'

'I'll still have your back even though I'll be away.'

'Good to know.'

'Who is it, do we know?' Harry asked.

'He's one of ours,' Dunbar said. 'DS Ricky Dawson.'

'Dawson?' Harry was shocked. 'He was on my team in CID. To be honest, young Presley and I were thinking he and Ian Pierce might have been behind the attacks on us. Along with Ray Walker.' He shook his head.

'Was he murdered?' Miller asked.

'Hard to say, cock,' Stewart said. 'The gin-tottering old bastard of a doctor they have on duty barely looked at him before pronouncing him a goner. He didn't elaborate or make an educated guess. He just came here to make up the numbers and get paid. Mind you, there's nothing to show Dawson was murdered, but the PM or the tox report will maybe show up something.'

'And there were two glasses on the coffee table with an opened bottle of whisky sitting there as well,' Evans chimed in.

'Just like at Ray Walker's flat. I wonder if Lizzie had a hand in this one too, Dunbar said.'

'There's a phone sitting on the coffee table,' Stewart said. 'Let's go and take a look.'

They went inside, out of the cold, and saw the iPhone on the table.

'I opened Ray Walker's phone by holding it up to his face,' Harry said.

'Using a corpse to open a phone. I like the cut of your jib. Evans! Get onto it. Make sure that van doesn't leave before you have a chance to open his phone.'

Evans, who already had gloves on, picked up the phone and took it outside. He came back in a couple of minutes later.

'I caught them in time. Phone's unlocked,' he said, slightly out of breath.

'How are you out of breath?' Stewart asked. 'You didn't use that phone to give your girlfriend a quick call, I hope? Or worse, take a dick pic with it.'

'Too cold for that nonsense, sir. Wouldn't want to give her the wrong impression.'

'Right, rumour has it you've got very little to impress a lassie to start with, never mind whipping it out in the cold. But enough of your bloody nonsense.

Get the phone opened and see who called Dawson or sent him a text.'

Evans navigated the phone like a pro, saying something about old farts under his breath.

'We're no' deef,' Stewart told him.

'I found a text from a Lizzie Armstrong,' Evans said, turning the phone to face them. *Can we meet? You know where.*

'Check for calls too,' Dunbar said. 'They knew each other. Maybe through her mother's job?'

Evans looked at the phone again. 'Yep. Same number.'

'Jesus, we need to find this lassie,' Stewart said. 'How old is she?'

'Twenty-one,' Miller said.

'Not so much a lassie as a full-grown young woman who's more than capable of killing men,' Dunbar said.

'What about her mother?' Stewart said. 'Do you think she'll be a target?'

'Who knows what's going through Lizzie's mind,' Harry said.

'Look at this,' Evans said, still looking at the phone screen. 'Very interesting.' He showed it to Harry.

'Christ.' Harry looked at his watch, then reread the message.

Let's finish the bastards tonight.

The message came from Ian Pierce.

FORTY-SEVEN

'Look at you, girl,' Lillian O'Shea said to herself. 'Friday night and you're at work, poring over some old files, instead of being out with a boyfriend. Having a nice meal, then going to a bar to unwind. Maybe a little dancing. But no boyfriend, nobody to go home to. Not even a cat. Just a TV and a half-drunk bottle of wine. You're pathetic. No man would want to be saddled with a workaholic.'

She looked over at another desk and saw Paddy Gibb sitting there. A hollow outline.

'*Listen to yourself, Lily,*' he said to her. '*We're Irish, you and me. We don't give up easily, and we don't put ourselves down. You're a beautiful young woman. Any man would be glad to have you by his side. I told you that many times. Just keep the faith.*'

'I know, Paddy. I know you've always been right. And thank you for keeping the faith too.'

'I've always believed in you, Lily. That's why I trusted you with the key. But not just the physical key. The key to solving this is in that box. You just have to look hard. It's there, started by a man a long time ago. A man who saw it all, and who left a legacy for solving a cold case.'

Paddy got up from the desk and walked over to her. She had put her head down on her folded arms and was crying. She felt his arm go around her shoulders, felt the comfort and warmth there as she cried.

Then she jolted awake, confused as to where she was for a moment. She thought that Paddy dying had been a bad dream, but the only dream she'd had was his being with her. Then she remembered his words.

The key to solving this is in that box.

She began to empty the box file of all the papers. A detective called Charlie Armstrong had started this investigation years ago and she was determined to finish it. There was something in here that would help them find the killer who'd taken the baton and was running with it.

One of the papers jumped out at her. The suspect, his name was Peter Torrington. A business traveller for a printing company. He was always travelling from Edinburgh through to Glasgow and all over the UK. A car like his company car had been seen near the bins at the Harthill Services. He had denied being there, and when they'd checked him out, his wife had confirmed his alibi. He lived in Edinburgh with his wife and daughter. Maribel and Elizabeth.

Lizzie.

She stared at the copy of the newspaper clipping. Torrington was thirty-six at the time he was questioned. Which would make him seventy-six now, give or take. She wondered if he was still alive.

She typed his name in Google and scrolled through the results. There. The headline jumped out at her: *M8 murder suspect commits suicide*.

She started spreading out the papers again, looking to see if there was a copy of a clipping, and sure enough, it was tucked away behind so many others. Nothing was in chronological order.

She pulled it out and read through it.

Yesterday afternoon the emergency services were called to a house in the Broughton area of Edinburgh where they found the body of Mr Peter Torrington, aged forty-four. He had committed suicide by cutting his wrists and bled out in the bath, which was full of water.

No reason was given for the suicide, but it is possible that being accused of the murders of three women had taken a toll on Torrington. His wife had left him a couple of years ago, his daughter said. Elizabeth M. Torrington, eighteen, said she was shocked by her father's actions and knew nothing about the accusations made against him.

Lillian looked down at the sheet of paper and wondered where the daughter was now. She typed the name in but got no hits. Nothing at all.

It was as if Elizabeth Torrington had vanished off the face of the earth.

Lillian gathered all of the papers up and put them back in the box file. She was about to leave it on her desk when she had second thoughts. She'd take it home. After all, what else did she have going on?

FORTY-EIGHT

Colin Presley cursed himself for not taking a taxi, but now it was too late. The bus was almost full and he was being squeezed in his seat by a fat bloke who smelled like he had spent a week in the office without going home to shower. He tried breathing through his mouth, but it was no good.

He rubbed at the condensation on the window with the back of his hand, promising himself that he would look at buying a car as soon as he could easily get in and out behind the wheel. His ribs still felt like they had been used by a circus elephant for balancing practice.

He and Harry thought it might have been Dawson and Pierce who were trying to kick the shit out of them, but why? Harry he could see, with his being ex-Standards, but why drag Presley into it? Harry said Presley was collateral damage, there to make it look like they weren't targeting Harry while that was exactly what they were doing.

Pair of bastards. But was Ray Walker involved too? There were three attackers after all. From what Presley had seen so far, the DI didn't move very fast, and the attackers could. Harry had sent him a text telling him Walker was dead. Maybe at the hands of the woman they were looking for, this Lizzie girl. If she had taken out Walker, how had she done it? There was no sign of violence, so she'd have had to get close to him. It was somebody Walker trusted then. And he knew Lizzie.

Presley got off the bus at the foot of Dundas Street. This had a benefit: it was close to the chippie. Amy liked a fish supper just as much as he did, and since he wasn't able to take her out to eat because of the pain, a fish supper was the next best thing.

He crossed over at the lights on Henderson Row and went into the L'Alba D'Oro chippie. The best in Edinburgh, in his opinion. He got the two fish suppers and had just stepped back onto the pavement when his phone rang.

It was Harry McNeil.

'*Colin?*'

'It is indeed, sir.' Presley wondered how long it was going to be before McNeil started calling him Elvis like everybody else.

'*How do you fancy a fight?*'

Fuck. Had the older detective been drinking? 'Not so much, sir, but thanks for the offer. You have a good weekend now.'

'*Not with me. With somebody else.*'

'And who would that be, if you don't mind me asking?'

'*Ricky Dawson's dead. You know how we were thinking we knew the three attackers? Well, now we know for sure that two of them are dead.*'

'Christ, were Walker and Dawson murdered?'

'*Not sure, Elvis.*'

There we go. Not as long as he had thought. The DCI had slipped over to the dark side, whether subconsciously or because he had stopped fighting it.

'And I'm guessing that I'm supposed to have a go with attacker number three?'

'*Not exactly. He'll be waiting to have a go with you.*'

'What do you mean?'

'*You'll see.*'

Presley started walking faster – well, as fast as he could without looking like he'd shat himself –

keeping a tight hold of the fish suppers. The phone call from McNeil made his heart beat faster and adrenaline had kicked in.

He turned the corner and walked down to Amy's apartment block, then into the entrance.

He had taken his phone out and was waiting for the call to connect. Then his girlfriend answered.

'Amy! Are you home?'

'Yes, I am now. You almost home?'

'I'll be upstairs in a minute.'

'Hurry,' was all she said before disconnecting the call.

FORTY-NINE

Lillian parked her car round the corner from where she lived, close to Harry's old flat.

Close to where Alex had lived.

She and Alex had started off on a rocky road, because Alex was pregnant when they first met and her hormones had been all over the place and it had caused jealousy to kick in. But they had talked and soon became friends.

Lillian missed Alex. Living so close, she had thought they could have gone out socially outside of work. Lillian didn't find it hard to make friends, but like Alex, she had found her old friends slowly drifting away since she joined the force.

That was why she was going to sit down with the

box file in her flat, glass of wine in hand, and read through every single article in there.

She walked into her stairway and up the stairs to her flat. She took her key out and let herself in to the dark flat. Then she stopped. Gently closed the door behind her and stood still, listening. There was nothing but the heating on. There were no ticking clocks in her flat, because that was something she hated.

Something else she didn't have any use for nowadays: perfume.

But she could smell perfume in her flat now.

She walked as silently as she could in the darkness to her living room. She noticed the curtains had been drawn.

The woman was sitting in one of her chairs.

'Hello, Lizzie,' Lillian said.

'Come in. Please sit down,' Lizzie said, as if this was her flat and not Lillian's. She made no attempt to put a light on, but Lillian's eyes were slowly adjusting to the dark.

She moved forward and sat on the settee, putting the box file down on the coffee table.

'I'm assuming that's the file that Paddy told you to get from the house.'

There was no point in denying it. 'Yes, it is.'

A slight chuckle came from the dark. 'I wondered what had happened to it. I knew Paddy had found it. He knocked something off the wardrobe shelf when he took it down. It hadn't been put back the same way, and I knew then that he'd found it.'

'Lizzie, you don't have to do this.'

'I know. But I want to. There have been too many secrets in this family. It has to end now.'

'And it has. We can go to the station and talk about it.' Lillian took her phone out and opened it, the screen illuminating her face. 'I'll text my colleague.'

'Ah, yes, Elvis, isn't it? He seems nice.'

Lillian was trying to keep an eye on Lizzie and text at the same time. Luckily, she could type fast using her thumbs. Texting was second nature to her, unlike the oldies.

In my flat. Lizzie is here. Help.

She hit 'send' and off it went. Lizzie hadn't moved at all.

'Who did you tell about the box file?' Lizzie asked.

'Nobody.'

There was a chuckle from the other side of the room. Looking at her phone had made Lillian's pupils dilate slightly, making the room seem even darker.

'That's funny,' Lizzie said. 'You're a cop. Paddy spoke highly of you, he really did. Said you would go places because you had a copper's blood in you. He was proud of you. But that doesn't gel with what you just said. You wouldn't have taken that file and read through it without telling anybody.'

'They all know. We discussed it at the station.'

'That's better. It's what I fully expected of you. Oh well, the game is over now. You'd better arrest me.'

Lizzie stood up. Lillian stood too, and now her eyes were adjusting to the dark again, slowly. She could make out Lizzie holding her clenched fists out in front of her, waiting to have the handcuffs slapped on her.

Lillian stepped forward and took the handcuffs out of her pocket. Just as she reached Lizzie, she realised with horror the mistake she'd made.

The smell of the perfume when she came into the flat was familiar to her. Now she knew why. It wasn't perfume at all. It was aftershave.

The knife that Lizzie had been holding in her fist was now in front of her. She grabbed Lillian's arm and thrust the knife into her side. Lillian gasped as pain shot through her. She was going to die, she thought. The knife would be rammed in again and again and her fingers would be cut off.

'Lizzie, that's enough!' a male voice behind her said. It was firm and carried throughout the living room.

Lizzie stopped and held the dripping knife by her side.

She let Lillian go and stood back, watching the detective fall to the floor.

'Come on,' the man said. 'It's time to go.' He stepped into the room and put his hand out for the knife.

'She's just one of them.'

'We tried. It didn't work. We need to get away instead.'

Lizzie nodded and turned the knife round, handing it to the man handle first. He gently took it from her.

'I'll leave the one with the other prints on it.' He had a backpack on, and he slipped it off one shoulder, reached in and brought out another knife. He walked over to where Lillian was lying, pulled her hand out of the way and wiped the knife on the blood seeping out of the wound. Lillian gasped and put her hand back as he let it go.

FIFTY

The man tinkered with the lock on the front door, pushing and twisting until the lock pins aligned and he could turn the handle. It moved easily and with little sound. The landing was well lit, but the flat was in darkness. Maybe the woman hadn't got up from the underground garage yet. Good. That would give him time to surprise her.

He had followed her from the hospital and had parked round from the entrance to the building. He had easily gained entry by pressing a couple of buttons and giving the resident who answered some spiel.

Now he was in her flat and walking along the lobby. What room would he wait in? The bedroom? Spring out at her? The kitchen? Jump out at her with a knife? No, he might end up stabbing her and it was Presley he wanted, not her.

The living room would be just fine. He could sit and relax and wait for her, then he could be holding her when Presley came in.

He found the kitchen first, then a bedroom. The living room door was closed. He looked round the edge, making sure there was no light coming from underneath.

It was dark.

He turned the handle and walked in.

There was somebody sitting in the chair.

He froze for a moment, thinking it was Presley, and he was about to rush him when he felt a shove in his back and fell onto the floor.

A light came on.

'Come in and relax, ya fucking bawbag,' Calvin Stewart said. 'Oh, I see you already have.'

Ian Pierce tried to get up, but Robbie Evans walked forward and stepped on his back.

'I said relax, Ian,' Stewart said. 'We want to have a little chat.'

'Get the fuck off me,' Pierce said.

'Dearie me, what kind of talk is that? We're only here to have a wee chat. No need to get all pissy about it.'

'Fuck you.'

'It's fuck you, *sir*. I'm DSup Calvin Stewart and this is DS Evans. We're from Glasgow, and you, my friend, are starting to grate on me. Now, I want to know why you and your cronies have been trying to give my friends a kicking. You have sixty seconds. Go.'

'I don't know what you're talking about.'

'And the clock is ticking. Now, once again, why were you, Ricky Dawson and Ray Walker getting physical with Harry McNeil and Colin Presley?'

Evans stood harder on Pierce's back.

'Okay, okay. It was Walker's idea. He said we could all get back at Harry McNeil because he'd been a pain in the arse when he was in Professional Standards.'

'So the three of you ambushed him in that flat in...' Stewart looked at Evans. 'What did he call that place again?'

'Dumbiedykes,' Evans answered.

'Aye. Dumbiedykes. You three ambushed him and Presley there, But tell me: was Presley part of the plan?'

'Walker wasn't part of the fight,' Pierce said. 'It was me and Dawson and the other bloke.'

'What other bloke?' Stewart asked.

'I don't know his name. Ray told us about him. Said he would meet us there. Ask him if you don't believe me. Ask Ricky too. They'll back me up.'

'No can do,' Stewart said.

'I'm not going down for this on my own.'

'You are. You see, Walker and Dawson are both dead. Whoever is pulling the strings is cleaning house now. They want you to get rid of Presley and then they'll pull the plug on you. Just like they pulled the plug on your friends.'

'What? You're fucking lying.'

'Again with the lack of respect, ya fucking nut-sack. You're in so much deep shite, you'll be breathing through a snorkel. Why Presley?'

'He was just there with McNeil so it wouldn't look like we were targeting McNeil,' Pierce said.

'Why are you here in Presley's girlfriend's house? She told us she was being followed from the hospital. Harry McNeil doesn't live here.'

'I just wanted to teach Presley a lesson.'

Stewart laughed. 'He used to be a boxer. You on our own would get your fucking arse handed to you. He wanted to be here, but I sent him away. I didn't want him killing you in self-defence. I wanted to have a chat with you. But I can get him back here in five minutes. He'd love to smack the shite out of you for following his girlfriend. But I'll keep him away if you tell me who else wanted Harry McNeil hurt.'

'I told you, I don't know who he is. Somebody that a friend of Walker's knew.'

'Who is this friend of Walker's?'

'I don't know. Somebody he was messing about with. I don't know her name. Lizzie maybe.'

Stewart and Evans exchanged a look.

'Right. My colleague is going to stand you up and arrest you. A patrol car is waiting downstairs, and you'll be taken to the High Street station, where you'll be booked in. And think yourself lucky. Those friends of Walker's have turned out to be anything but.'

Evans hauled Pierce to his feet.

'Just a word of warning,' Stewart added. 'My colleague there was also a boxer. Try and stick it on him and he'll clean your fucking clock.'

FIFTY-ONE

Colin Presley wasn't waiting downstairs, not after receiving Lillian's SOS text. Once the two patrol cars turned up and he was sure Amy would be okay, he'd been picked up by Harry, Miller and Dunbar, and they were now shooting along the road to Comely Bank.

'Lizzie must have found out that Lillian had the box file with all the cuttings about the M8 killer in it.'

'Why would that bother her so much?' Presley asked from the back seat, wincing.

'There's something in there that's incriminating and she doesn't want anybody finding it,' Harry said from the front.

In a few minutes they arrived outside Lillian's

flat. They parked, got buzzed in by a neighbour and ran up the two flights.

Lillian's door was ajar. Harry went in first, followed by Miller and Dunbar. Presley brought up the rear, in a keep-your-eyes-peeled capacity.

They started slapping lights on and quickly found Lillian slumped on the living room floor, blood seeping out of the wound in her side. Miller got on the phone for an ambulance as Harry and Dunbar made her comfortable.

'Get a towel, Elvis!' Harry shouted, and the younger man scuttled through to the kitchen to find a towel. He brought it back and Harry applied pressure to the wound as Presley went to find another one, sure they were going to need more than one. He came back and stood with it in his hand.

'Lillian?' Harry said. 'Can you hear me?'

She groaned and her eyelids fluttered and then she started to panic.

'Lillian, relax, it's me, Harry. You're okay now. You're safe. I've got Jimmy and Frank and Elvis with me. You're safe now.'

He saw her visibly relax and her eyes opened. 'Harry?' she said, her voice a dry whisper.

'Yes. It's me. Help's on its way.' Harry looked at

Miller. 'Tell them an escort's needed for the patient. She's one of ours.'

'Got it,' Miller answered.

'Lillian, do you know who did this? Elvis said you sent him a text telling him it was Lizzie. Is that right?'

'Y...yes. It was Lizzie. But not Lizzie.'

Harry looked at Dunbar, who was kneeling next to him on the carpet. 'Lizzie but not Lizzie?'

Dunbar shrugged. 'Maybe she's delirious with blood loss.'

'Not...delirious,' Lillian said, her face getting paler by the minute. 'Lizzie. In the file. Look...in the file. Paddy...knew. She killed him. He had to be... silenced. In the file. I...copied it.'

Dunbar stood up as Harry kept the pressure on the wound. He walked past Miller, who was still on the phone, to the box file on the table. 'I wonder why Lizzie didn't take the file?' he said.

'What good would it do her?' Dunbar said. 'If it's just a copy, then she knows the other one is at the station. Even if she took that one, the other one is with us, where she can't get to it.'

'True.' Harry looked through the papers on the coffee table and saw the one on top. 'Peter Torrington was the only suspect, but his wife had alibied him and he was no longer a suspect,' he said. 'Then he killed himself eight years later, leaving behind a daughter. Elizabeth M. Torrington.' He looked at Dunbar. 'Lizzie.'

The ambulance crew arrived and took over from Dunbar. There was a rush of activity in the flat, then they got Lillian on a stretcher and took her downstairs.

Harry found Lillian's keys on the coffee table. 'Elvis, you go with her to the hospital. We have to go and talk to somebody about Peter Torrington.'

FIFTY-TWO

The bingo night had finished at the church and the old folks were leaving, saying goodbye to each other, the sound of laughter ringing in the cold air as they went to get the bus just across from the front steps.

Frank Miller slipped past them, Harry and Dunbar behind him. They'd thought it best if he go in first.

Reverend Michaels was near the front of the church, talking to some of the parishioners, as the three detectives walked past. His face changed slightly, but they ignored him, continuing towards the back of the church, to the garden room.

Inside, some of the stragglers were still putting their coats on, and they made quite a noise as they cackled and laughed and chatted amongst themselves, in no hurry to get home to a cold house that they couldn't afford to heat.

Miller found who he was looking for, chatting to an old man. She turned to look at him.

'Frank!' Maggie Parks excused herself from the man. 'Is everything okay? Did you find Lizzie?'

He looked at her for a moment, thinking about his friend lying in the hospital mortuary, waiting to be picked up by an undertaker. Thinking of the laughs they'd had.

'We have.'

Maggie put her hand over her mouth. Then she saw Harry and Dunbar standing behind Miller, and then Tom Michaels rushed past them as the last of the old folks left.

'What's going on?' he asked.

'They found Lizzie,' Maggie told him.

'Thank God,' Michaels said. 'Where is she?'

Miller stood in front of Maggie and made eye contact. 'I'm looking at her.'

The only sound in the room was the distant laughter of the last bingo patrons. Then that faded, leaving only silence.

Michaels broke the stalemate. 'What do you mean?'

'Do you want to tell him, or will I? Oh, wait, you

already know.' Miller looked at Michaels, turning sideways so he could address both him and Maggie. 'It was the box file, wasn't it, Maggie? Or would you prefer I call you by your original name, Lizzie Torrington? It was all there. How you were the M8 killer's daughter. It was him, wasn't it? Peter Torrington. He was their main suspect forty years ago because a witness put him at the scene of the dump site at Harthill Services. But your mother gave him an alibi. He travelled for business and often stopped there, but crucially your mother gave him an alibi for the night of the abduction of one of the women. What was it that made her do that? Fear? Loyalty?'

'You don't know what he was like,' Maggie said. 'He was a bastard. He made me and Drew do some horrible things.'

'Ah, that's right, your brother here. Drew Torrington. We also found your name when we did a search for name changes. Drew Torrington became Tom Michaels. Lizzie Torrington became Maggie Parks. Was your original middle initial M for Margaret?'

Her silence answered in the affirmative.

Miller carried on, watched by Harry and Dunbar.

'I'm guessing that you changed your names because you didn't want to be associated with him?'

'Yes,' Michaels answered. 'You see, our father was living a double life. He had two wives, but technically he wasn't married to my mother, just lived with her. He had me with her, and Maggie with her mother. And she's right, he was a complete bastard. We didn't know each other back then when we were kids; it was only later on in life that we connected. But he used to take us along when he met those girls. He made me watch him kill one of them, and I'm not talking about one of the three victims. There were others that he didn't display. Others that he buried out in the woods. As I got older, I wanted him to stop, but he wouldn't. He made me help him bury them and then told me if I went to the police, he'd tell them I killed them. Or at least helped him kill them.'

'What about you, Maggie?' Harry said. 'How did your father treat you?'

She was smiling then, and her eyes were glazed over as if she was reliving it all. Then she snapped back to the here and now.

'Much the same way. He never killed them in the same place, but he took Tom hunting with him through in the west, and took me when he was back through here. He would make me watch. But unlike Tom, I got a kick out of it. I can't tell you why, but when I saw him doing it, it was like Christmas morning. I felt a shiver of anticipation run through me, that jolt of excitement. He could see it in me and let me help. I enjoyed every minute.'

'Did you kill him?' Dunbar said. 'We read about him committing suicide.'

She laughed. 'Of course I did. He didn't like it when I was going to go away to university. I wanted to make something of my life. My mother had died and it was just the two of us. He said he would tell the police if I went away. So I slit his wrists and put him in the bath.'

'Then you met Charlie Armstrong. How did he pick that cold case to look into? Bit of a coincidence, don't you think?'

'He was a good detective, Charlie. I don't know if he suspected, but I think he did. Some things just didn't add up, despite me lying to him. I think he just got more suspicious over time. We had got married and moved into the flat next door with his daughter, Lizzie. I didn't even know about the box file until recently. I couldn't see on top of that shelf and it was away at the back. You wouldn't know it was there unless you looked for it.

'Then after Charlie died, I met Paddy and he moved in. And one day Paddy asked me if I'd seen his old camera. I hadn't, so he went looking for it. Later I noticed he'd dropped something off the top shelf, so I got the stepladders to put it back and then I saw it, the file. I took it out and looked through it. I thought Paddy had been looking through it, and then I knew that he knew I was Lizzie Torrington. I couldn't take the risk he'd told anybody, so I pushed him down the steps.'

'You were in here, but it was easy to slip away after Paddy sent you a text saying he was going out. Your brother here would cover for you.'

'That's right. I went out and Paddy was near the top of the steps. I pushed him back down and he hit his head hard. I came back in here.'

'And left him to die,' Miller said, his voice catching in his throat.

Harry stepped forward. 'What about Tess Grogan?' he asked Michaels.

'I made the mistake of telling her years ago about who I was. Our relationship was going sour and she wanted to mess around with other men. Clifford Dunn was one. I had to pretend I liked him so she wouldn't divulge who I was to him, so Maggie killed her to protect our identity. She took the fingers through to Glasgow. We knew Dunn was planning on having two goons throw blood over the statue, and he talked about where he could get it so Maggie put the fingers in the buckets.'

'What about April Donegan?' Dunbar asked.

'Tess said April was her best friend, that she told her everything. Maggie and I couldn't take the risk that Tess had told her. We were going to frame Dunn for her murder.'

'I'm confused,' he said. 'Where did Ray Walker and the other two fit into this?'

'I was having an affair with Ray,' Maggie said. 'I'd known him since way back when he worked with my Charlie. I told him that Harry was planning on taking him down. He was livid. I made it up, of course, because I wanted him to take you out of the picture in case Paddy had told you what he had found. Ray couldn't do it himself, so he got two detectives to help him, Dawson and Pierce, who'd both been investigated by Standards in the past. They were keen to give you a kicking. It didn't go according to plan, though. So they tried again.'

'And you set up your own daughter to take the fall,' Miller said, his voice a croak.

'It had to be done. Andy would do anything for her, so I used her phone to text him, and then when he got home, I ran him down. I would have killed him too if that other car hadn't appeared. I was going to reverse over him.'

'You killed Ray Walker too.'

'They'll find a pinprick. Heroin overdose,' Maggie said proudly.

'Being the head of forensics, you know how to process a crime scene, so you made sure your tracks were covered,' Harry said.

'I did. Same with Ricky Dawson. Ian Pierce would have got the same treatment later.'

Harry could see behind the mask now, see the insanity that was lurking there – whether from being born with it or being around a serial killer he didn't know, but it was there.

'Where's Dunn now?' Harry asked.

'And Lizzie?' Miller added.

'Maggie, run!' Michaels said, grabbing hold of Dunbar and throwing him at the other two men, knocking them over. Maggie ran out of the other door from the garden room into the church.

Dunbar rolled over in the heap and tripped Michaels up as the reverend tried to run. The two men got to their feet at the same time, and Michaels pulled back a fist to launch a punch, but Dunbar head-butted him and Michaels hit the deck.

Harry and Miller got to their feet.

'Bastard,' Miller said.

'Go get her, Harry,' Dunbar said, twisting Michaels' arm behind his back.

Harry and Miller ran out of the garden room into the church, but Maggie was nowhere to be seen.

'Do you think she'd have run back to her flat?' Harry asked.

'Let's go and look.'

They ran across the open floor of the church and opened the heavy main door. Outside, a small group of men and women were standing there, chatting.

'Did anybody see Maggie Parks come out here?' Harry said.

'No, son,' one of the older men said.

'Nobody came out here,' a woman confirmed.

They went back into the church and back into the middle, where they could see up to the balcony.

'I'll check it,' Miller said.

He ran into the vestibule and up the stairs to the balcony. There was nobody there. He came down the opposite stairs.

Dunbar had Michaels on his knees.

'You okay there, Jimmy?' Harry shouted.

'Just grand here, Harry. If Baw-Jaws starts his pish again, he'll be going to visit his bollocks in the museum of surgeons. He's cuffed and back-up is on its way. Just find Maggie.'

Miller ran back in. 'She's not up there.'

'Right, let's check the office.'

Harry and Miller ran over, but that too was empty. The kitchen, conference room and the room where the cots were set up were all empty as well.

'Where the hell did she disappear to?' Miller said.

Then they saw another door behind the pulpit.

'What's through that door?' Miller asked Michaels.

'Fuck you.'

Dunbar yanked the man's arms further up his back until he squealed. 'Okay, okay! It's the basement.'

Miller nodded to Harry. He opened the door and saw a set of stairs leading down. It smelled musty and ancient, as if it was an old tomb that had just been opened after being closed for a very long time.

It also had a smell that was very familiar to them.

Harry flicked the light switch, but nothing happened. The light from the church interior lit up only part of the stairway and they could see the smashed bulb. They took their phones out and switched on the torches in them and shone them down the old stone steps. The time for stealth was gone, and they both took out their extendable batons as they went down.

'Maggie, it's over,' Harry said, leading the way. It was at this point that it occurred to him that Miller was younger and fitter and should have led the way, but too late.

They reached the bottom of the stairs and shone the lights about. The basement was old and it stank. Evidently, it was the last resting place of the old pews that had been ripped out when they had put in the new seating arrangement upstairs. They were covered in dust. Other old furniture had also been dumped there, including desks and chairs. Harry's light illuminated what looked like dark hair sticking up from a chair. He crept forward, his heart racing.

He gripped the high-backed swivel chair and the smell was worse. He turned it round and involuntarily jumped back as the dead face of Clifford Dunn looked back at him.

'Fuck me, Frank, it's Dunn. He's dead.' No reply. 'Frank?'

He turned round and saw Miller standing still with a knife held to his neck.

'Move and I'll kill him. I have nothing to lose,' Maggie said.

'Okay,' Harry said, 'you don't want to kill Frank. Just take it easy.'

'Throw the baton into the dark over on your left.'

Harry did as he was told. Then he heard Miller's being thrown.

'You two are just a pain in my arse, you know that? But you're right, Harry. I can't kill Frank.' Maggie took the knife away from his throat and shoved him hard. For the second time that night, Harry and Miller went clattering to the floor. The phone was knocked out of Harry's hand and went skidding under a pew.

'She threw mine over there,' Miller said as they quickly got to their feet.

Harry fished his out from under the pew. 'Jimmy! Jimmy! She's heading up the stairs!' he shouted at the top of his lungs, running for the stairs, followed by Miller.

'What's all the shouting about?' Calvin Stewart said as Harry and Miller reached the top.

Maggie had been wrestled to the floor, kicking and screaming, by a few uniforms.

Then Evans appeared, running towards them. 'Her daughter, Lizzie, is safe. She was being kept upstairs in the small flat there. They'd kept her hidden in the basement before moving her up there earlier. She's scared out of her wits, but she's fine. She'll need therapy after this, that's for sure.'

'I think we all will,' Dunbar said, coming up to them as more uniforms led Michaels outside.

'Clifford Dunn is dead on an office chair downstairs,' Harry said.

Dunbar just nodded. 'I don't know about you lot, but I'm going to need a pint after all the paperwork is taken care of.'

Nobody argued.

FIFTY-THREE

Ten days later

Harry held on to Kelly Gibb as the undertakers brought her father's coffin over.

'I didn't want the bairn to see this,' she said, explaining why she had come alone.

'It's not something that you want to make an impression,' Harry agreed.

He looked over and saw Morgan Allan standing in black trousers and a heavy overcoat. He wondered if she was thinking about her own husband's funeral, but if she was, she didn't show it. She was standing beside Lizzie Armstrong, who looked like a train wreck, but with Morgan at her side, she would cope so much better. Lizzie had started seeing her already.

On Harry's other side, Jimmy Dunbar stood with Robbie Evans. Miller was on Lizzie's other side, his wife, Kim, beside him. His own little girls weren't there either.

Lillian O'Shea was next to Elvis. Harry had promised himself that he wouldn't get sucked into calling the young DC by his nickname, but he'd caved. Calvin Stewart was standing beside Lillian.

Snow had fallen a couple of days earlier and remnants of it remained. Now, a cold wind shot through the cemetery, and Harry wished that Paddy had gone for cremation instead, but it wasn't meant to be. He reminded himself that a man was dead, and he kept a tight hold on the hanky in his pocket. For some reason, the cold weather always made his nose run.

The minister gave the eulogy and Paddy Gibb was lowered into the ground. Kelly wept and Harry kept his arm around her shoulders. His mind went back to the charges Maggie and Michaels were facing. They had been remanded in custody until the procurator fiscal's office finalised the charges.

When the funeral was over, they met up at a

local hotel and gathered in a function room to give Paddy a good send-off.

'I didn't know your dad personally,' Stewart said to Kelly, 'but I heard he was a damn good bloke and a fine police officer.'

'Thank you,' Kelly said.

Stewart left to find Dunbar, and Morgan came over and filled his seat. She spoke to Kelly for a while, and then the young woman made her excuses, saying she had to go talk to an old aunt of hers.

'Two days until Christmas,' Harry said to Morgan. 'Got any plans?'

'Well, since my in-laws all blame me for my husband's death and I have no family of my own, it's going to be like every other Christmas: a turkey sandwich, sitting in my sweats and watching a soppy film. How about you?'

'Jessica is going to Spain tomorrow. The nursery is closed for the next week or so, and a group of girls are going, so I told her she should go. I'll be fine with Grace. I put in for some time off.'

'Good for you.'

'I'll have plenty of turkey, if you would...well... what I'm trying to say is...'

'Are you inviting me over for Christmas dinner, Harry?' She smiled at him.

'Yes. Sorry, I got a bit tongue-tied.'

'I'd love to. Thank you.'

They both had spouses who weren't going to be around on Christmas Day. Maybe this would be easier for both of them.

'I have to warn you, though: I don't wear sweats,' Harry said.

'That's fine. I'll leave mine at home.'

'Deal. Now, how attached are you to watching a soppy film?'

'Why? You got a better suggestion?'

'I have actually,' Harry said. 'Now, a lot of people don't think this is a Christmas film, but I do, and so do many others. *Die Hard.*'

'What? No. *Die Hard*? You've got to be kidding.'

'Nope. It's one of the best Christmas films ever made...'

AUTHOR'S NOTE

Thanks go to my wife as always. And to my daughters, for their support. Thanks to Jacqueline Beard once again for her eagle eyes. She's a wonderful lady. And a huge thanks goes to Charlie Wilson, my editor. She truly is a star, and without her, these books wouldn't make it out in one piece. I raise my glass to you, Charlie. Thank you once again to my niece, Lynn McKenzie, who takes on the role of detective superintendent. And to the real Lisa McDonald.

And thanks to you, the reader, who makes it all possible.

If I could ask a favour before you go – if you could see your way to leaving a review on Amazon or

Goodreads, that would be terrific. It really helps an author like me. Thank you.

Stay safe, my friends.

John Carson

New York

April 2022

To Liz

with best wishes
and thanks

Nigel [signature]

Drury Arts
May '10.

Chora

by the same author

Collections:

At The Waters' Clearing
Flambard & Black Mountain Presses 2001

Songs For No Voices
Lagan Press 2004

Blood
Bluechrome Press 2005

Dissonances
Bluechrome Press 2007

Nigel McLoughlin

Chora:
New & Selected Poems

Templar Poetry

First Published 2009 by Templar Poetry
Templar Poetry is an imprint of Delamide & Bell

Fenelon House
Kingsbridge Terrace
58 Dale Road, Matclock, Derbyshire
DE4 3NB

www.templarpoetry.co.uk

ISBN 978-1-906285-39-5

Typeset by Pliny
Graphics by Paloma Violet
Printed and bound in India

For all those who have been midwives to the craft

Acknowledgements:

Acknowledgement is due to the following journals, anthologies and radio stations who have published or broadcast poems contained in this collection: *Acumen, Agenda, Anna Livia FM, Black Mountain Review, Books Ireland, Breaking The Skin (Black Mountain Press), Burning Bush, Cordite (Australia), Cork Literary Review, Cúirt Journal, Cyphers, De Brakke Hond (Belgium), The Echoing Years: An Anthology of Poetry from Ireland & Canada (WIT School of Humanities Publications), Electric Acorn, Envoi, Faultline (USA), The Fifteen Project (USA), Fortnight, Free Verse (USA), Frogmore Papers, The Guardian, Honest Ulsterman, The Independent on Sunday, In The Criminal's Cabinet (Nth Position Press), Iota, The Irish Times, Journal of American, British and Canadian Studies (Romania), Journal of Irish Studies (Japan), The London Magazine, Magnetic North (Blackstaff & Verbal Arts Centre), The Moe Green Poetry Show (USA), National Public Radio (USA), New Writing, New Soundings (Blackstaff Press), The New Writer, Nth Position, Orbis, Outposts, Poetry Ireland, Poetry Review, Radio Foyle, Radio Ulster, Review of Postgraduate Studies, The Shop, Snakeskin, Spondee (USA), The Stinging Fly, The Sunday Tribune, Thunder Sandwich, Ulster Tatler, West 47,* and *Words (Canada).*

Contents

from *At The Waters' Clearing* (2001):

from *Songs For No Voices* (2004):

from *Blood* (2005):

from *Dissonances* (2007):

The following abbreviations are used in footnotes to the poems:

(Ir.) – Irish language
(Hib.) – Hiberno-English dialect
(colloq) – colloquialism or slang
pron: – pronounced
lit. – literal translation

Preface

I believe in poetry as an aural art. A poem exists primarily in the mouth and in the ear and in the resonating space between them. I tend to compose orally. The poem only appears in written form after a period of hearing the poem in my head and speaking it out loud. By the time the poem demands to be written down, it is already at an advanced stage of completion. What remains is usually tinkering with shape and line breaks.

I chose *Chora* as the title because it has the triple sense of ideas with which I think my poetry engages: It has that sense of permanent other; it is that which is outside the *polis*. It is has a sense of relation to the land and landscape. It has the sense of creative flux in which things shape themselves and find birth. My poetry has always concerned itself with the land and landscape and those who work it; the oral tradition, the outsider, the cultural erosion of the periphery; and the spaces where things form themselves. I think perhaps because of that, my work has found for itself a sense of belonging to a tradition posited as other to the middle class urban cool of the mainstream.

In its Derridan and Kristevan senses, *Chora* offers itself up both as a creative and nurturing space and a receptacle that can hold but not become part of that which it holds. It is both a vehicle for poetry and the void from which poetry emerges. It is a womb-like space that is analogous with the preverbal stage of composition where the poem has not yet found differentiation and separation from the amnion that surrounds it. It is a pre-lingual, pre-symbolic stage close to the materiality of existence, or 'the Real'. Poetry as an act is at least partly an attempt to communicate that.

The poems selected here have been written and rewritten over eighteen years. I have revisited the poems from my earlier books and rewritten many of them; some have been significantly cut or changed, because with the benefit of hindsight and development, I think I can help the poem do what it does a little better. Sometimes the change is little more than tidying up a word or line break that interrupted the flow as I read the poem. Reading to an audience is a crucial test that helps to identify a misplaced line break or an extraneous word.

In many respects my poetry is concerned with my desire to privilege the 'eye' over the 'I'. I have, over the years, noticed a development in my poetic philosophy which tends more and more towards the extinction of the poetic 'I' as 'ego' and a desire to foreground what that 'I' observes and experiences. A metaphor might be to think of the poet as positioned beneath the reader's view but holding up the image (and the speaking subject) above himself so that the reader's view is concentrated not on the 'I' or ego which writes but squarely on what and who is being written about. This does not necessarily mean the extinction of personality, but rather it constructs the 'personality' or the 'I' of the poem through an empathic act and offers a lens through which the reader may apprehend the subject /narrator/image and draw their own conclusions.

Nigel McLoughlin

April 2009

Chora never alters its characteristics. For it continues to receive all things, and never itself takes a permanent impress from any of the things which enter it, making it appear different at different times.

Plato, *Timaeus* 50-52

Some Go Dancing

'Some who go dancing through dark bogs are lost' - Louis Mac Neice

There could be emeralds
topaz, amethysts in the sky
where the setting sun
makes a tiger's eye
of the horizon.

The light sublimes
under night's arced wing
like a jewelled shock
of hair that springs
from mountains.

Nights like these she comes
a fickle witch, her red hair down
drawing me to the hills
that lie outside the town
and takes me dancing.

I have danced with her
where the moon sings
impaled in branches, or drowns
in streams that dragon wing
the hillsides.

There are nights she leaves
me to find my own way home
and I have danced down mountains
through dark bogs, have never known
that I was lost.

Foreland Heights in the Age of Mechanical Reproduction

Whiskey glass on the table. Tan on black marble (imitation).

I knew a guy once, drank lighter fuel, lit a cigarette. Immolated from the inside out, over a woman.

Lip sweet the liquid, burning in the throat, the stomach. Can I buy you another?

The woman at the bar is hitching her skirt, enticing me over. She needs a light.

And what if I stay with her tonight? Who knows? I find the grinding music of her stimulating somehow. Yes, I could be with her tonight.

My glass is empty. I push it over the bar to the brown-eyed waitress, waiting to be served. I can tell she's in no hurry.

My lips will be wet soon enough. I strike a match and conversation flares between me and the woman to my left. Her skirt is half way up her thigh. I eye her legs.

I leave with her, the easy swing of her hips in time with mine. Her eyes deceive me closely.

In the morning we will both wake early, make some excuse to
leave.

Subjects

I

He's keeping time with a pencil
on the page to the slow air
the fiddler bows. Drawing her.

He flicks fine hair across her neck
shading her cheeks, her hands
eyeing her, eyeing her constantly.

He's measuring her, all thumbs
angling her with pencils, stopping
sometimes, proportioning; divining her.

II

There is a feel of 3B about
her soft graphite eyes.
They never stray, remaining
fixed to the back wall, lost.

Her hands dance across
the fiddle neck, trimmed
hands with a scrubbed look
feline in their fall across strings.

Her face has a high colour
like an afterglow or blush
perhaps from the effort of playing
perhaps aware she's being sketched.

Firesides

Each Halloween
she'd sit spinning yarns
teaching the art of divination.

Her chosen medium, hazelnuts
licked by flame, drowned in ash
would spit and fizzle on the fire.

In the end they'd burst
as we eyed them one to the other
waiting to find out who'd die first.

She was full of old wives' tales
of bean sídhe, madadh mór
cóiste bodhar, well versed in portents.

She was at home in these dark days.
When her shell burst first
I'd catch her smiling, proven right.

At eighty-four she left an empty hearth
without a sound, no yelping dogs
no coach wheels, no keening.

Quick, like a shell splitting
a short hiss of kernel, absolute
as one who had known all along.

madadh mór (Ir.) – pron: madoo more – lit. great dog
cóiste bodhar (Ir.) – pron: coastye bower – death coach.
bean sídhe (Ir.) – banshee – all three are portents of death.

4

Image

Suited up for Sunday
before they took you
dressed you in khaki
and sent you rifled
to the Dardanelles.

I got your name second-hand
passed down with details
sketches of your life
your death in the military
hospital in Wales.

I know nothing of the dreaming
years before the barbed wire
bullets and the mines left you
in a regimental plot
none of us have seen.

I could even doubt you
put you down as a family
myth were it not for this
photograph, the sole survivor
I keep as proof

and to imagine what was
going on behind your
familiar familial eyes
why the day you left
you were smiling.

Breaking Clocks

Beginning each identical grey morning
the only blue the bus that passed him by
his life is beaten out, repeated
in the seven-second cycle of his machine.
Nightly, he oils his throat down at the local
talking football. Even that's no longer an escape.

When he dreams his way above the thicket
out past the landfill of his life
then the sky unmapping into mountains
opens up a clearer kind of eye.
Here he can unravel any colour.
He can put the roof upon his half-built life.
He can feel the clocks have all been broken
feel the sky rush through the flight of birds.

In Falcarragh

The wind soughs at the gable
sings to the creeping damp
where the moon's cold flag rises
over Machaire Rabhartaigh. A pallid
light bends the tide from Toraigh
crossed by a flicker regular as waves.
It's as though the windows breathe

to the cold hearth and I
weather out each gust, proof
under blankets to my chin.
Only the occasional star intrudes
like an eye in the glass pane
and I know this roof will stand
the blast and bar the wind.

I decamp and close the curtains
fill the room with a dark tide
return to snuggle close to the balm
of skin shining through the dark.
I reach for her face and drift and kiss
the mouth beside me and forget.

Machaire Rabhartaigh (Ir.) – pron: Maheraroarty – lit. Roarty's Plain – place
name in Donegal.

Toraigh (Ir.) – pron: Torree – Tory Island.

Cat at my Window

A black cat with cyan eyes
watches me from my window.
A buckle-back arches hair
to heaven and a pink slit
is bitten out from teeth.
The face is feminine
too small to be intimidating
yet she looms at my window.

A shadow on the night
the borders of her body
blur into the outside until
she becomes as massive as sky.
The cyan eyes wax and pulse
lights in the huge beast of night.
Her soundless mouthings under glass
lost cries at her changing.

Earthed

Just a foretaste of storm to come:
winter in juvenilia, playing, testing
its strength or the strength of walls.
The wind gives voice to gables
and trees are singing, soon
I think, it will tear down the eaves.
The rain is a burglar, stealing
in through the window seal
and the glass is melting slowly.

I have seen the storm full grown
lay trees across roads like ladder rungs
leave wires sparking in the sheugh.
I have felt it bellow me to the fireside
when the sky lit and thunder tore.
I watched my mother run to cover mirrors
draw curtains across windows
remove the tongs, render the hearth safe.

I don't believe these old wives' tales
of lightning bullets that ricochet.
Electricity seeks ground not glass.
Still, I won't stand at windows
to watch lightning, to face down the fury
for even though I'm not the tallest standing
arrows miss their mark; accidents happen.

sheugh (Hib.) – pron: shuch (where ch is as in 'loch') – drainage ditch

Darkling

I

You could see the old latchico
any day, perched on the park
bench, paying out the hours before
sunset on beads of bread he fed
to birds. He appeared half-sídhe
half-saoi, speaking to the pigeons
and the air.

He told me once he came
early to the outside of this world
that he had always known
he had no share in it. He hid his fear
behind his closed mouth
his unransomed loneliness.
He died there.

I went to his wake, one of the few
willing to associate and kneeling in the dark
between two candles, I think I found
the word that stiffened on his lips, what
prayer exhumed from the weeping wax.

latchico (Hib.) — an undesirable
sídhe (Ir.) — pron: shee — bewitching (possessed of the glamour of 'the gentry').
saoi (Ir.) — pron: see — head of a monastic or poetic school

II

He had eyes that could be tears
in tallow, could guide him
through the darkness under
the lios, where the night
danced like lovers' fingers
on the skin. It was his:
the entire yielding element.

It had named him early for its own.
It lingered on him still, a salt kiss
on those wax lips, as though his words
might rise and fill the room:
the dark is a woman with soporific skin.

lios (Ir.) – pron: liss – enclosure or fort often associated with the sídhe

Songs for the Years' Turning

I Imbolc

Knitting words into silence
incanting at the hearthstone
fire lights the hag's eyes blind.
She's remembering each noviciate
gathering rushes by the shore's edge
each woman weaving crooked crosses
the low moans around gables
every bean sídhe. She's remembering
all the things she's been
and keening for the years' turning.

II Beltaine

The snowdrop pushes soil
screams out rebirth
as juices ooze upward
in a slow sexing under eaves.
Under the bark, fused
to the explosion, the bursting
of the buds is almost audible.
Take all of this, each landing
and leaving time, and dedicate
it to death and change.
With each dive and circle
birds are flinging to the sun
their songs for the years' turning.

III Lughnasa

It's a short journey
from a borrowed throne
to the sage's seat.
For a master of all the arts
there is only dissolution left
sweating groundward.
The air reeks of elder and heat
where the dogs are lying
fleas cracking in the sun
and each movement labours
like slow music
at the year's turning.

IV Samhain

The mind aquaplanes
into mist, free falls
to omens, portents, ghosts.
These are the dark days'
blurred borders.
That first wind that cuts
the sallies names it:
night of the world's dreaming.
The hooded crows cloak
their black secrets from the moon
and forgotten gods are gathering
around fires in the hills
where the Morrigan is dancing
to the song of each year's turning.

The Green Man
from the Irish of Cathal Ó Searcaigh

You ride in from the outback on the back of the wind
loose-limbed, hob-nailing a storm. I smell whin fresh
on the gale of your breath. The ooze of the bog drips
the green sod of your tongue, flocks of birds sing like leaves
in your hair's cowl. You come inciting seed, the roots'
fingering and bidding sun's lustre to the grey face of April.

The clouds are tangling in your limbs and birds nest
in your chest's heather, settle in the hedgerow of your loins.
Yet you come scouring, pelting the cuckoo out with rain
that drives a sheen on weed and bush and blackthorn.
And when you stretch the spring of your bones
there is a bleat in the field and a crake in the meadow.

Here, in this mountain pasture, the green light of your eye
dives into our clay and hope is full in bud and feather.

Restoration

Lightning. Rain crashes on the window pane, to wake me
and keep me writing. I'm drawn to storms, to the darkness
of the tree that looms across the lake.

You can still see the scars on the trunk where the car hit
they've grown over now, faint reminders of deeper cuts
in the softer pith.

The night after the car wreck I walked the road beyond
the tree at two or three o'clock in the morning. Winter
with my crombie coat tucked about my chin, head down
into the wind and rain. I pushed myself home.

Nights later, I passed a poppy wreath blowing between road
and ditch, thinking it would not be found come morning
but returning home just after dawn, I saw it thrown back
beneath the tree. A chance act of the last gust.

Kilmakerrill

Between Manorhamilton and Glenfarne
there is a place just off the road
whose name rings out with loneliness.
Kilmakerrill – a burial ground
where graves are cut from granite soil
and the stone is rough.
A thousand years of bone and rock
(and maybe a thousand more)
lie in that uneven ground.

Generations of my ancestors
lie line on line
in close-knit family groups.
Within the rough rock wall
the gravestones grow
like dragons teeth.
On this wind-lashed plain
there bleeds true freedom
and all who lie here know
the cruelty of real peace.

Unearthly at night, no church
no God gazes down.
You can hear the grass whisper:
here a man can be truly dead
and a corpse completely cold.

Funeral

Accelerating years plunge
from birth to earth
like a hurtling bird.

Ground approaches,
sudden as a bullet impact
or the stopping of a clock.

Those eyes on me
as my tear-dried throat
stumbles over Aves.

Aware of the gaping grave
its need for filling in
I hold the little ground I have.

Later at the graveside I unroll
words like a carpet, even
and unafraid warming

my communion alone and in the dark.

Aves (colloq.) – Hail Marys

The Gift

Smiling to yourself somewhere
between the purse of a slow air and the belt
of a reel as though you know that wood
is not the true instrument and music
is sparks in the head forced to look
for a lightning rod.

At the point where the tune took off
you'd close your eyes and disappear.
Fire spat through wood. You'd wring
tears from timber, turning and turning
the tune through the furrows of your head.

I picture you in a maze of melody
notes like flames around your head
and your eyes closed, at once lost
and unified with music, fingers
raised to dance the air in the semi-dark.

Here, this long night I offer this:
a rod for grief's cold lightning.

Crossings

I'm sure I saw a fug of fox
high-tail to the dark and green-
eyed ditch under the fog and out
of the corner of an eye. The road
bent and the lights caught the lake
on the fall and a fish split
the surface for a second
in a small shingle of light

where the eye of the lake stared
through a lens of frost and fixed
the colour-blind moon in focus.
Trees groaned under the weight
of black air that draped
on the rumpled sheet of hills
crowding back to back in coats
and shawls as though the world
was nothing but a lake of shadows.

The morning brought a white rime
and a dagger wind that cut me blue
as they put you down. The rosary ebbed
and flowed and finally abated and I drove
the same road home in daylight. The world
was nothing but a lake of mist.
I'm sure I saw that same fox high-tail
to the ditch and turn red eyed to face me
at the waters' clearing.

Deora Dé

"See them?", she said
and pointed to a yellow
flower blotched with red
"They grew below Christ's cross.
And see.....", she said, pointing
to each stain, "the seven
drops of blood."

"See them?", she said
pointing to the unopened
fuchsia earrings in the hedge.
She lifted one and nipped
and broke it where the flower
meets the pod and prising the top
end: "Taste!" she said.

A single drop
of nectar fell on the end
of my tongue, surprising
me with sweetness.
"When God cries," she said
"His tears are sweet
and red."

I picked an opened version
and did the same.
"See them?", I said
"Them's little ballerinas
red skirts, red tights
and little purple knickers."

I giggled, twisting each dancer
into a turn and turn on a green
backdrop – six pleated
blurs on the stage of a wall.
"You'll never make a priest."
was all she said.

Deora Dé (Ir.) – pron: jora jay – lit. tears of God – fuchsia bush

Catching Fire

She maintained only one right way
to clean the flue: fire shoved
up to burn it out, drive sparks
from the chimney stack and smuts
into air. Each bunched and bundled
paper held till the flame took
and it flew, took off on its own
consumption, rose on its own updraft.
I stood fixed by her leather face
dancing in firelight, her hands
clamped to the metal tongs.
Eyes stared black and wide, rims
of blue that circled wells, pools
that fire stared into. I watched
her pull from beneath them black
ash and a paper smell I love still.

She told me she saw faces in the flame
and people, places, things take place.
She'd spey fortunes there. Told me mine
but I saw nothing more or less
than the dance of flame, the leap
and die, the resurrection of yellow
cowl and dual change of split-
levelled flame that held within it
a dance of words, a ballet of images.
I heard only the music of burning
a soundless consummation of persistence
imagined a vision of my hands reddening
felt my knuckles braising
my bones in tongues, flaming.

Quarterlights

I Garden

Just a short walk from mist into the dark.
A statue's head peeps over a wall to frighten lovers.
Telegraph poles stand like gibbets
and birds whistle in the dark.

In the mist branches grow vernal with verdigris.
A garden of remembrance never planted
a grown-over bomb site; a half-demolished
building; a monument covered up.

The car park's chasm is overrun with *Beetles*
and haloed trees stand as unknown soldiers.
The only sound remains my feet
and the echoes in the silent places.

II Town

A street of palaces and pubs
a courthouse crumbling and the church.
Hairdressers, whorehouses, leaded windows
lattices and lechers, levity and debt.
This is Ireland.

Artificial arches, wallpaper and weeping
defunct post-office, townhall, death.
Chemists, chandeliers; litterbins and layabouts
dolls houses, dole offices, marriage, drink.
Buttresses, bomb sites, banks, and bridal boutiques.
Everything with shutters down.

Toyshops and graveyards, taxis and takeaways
hardware, software, charities and change.
Bank machines and bridges; bread and breakdowns
jewellers, general stores, butchers and tourists
one bookshop, one town centre, all ivy and atrophy
and in the middle of it – mist.

III Hill

Sky blue-black near dawn
and mist pervading pockets
of full-moon light.
The town lights, pale red
and yellow, pin-pricks of sadness
on the mirror of the lough.

Orange and white bouncing
from the upper veils
of valleys filled like cups
under breasted hills and paths.

I can taste the air
light as star-glow.
I breathe.

IV Lough

Standing on a bridge, below a graveyard
one step away from being entombed
in mist lying six feet deep over water
where skin-creep and moon glare
light candles of recognition.

Two lovers twisted like beech saplings
lean inward in mutual support
against a brace of black topped buildings
brightened by the moon and moisture.

Reeds rustle. I sit at a table damp with dew
topped with beer cans, lit by the moon's corona
all hues and glows and mildew. I strain
my sight to see ten yards ahead.

V Nightclub

Car radios beat steady as hearts:
rhythm regulating engines.
Headlights under mist beam yellow
under paler yellow streetlights
dogs bark as a jaundiced sun is rising.

Existing only in shades of car-light laser
distant shouts as the nightclub
throws out its last hoard of drunks.
Cigarettes, Zippo flames, metal, glass
and an ambulance swells against the night.
A bird sings to the light of the KFC.

Caha

You could crack a match
on the rock inside these tunnels
when they were first chiselled.
Sledgehammers, bits and wedges
drilled through the years before Nobel.

Moveable forges kept the metal true
roasted spuds once daily
halfway between dawn and dusk.
A navvy army hammered away daylight
fought blow by blow through mountains
heard hammers even as they slept.

After chipping away choking summers
in the dust, battering away winters at the forge
it must have been like birth to strike
that final blow and let the air come dancing
through the gap.

Stones

Passing Milltown on the last bus home
the gravestones flicker-flame
flare into life, just for seconds
as if to say...

Remember how we buried truth
under martyrs, under blame
when God was which and who.

The lights of The Maze play in lines
dancing chains around the gaol.
Our dead rhetoric returns
in sentences, parsed with guns.
it echoes off walls...

Haunts our silences, in these places
where those we've shut up, put
under stones, form monuments
in years, in tears, in flesh
bagged by the hundredweight.

Lines

I

The lines were run in circles
into boxes, measured out in yards
each hook checked and spanned
breastbone to fist for the next
cursing the barb-bite of a stray.

The lines were lifted early, set late.
The time between, a fury of mending
checking, baiting, and driving drums
to the Dutchman to be weighed. Lunch
was eels, fried still moving on the pan.

II

Lines of eels thrown lithe-live
into an oil drum in my uncle's boat.
Once, I tossed the drum
screamed under their oozing mass
and always after fished for pike.

III

The little ones I carried home
forefinger and thumb in either eye
larger ones were middle-finger
gaffed under the last gill, taken
to be gutted, skinned and fried.

Jawbones of the biggest, boiled
and bleached, I kept for trophies.
With my fingers slashed by gills
of ones I *nearly* killed, I spent
summers dodging water-rats.

IV

Each assassin tempted out of reed-clumps
with live bait. Sink and draw, drawing out
the fight to complete capitulation on lines
without trace-wire. My landing net
was a cold slapping on concrete piers.

V

Of the men who fished Lough Erne
professionally, few could swim
and none would fish at Whit.
The lough takes three a year

a sacrifice to the old god
who hides two miles from shore
in the pit of the Broad Lough
where light stops and weights
have failed to hit the bottom.

I stood on piers, cast a line
where I would not venture
pulled pike for fear of eels.
I stayed well away at Whit
out of respect, fearing a slip.

VI

I've seen an eel cross land
snake its way to water with
a muscular will to live. Even
with the head cut off they thrash
for hours and if you poke a finger
into the headless gullet, you can feel
the suck as it pulls towards the stomach.

VII

"A peaceful death?"
That's a lie that fishermen tell
to comfort relatives of the bloated corpse
they drag mangled from lock gates
or the net's mesh, mouth wide

in a watered scream, hands full of grass
they gripped so tight the fingers must be broken
to release it. You drown by thirds, three chances
to be caught and dragged thrashing back.

Three breaths before water sucks your dream
and thought dissolves, before everything is water
your eye wide and cold as the pike's.

VIII

I learned to swim when I stopped fishing
left my singing reel, left my line to rot.
The only thing I could not leave:
the lough, the water, called me back
as a mother would a straying child.
I never left it long. There is a bond of blood
that pulls me to it: several ancestors
dead by drowning.

IX

These days I run my lines by metre
not the yard, but still I circle
box them in and check the hooks.
I run them shore to shore, have pushed
apart the weight, the float and set
my lines to fish the deeper water.

Epicedium

At four years old I'd turn up and stand and watch the line
shoot, a yard at a time, into a perfect circle in the box
how you'd lash hooks with finger twists too quick to be a knot
or when you sat, a cross-legged magician, mending nets
all wrists and teeth that somehow missed the flying needle.

I'd let fly with a head-full of questions. You'd answer
with a wink and nod to Ned or Paul and I'd believe you
for I knew you knew all the green secrets of the fish
every cold vector of the lough, the shallows and the depths
where all the black eels hid and the hook-jawed, monstrous pike.

Always, you'd take me in and guide my hand slowly through
the making of a knot, again and again, until I'd get it right
or show me how to patch a broken net before you'd go.
And I'd watch you all down the road, making for the lough
where I knew your boat was waiting and ready for the water.

The Vase

I have never been one for buying flowers:
you bought your own and brought them back
tiny yellow buds that floated in a sea of flock.
The sugared water you put in kept them fresh
and after a few days their heads opened.
Fold after fold of yellow petals spilled
above the neck of an off-white vase.

I had never noticed it, the vase I mean
I disregarded it daily as it sat slightly
to the left and a touch behind the television.
But now as each set of flowers pass their best
and end up in the bin, it sits in the room like a gap
or staring at me as a stranger might
ushering me out to buy more yellow roses.

Forty Shades of Fuchsia

I could show you three pictures from an old man's head.
I could show you that they lasted him a lifetime.
I could show you the last tree on an island
and the men breaking their boats to bury their dead.
I could show you a sky at evening.
I could show you forty shades of fuchsia.

I could show you bodies wasting into long shadows.
I could show you men dropping where they worked.
I could show you the road to no-where
and where they say there is hungry grass.
I could show you a field of wild flowers.
I could show you forty shades of fuchsia.

I could show you a son standing over his father.
I could show you the grip slackening on his arm.
I could show you the plea in his eyes at his last words:
"Ná bí ag briseadh baidí ar bith domsa."
I could show you a host of boats at sail.
I could show you forty shades of fuchsia.

Ná bí ag briseadh baidí ar bith domsa. (Ir.) – pron: Nah be ig brishoo badji ar beeh
doosa – lit. Do not be breaking any boats for me. – Be moderate in your grief.

Half Remembered

A shivering boy
incoherent
in the dark
sweat soaks the sheets
the flannel pyjamas
curls slick across cheeks

in the distance
an opening door
familiar footsteps pace
towards him like a heartbeat
a soothing hand
a few soft murmurs
descending in a kiss
sleep

and somewhere in the darkness
a fever breaks.

Late Snow

Drunk, we brushed away the years
into snow that lay knee deep
soft as talcum, dry as powdered bone.
Three of us, children
numb-fingering snowballs into ice.
We pelted ears already singing
from the cold. Faces beetroot and maroon.

Tomorrow, we'll grow up again
trudge respectably through slush.
Tonight, while the trees are all moon-
feathered; the hills are daylight bright
and fluorescence is blinding off the snow
tonight, one last time, we'll deflower
the virgin of our imaginations.

Re-inventing the Light Bulb

The mouth gapes at the dark
inside it, flying in filaments
circling in like paranoia
breaking like a virus in the cell
of the head, shining out from a black
ecstasy of terror.
                    Soon you think
it has to burn out and pop, shattering
the brush-stroke tension
forcing outward in a scream
to batter the walls of the gallery
become the colour of total extinction
consuming itself in an island of light.

Song for No Voices

The words I loved are gone, my mouth stopped
with this slack tongue, my jaw locked with rigor.
I remember how my outstretched arm would circle
the nape of your neck, your head lolling forward
full of sleep. The sweat on the curls below your jaw
a breast-brush on my thumb that timed your breathing.

I remember feeling the foetus stir beneath your skin
under my hanging hand, how your legs encircled mine.
Hot tears on my cheek and warm kisses. It's these things
I'm willing you to remember, willing you to forget.
I left you to batten down your grief; give sorrow to the warm
wood and tell our child, that I never knew, I never knew.

Pipe

Remember that grinding action
as he twists the knife into his palm
chips, screws and gradually softens
the block of *Old Warhorse Walnut Plug*
in that brown hand of his, and its heart
as hard as the barrel of his pipe.

Remember how he holds the pipe
in his mouth as he mixes his mortar
grips it occasionally in that claggy mitt
narrows an eye, and gently tamps
his plug into the barrel just loose enough
to such great teeth-gritting lungfuls back.

Remember how the smoke is released
with a smile from the prison of his body
how breath will come wriggling between
the bars of his teeth, find the air and dissipate.
He'll turn back to his work so you won't see
the plougher that wracks him, the rusty spit.

plougher (Hib.) – pron: plucher (ch as in 'loch') – rasping or wheezing cough

Cut Up

Silver screams lost in a cloud dungeon
church this crimson gloom to sunrise
shiver the mist that is necking our room.

Say: 'nightmare' and I rattle like a mirror
moon all the spider night to seize a storm-
ghost, the black angel of your blood.

Bury this candle breath coffin dark, down
here, where we empty tears with cold velvet.
Come make a grave – haunt me if I cry.

Baile an Easa

She likes to go walking late at night
and the hooded figure that I pass
on the road might well be hers.

The laughing murder of crows amass
and almost break the branches
with dead weight. Burning sky blackens

into monochrome. The middle ground
becomes a series of grey shades.
Gorse burns. The moon drips a rheumy

eye through sackcloth, gibbous, changing
like the pupil of a cat. It darkens
off wet roofs where the glint of bulbs

are moons in windows. The sodium light
yellows everything, the tree, the house
the pillar of the road. Crossed by beams

of a car, animal eyes redden in the night.
The moon has become a bull's eye
reddening in Taurus, unsilencing this place

loosing the hush and rush that named it.
The back of my neck quickens
nerves goosepimple, hair stands. I feel

shadows cross where there is no light.

A Present from Pompeii

Shocked in a shell
shaped paperweight
a sea scene, simplified
to a sea-horse, stones
starfish, weeds, shells.

A manufactured memory
a light-weight, imitation Pompeii.
I expected pumice lovers fused
and real life ashed out.

The sea-horse swims forward
as if wanting to be asked:
what Vesuvius poured over
entombed him under glass
painted his background black?

Crows

Glaucous ruptures of air
turn impossibly on updrafts
skim imminent ground.

The unlucky plummet
become a bolus of feather
and bone, grow maggoty with life.

Tragedy is beautiful
from the outside
death is sweet
as silence in the throat.

The Morning After

A sackcloth morning sky
is looming through my window.

I can smell the petrol
feel the soaking of the rags.

Beacons burn their warnings from the hills
I can feel each coffin shouldered.

The day comes too late
too late the penitent ashes.

Poitín Maker

Elfin renegade in the hill, turnkey
to the secrets of the worm
maker of good mash, lighter of fires
under stills. Consistent in his humour
as his whiskey, a man who can speak
volumes with a wink and a smile
who avoids conversation like excise.

Underneath all his tight-lipped
bargaining, there is total surety
of all the heart's distillings
drilling through copper
dripping off tongues.
See it burning in his eyes
clear blue, like flame.

poitín (Ir.) – pron: potcheen – illicit whiskey

In the House

Errigal is violet with snow and light
and the falling air drags smoke down
from chimneys to slacken at eaves.

Silence blackens like the fire back
where I pace my grate impatient
for kindling. I cold-shoulder

the January air to the far poles
of the house with fire, drive
blocks of wood into embers. Light

catches my eye from the white
night outside like a face
at my window. I startle briefly.

Without the wind's low murmur
it's easy to be lonely. Too lazy
to trek to the car, I settle

for the kettle and TV, the pub
attracts me less these days
I seldom show my face.

It's bitter out, even though it's just
an inch or two of snow. The log-pile
across the yard is frozen, but I go

return, arms full, sliding on the hard
patch at the door. Opening it, I hear
the mobile ringing, I dump the logs

in the wood-box, jump across the chair
and grab and answer just in time
"Hello," you say, "Where are you?"

without thinking, I find myself saying
"I'm at home."

Drawing Blood

Your hand in my left
my right fumbles the dummy in
and the nurses grip

while the doctor inserts
the cannula in your head
for a second time.

I am proud of the fact
that it takes four of us
to hold you down.

All this for two drops
of tiny blood that ooze
into a plastic bottle.

I smile and kiss you
try and make you understand
that *this* pain is temporary.

When I let go, the screaming
starts in earnest. I see the fear
and blue fury in your eye.

The hair the doctor shaved
is lying on the sheet.
Your mother gathers every one.

I hand you over to her
leave the room, where my stomach
turns like a traitor.

Meningitis

1.

One elbow hooking the back
of your knees, the other
clenched around your neck
the idea being to bring
them both together, immobilise
the six-week-old base
of your spine. I cannot watch
the needle go in. I bow
my head and pray for good aim
and clear fluid. (Any blood
contamination means delay.)
I kiss you. You do not cry.

2.

Your mother and I know
what it is to curl
all our hopes up in a ball
and make a fist of them
and do nothing but
watch the peak and trough
beep across the monitor
and not dare speak
or break the faint contact
with your skin, but squint
through the dark as numbers
change and you slip in and in
to sleep. Poets wish
a thousand things for children.
I wish you complete ignorance of this.

Estuary

A curve and arc of laughter
over stones. A fall and drift
to flattening sands where salt
and water mix in the mouth.
This is where the sleeping
tide lulls in a trickling over
beaches, where they fall in
and rise out of one another.
A marriage, where the stream
beds down with the sea
and both are neither.

The Song of Amergin

Translated from the Irish

I am poetry – I am fire on the brain
I am sea-wind breathing you to paradise
I am inundation – I bring doom to your plain
I am breaker tearing at your rock
I am salmon strong in my element
I am seven pronged antlers sharp from the rut
I am molten tears – I am the sun's extract
I am boar – I bleed savagery
I am hawk keeping watch on a cliff
I am thorn nailing the incomer
I am queen in the hive – I am the centre
I am prodigy – I bring flowers

I am one with the tree and the lightning
I am the secret of the gravedigger's working
I am signal beacon spreading over the hills
I am shield who will shelter you in battle
I am spear – temper me in blood
I am the sun's bed – I am the moon's face
I am sea and sky, river and mountain
I am the shape shifter – I am endless
I am the source – I am the author

Excavation

III

How do I tell my people their gods are dead?
I don't – if I want to keep my head.

I'll say that these were a band of peaceful traders
butchered by the savage native raiders.

It is easier (and safer) to manufacture
an enemy and send the soldiers into action.

The feel-good factor from our victory
will offset any possible bad publicity

generated by liberals giving it the vocals
while we get on with wiping out the locals.

Fire

I

I spent the night staring at the fire
watching the red and silver disintegration
of the wood, how the flames never touched
their fuel but consumed it nonetheless
as though they sprang from within the tree
were always in it, hid, until spark and tinder
took and released them, how the different types
of wood brought colour from the flame, blue
orange, green, yellow, violet, transparent as poetry.

Fire draws the eye in, the crack and pit
of bark holds until the wood becomes
a breathing ball that makes
grey silk on the surface lift
like skin flayed from flesh and bone.
I watch the pulse of heat bleed its way
across the inner surface, darkening
and brightening, rushing in and out
of the fire-heart, blushing over its face.
Each infinitesimal change more beautiful
for its brevity, a living blur, where I became
as lost as many are in the sea.
It warmed and consumed me
reddened my hands.

II

I stepped ashore to bless this place
spoke my incantation, claimed the beach
and the headland, the valley and the mountain
claimed the tree and the bird, grass and calf
stone and wolf, lake and fish, crow and hare.
I immersed my hands in the sea, the sand
the earth, claimed all their borders.
On reaching the marshland I baptised
my hands, withdrew them red and dripping
the rusty water hanging on them like cold blood.

I divined that this was a land full of blood
knew that it had tasted it early like a pup
that plays among the sheep, until one day
it nips too hard, draws blood, finds its red-
toothed craving. I washed and washed
that omen from my hands, but here it is
returning in the last light of the fire, burning
like the approaching dawn, red as tomorrow's
blood, red as battle, as shame, as persecution
red as bigotry, as hate, as blind fury
the monstrous red we paint our enemies
burning, red as we picture devils

red as our hearts, red as pain
red as history read as the future
red as a child's scream burning in its throat
as the child burns in its bed, burning red
as remembrance for the bodies never found
for the sons and mothers, for the fathers and daughters
burning for everything done, and for everything yet to be
done

for all of it, for the end of it, for the start of it
burning for invasion, red as displacement
burning knife-sharp in the belly, red as starvation
burning like a tongue ripped out, like the death of a tongue
red as tongues of fire that appear not to touch but still destroy
red as protestations of innocence on a stone ear
burning like the cry of powerlessness; red as futility
burning like the need to speak out, red as the fear of speaking
                                                                    out

burning red like responsibility, bloody as all our hands.

Harvest

The battle was fierce. You should have seen the ground
after the spillage. We came to claim our own for burial
but found it hard to tell ours and theirs apart, harder
still to claim for certain corpses of our sons, brothers
fathers and husbands. The enemy left their dead
where they fell, for wolves to tear and hooded crows
to pick apart. We threw them in a trench and filled it in.

You'd think that nothing would grow again on ground
sodden and contaminated by blood, but grow they did:
for years after, a mixture of wild flowers and grain
a rainbow springing from the pit, sprouting in clumps
from the bodies of the dead. We refused to put plough
to a bone-yard, but still a crop grew from seeds and tubers
the dead men carried in their food-pouches, blossomed
from the bags of their stomach, resurrected from the guts.

In a generation or two people can forget taboos, this land
will be opened up again and other invaders will settle
and die out. Still more will plough the same ground
plant new seed, reap, will have their fill of the field of blood.

Removing the Tongue

There is no need to be crude about it.
No call for twisting and gripping.
Shears and pliers won't be necessary.

All that need be done is a couple of swift cuts
right at the base of the muscle, sever the tendon.
There will be surprisingly little blood, minimal pain.

The tongue is rendered useless, it lolls
along the pallet and refuses to move.
Then there's just a short period of mourning

after that...

Terzanelle for a Killing

There I was, standing on the height
squinting toward the sun, my sight
blurred by the constant strain

my tears rainbowed by the light.
I saw a hawk gyre round his game
catch the air, stand at eye-height

not twenty yards distant. I swear
he plucked the bird clean and banked right
strained his body to a blurred stain

in his dive as he stooped and righted
turned and sped sunward like a ricochet
and left me standing on the height

astounded, short of breath, asway
(until I found my feet), delighted
that I had not stained my blurry brains

on the rocks below. With all my might
I flew down that hill like a man astray.
An understanding carried from that height
and blurred inside me like a muted strain.

A Storming

Often she would sit beside the fire
when the wind was rife
outside and rucked the trees
and hung among the tresses
of the grasses.
She would sit and listen to it all
as it rose and fell
about the roof; a storm
that pulled at the mortise lock
and shook the door, or squeezed
between the gappy wood of eaves
to invade the house.

Sometimes, I think, it raged
inside her too and dragged
the fire in her eyes like bellows
into life. Until, full blown
in its broiling, she'd go out
into the night to face it down
and I out after her to lead her home
would find her laughing (as well she might)
and her silver hair raging at the night.

Account

First, the flu-like symptoms, the minor annoyances
of phlegm and mucus, the aches and agues
of joint and muscle. But these soon give way
to gradual disintegration, a slow creep of fluid
swellings at the neck, knees and ankles, restrictions
on movement and speech. In the middle stages
the fever comes, brings with it lumps, solid in groins
and oxters, the knives of pain if these are touched.

By this time, it has you bed-ridden, raving and incontinent.
Then it comes: a rash that breaks to sores and screams
leaves you stuck to the bed-sheet with your own blood
moves from the skin in, and by the way the flesh melts
like tallow from your bones, you know you've taken
the disease, and it you, straight to the marrow, home.

oxters (Hib.) – armpits

Signals

She carried beauty as though it were
a gun, shot eyes all eider and ice.
She was a star I reached for in water
an answer I looked for again and again
like a lighthouse sweeping a bay.
Somewhere the meanings all got lost
or melded into myth or Morse or hieroglyphs
and the world forgot them.

Blind boats steer out past rocks
the surf crashes and the wind sounds
like a low moan across the headland
while I stand here on the shore, turning
again to hob-nail my way through all
the ploughed lands of language.
She dances the fallow field of my dreams.

Into the Dark

This place is as treacherous
as an asp in an orchid.
I have seen its gilt-
lit heather turn
to a blind snow of fog.
I have picked my way
with headlights
inching the verges
that disappear in the dip
and rise of the road.

I have lunged in the dark
and felt that momentary lapse
into air, the surprise
of landing safe and sudden
in the cornering darkness
felt the wind tip and yaw
across the valley floor and lift
pitch me forward to the wall's
turning; felt the bordering control
of it and me; the drop homeward.

I make it my business
to dance on bog, to heel
and toe the line between
the mountain and the sky
to pitch myself and dive
blind, through gaps
between the inanimate pig
of life's dark treason
and the waking myth
of the obstinate truth.

Trees

Gnarled and knotted as language
they form the line of the road:
contorted crucifixions
with suffering etched in every ring
hanging on their rough faces
obstreperous as Gaelic curses.

These are the lampions of the terrible fog:
generation upon generation hanging on
the broken children of the rock.
Each geocentric root is fed on metal
bred pig-iron hard through stock
and branch, bred pig ignorant to weather.

These are grown to wait on lightning bolts
to cackle like hags elemental in the wind.
Brittle-beautiful their fingerings
their black bracing of the dark that grasps
at earth and heaven, keels to snatch
and whisper news of the strangers' coming.

These are the last of their line, would-be spears
or Celtic brooches pinning sky and dark
and rock in place. Stunted runts that clawed
and stabbed and kept the invader out for centuries.
What rises in their sap? Long nights of lightning
that put fire in the wood and seasoned them.

lampions (colloq.) – fools (as in jesters).

Bridge of Tears

"b'anseo an scaradh
Seo Droichead na nDeor"

An epitaph cut into the stone block
marks a bridge in the middle of nowhere.
The stream it fords is far too small
to carry a name and the stonework slung over it
looks out of place. Beneath it is a scar
excised by the trickling waters, a red gully
in the bog, a valley's parting.

The rock commemorates the thousands who left
taking the long cut out for Glasgow, England
the States; where both sides turned their backs
and parted; became dead to one another.
The valley recalls it in the spring melt-waters' rush
the sluice of juice where the sleán struck; the blood
the scar and the healing

standing like a plea in the last letter home:
come meet me at Droichead na nDeor
and walk with me again.

Translation of the Gaelic epigraph:
"Here was the parting
This is the Bridge Of Tears"

sleán (Ir.) – pron: shlan – turf spade

A Chinese Woodcut

Wood and metal in the eye mock
stone and earth on the slow drive
through a gap in Donegal where
the sun is molten in the stroop
of mountains and the lake seems
to gleam and tarnish like sodium
cut and cut by a pocket-knife wind.
The trees stand rigid as scuts
of pig-iron out on the corroded
copper headland and gorse is brass
on the mahogany mountain.

I am following a man I hardly knew
being driven to his wake thinking
in his blind eye, which of the two is alien:
to know that in a foreigner's eye everything
can be seen in terms of metal and wood
or to realise that the day after you die
a stranger sees why the crane flies west.

Tongs

Years nailed to the wall as an ornament
the tongs grow clatty, plastered with lime
and disuse. Once, they would be taken down
to cross your cradle with at night. Blessed
and blanketed and doused with holy water
their lightning metal hid from thunderstorms.
They could cure or curse and knew their own.

The long years cut the shape of crooked fingers
on the handle, have sooted them full-way up
the shafts, burnt the claws to blackened stumps
dark as her eyes, dead as the ash in the fire.
And when they take the coffin out, and before
the house is sold, or tossed, or the roof falls in
take them out across the threshold; bury them.

clatty (Hib.) – encrusted with dirt.

Elevation

From this height the land rises out to meet me
the ship-wreck lists and leans its crippled way to shore.
It was here the crew drowned a stone's throw
from the dark side of the ship and yards from land
a century ago when water doused their lanterns.

From this height the friar leapt to avoid the hell-hounds
baying at his heels, threw himself head-long and trusted.
It was here an island brimmed and hardened in the dark.
The monastery he built stood in thanks four hundred years
until the Viking's navigation doused its lanterns.

From this height a madman saw three stone carvings
turn and turn and turn on Easter night, believed
it was the work of angels, died disbelieved until
they found his body in the boat – no-one explained
the strange lights in the sky, lighting water like lanterns.

From this height the water called her down to fly
windward to the cliff-side, and the land rose up
to meet her and brimmed and hardened in the dark.
It was here she tasted the fire that fills and fuels
darkness and her face lit the water like a lantern.

From this height I watch the tourists take the boat
making for the island and the church to attempt
three turns inside the little coffin, reassurance
that they won't die within the year. And all the smiles
and all the laughter darken like a lantern lit by water.

Amergin's Song

There is nothing linear here:
birds beak silence to the wave
that doesn't reach the beach.
The governance of time stands
impeached by the 5am drip
of moon and star into lazy sun.
Time is relative – light bends.

Amergin, shown everything
in an instant, sighs in a trance.
The ink of his mind opens, spills
to take wing from a cliff field
to soar his words, wish them
to a high wind, where they scatter
to a different syntax.

Carried where the word carries
power of itself, driving
meaning to the stuttering
engine of the brain, sparking
until what we hear is meaning-
less and silence shouts unheard
words to flesh, soft and bloody

in the mouth; until we taste it:
a prism full of colour and uncolour
the upper and lower registers
of light, sound, language
until it burns clear
fire in the mind, drunk, ecstatic
until the music is the instrument

vibrating in sympathy; pulsating
until the word and the mouth
find unity; build in series
until we become words on the wind
scattered to sky, tree, land
until they become body and blood

until we eat, drink, believe.

High Water

Day and daily I have come to this ford
loaded down with rag and ronian
have pitched them down and dowsed them
and hopped them off the stones.
My fingers are flint and my palms
sandpapered, cracked and hacked
from the constant hard water.

Day in and day out I bring them
other people's clothes, as my mother did
as my young child will when I'm too old.
This is a family business.
I've cried, now and then, when the ache
in my hands gets too much or when
a hack cracks open and stains
some new-washed garment red.

That's what happened yesterday
as if I hadn't enough to do
without washing simmets twice.
I was in tears, scrubbing and rinsing
and working myself into a temper.
As I lifted the clothing to the light
to check the stains had gone
they caught me by surprise.

The leader gave me the strangest look
I caught it out of the corner of my eye
he turned sour-faced and pale.
I thought it better to be off
those men were trouble – I knew
them from their South Armagh brogue.

I heard their leader died a short time later
lashed to a pole with a crow on his shoulder
and now the Ulstermen are saying I'm bad luck.
Come hell or high water I'll be back again
tomorrow, for there's another bundle ready
and you'll find me here, sousing and dousing
wringing out the blood.

ronian (Hib.) – small piece of clothing
simmet (Hib.) – vest

After the Battle

Night cursed its way along the valley
lay like a malartán in the cradle of two hills.
The moon like a burst of ore had shot through
the streams' seep between the stones
and sifted ferric flakes downhill
from the battlefield where the weapons
rust their way to an oblivion
of soil and shattered bone.

Even the grass is vaguely ferrous
the sharp blade hides that underhand
green, flicks it from the frosty
underside like a switchblade of colour.
Dew shod, I make my crossing
across a treachery of stones
my feet defy by gripping
before the crack splits the blue air

wide open and through it something
vast and dark at the corner of my eye
approaches, flutters, passes. Again
and I look down into the whiskey-
coloured water a long while before
I realize the ore that colours it. I drop
my gun – a splash – a crack off stone
I feel the iron heat half-cauterise my side.

Who'd have thought that blood
could have been *that* colour.

malartán (Ir.) – cursed thing or changeling

Civilization

You shattered my language
until it stuck in my throat

I spat splinters of words
back at you like nail-bombs

You made a slave of me
and left my culture in rags

I became naked aggression
I became the barefaced brick

You turned a blind eye
while your soldiers ransacked me

I became the bullet
I became the hijacked plane

You would neither talk nor listen
you told me justice was blind

I became the terror you couldn't deal with
I became your waking fear

You told me I was capable
of every sort of savagery

I will pull the pin beside you
and explode

Split Second

Forward and back
Forward and back

The man is rocking

Forward and back
Forward and back

His lips are moving
Maybe he's praying

Forward and back
Forward and back

His son at the window
Is seven years old
He sees his father

Forward and back
Forward and back

He's saying something
While he's rocking
You can barely hear him

Don't go to sleep
Don't go to sleep

Forward and back
Forward and back

His son is pulled

Out of the window
A woman is screaming
They see the blood

Don't go to sleep
Forward and back

Don't go to sleep
Forward and back

The stumps of his legs
End in the wreckage
Melt to a puddle
Of blood in the metal
The man is muttering

Forward and back
Don't go to sleep

Forward and back
Don't go to sleep

She comes out running
Dives at the car
O Christ O Christ
Look at the blood
He keeps rocking
I love you I love you

Forward and back
Forward and back

Don't go to sleep
Don't go to sleep

Sirens roaring
Police come running
Guns are cocked
An ambulance screeches
Swings in beside us
Move yourselves back!
He's rocking slower

Forward and back
Don't go to sleep

Don't go to sleep
Forward and back

From every direction
Shocked faces running
The medics keep working
Staunching the blood
Stopping the screaming
Killing the pain
The crowd gathers in
See he's stopped rocking

Forward and back
Don't go to sleep

Don't go to sleep
Don't go to sleep

They manoeuvre him out
Onto a stretcher
And up through the doors
From out of the crowd

A hard man is shouting
Hey UDR bastard
You forgot your snap

Forward and back
Forward and back
All our histories go
Forward and back
From this point onward

None of us sleep

snap (colloq.) – lunch – an allusion to the fact that bombs were often packed in
lunchboxes for ease of attachment to a vehicle.

Bomb

They're washing away the blood today
and tomorrow the funerals will start.
The rumour mongers have fallen into
an enumeration of bits and body parts:
all that was found of so-and-so
what him up the road was missing
the difficulties in trying to identify
and separate what belonged to who.

I sing dumb and tut and shake my head
or try and change the subject. I know
the process you have to go through
looking at scraps of clothes or a shoe
for some form of final proof, but I can't
tell them. Sometimes it's better not to know
that in the end you bury nothing, or next to.

Seanduine

I soften for you. Your toddle
and "how-do" short-legging it
along the path, conniving
to be last in line, hands
clenched behind your back
or relaxed into a wrist-
and-kidney strut, you come
with a reverse kiss
the da-da da-da syntax
urgent with no words.
Your head and heart are full
of all the things you can't say yet.
You contrive. You mean like hell.
And so do I. And so do I.

seanduine (Ir.) – pron: shandinnya – lit. old person – used for precocious children
and historically as a term for babies.

Chorus

A thousand webs barely contain the green thrum
of the hedge and the night-drop dregs of silver
burst in the mouth; reek like zest. The eye irradiates
with a clamour of birds blackening into horizon.
Colour begins a slow thunder across the sky, multiplies
and changes; sings in bird-throat to the beat of wings.
The air hives with birth, vibrates out of shadow.
Everything burns, everything rings, including me.

The great bell of the world vibrates and I am drunk
with winter-shine. The concrete blazes. The red tang
of seven o'clock and the vein-belt of walking brazen
to the frost leaps through me. An hour before petrol-stink
and the shrink of people diminishing into a rush, here
in the open-throated song of morning, I am in the clear.

After Rain

the blue arch of the wind
makes the catkins ripple.
One falls and stipples
across a puddle. Lead peels
like bark off a steeple
and evening flattens
on a park bench.
Everyone is under cover
huddled below eaves
and behind shutters.
A car pinks by
the exhaust stutters
a plume of smoke
thunder coloured.
To the west, a clearing
opens up to the silence
left behind. The street
swings into motion
black umbrellas gleam
against the ocean
of a whitening sky.

A Hill Farmer Speaks

No-one envies me my spire of fields
when the sun barely creeps above the maam
in the bowl of winter, the whirlpool of early spring
and I'm out pounding the land in all weathers
climbing up the sheer face after sheep
or up to my oxters at lambing time.

Not even the hill walkers want
to cross my bare quarter, under
the brooding bulk over Doire Uí Fhríl
where the wind sheers in from Toraigh.
It's no wonder I took the second job
to see the animals foddered over winter.

No-one understands why I stay
why, day in and day out I hob-nail
my barren acres, where I know every stone
and own each knuckle of ground.
The dark mass of the hill
is mine to the bone.

Doire Uí Fhríl (Ir.) – pron: Derryreel – lit. Friel's Oak Wood – placename.

Crosses

I go up to cut the lengths of rushes yearly
hopped up warm with clouts and the last
air of January condensing with the morning
on my coat. The wind slices across Pollagull
all the way in from the shore and white horses
batter out on Harvey's Rocks as the tide turns
from the slack of low water.

My small knife is fresh from the whetstone
and between the blade and my thumb I nick
the rushes at the quick and gather them up.
By mid-morning I'm back beside the fire
and the day twists and turns its green length
on the four sides of every cross. Even at seventy-
odd my fingers are nimble enough to turn out
the best crosses in the townland.

I make one for each room, one for every
neighbour house, a few for all of my five
children (though they never put them up).
Each year I seem to make a couple less.
Tonight, I'll go round every room, taking down
the dry brown crosses, putting the green ones
in their place. I'll burn the loose old rushes up.
The last thing that I do is tie my Bratach Bríde
to the outside latch, say a prayer for rain.

Bratach Bríde (Ir.) – pron: bratah bridje – lit. St. Brigid's Rag – a piece of cloth
(or sometimes a belt) left out on St. Brigid's Eve is believed to have curative
properties.

Cailleach

You barred the chapel door
with your body's huddle
under the black weeds

stretched your arms out
as straight as you could
and shouted at my face.

It took a while to figure
that these contortions
were a way of voicing

the sacrilege of my bare chest
and when I slipped a T-shirt
over my head, you side-stepped

and relented. On the way
back out, I saw you crouched
and hunkered in the corner

under an arch at the door-side.
You sat gumming bread softened
by a small pawnger-full of wine

and stared at the tourists with
a face like a bolted door
shut against all the sins of the world.

cailleach (Ir.) – pron: callyach – lit. old woman, hag or nun

Crab Apples

August. The first knuckles swell
and harden but do not thole long.
They drop with every breath
until the concrete becomes a carpet
of clots, arterial and dangerous

and a perfect counter-balance
to April's electricity. Smithereens of pink
blossoms slinking branch-long needle
at the eye while even the air greens
and erupts against a thunder-weather sky.

Between, mid-winter gnarls and mists
as a poet stares out at the twisted muse.
It stares back twice as bleak. Bemused
the poet turns away and dreams of fruit
beautiful, futile, bitter, amaranthine.

thole (Hib.) – to endure.

Electricity

The gathering dark looks in at me
as I light the lantern in the porch
turn off the electric light and see

my reflection disappear. The red
night dancing in the window fractures
across droplets in the misted up pane.

It's as if it asks me to approach
to meet it mouth to mouth, to close
in on the solid absence of light

and look deep outside, where black
shapes move against a dark background.
Something darker-looking moves inside

forces me to retreat away short-breathed
to the kitchen, make some excuse for tea.
I grasp the light switch in an urgency

to see again, the soft yellow eye
of the light bulb, to lie my way out
of that element which fuels me
runs me like a turbine in my blood.

After Effects

At the point of submergence
what ever it is will rush in
when the mouth opens
and sinks

the vessel disappears
leaves a ripple
that might just make it
all the way across

and sometimes if you're lucky
you are left with the measure
of the gap.

Snapshot

The light changes. It
flashes the road to sepia
in the mirror. A backward glance

at the kids shows they're sleeping
and an old man pushes a bike.
The light changes it

to a skeleton of black lines
changes him to a black line
in the mirror. The backward glance

of sunlight off the road glares
the whole picture into a monochrome
the light changes. It

changes the old man, bends him
into his grandfather, a picture-postcard
in the mirror; a backward glance

a hundred years ago. Nothing changes.
Time fragments like a flash and gleam
in the mirror. A backward glance.
The light changes it.

Family Tree

You stayed behind
all that April, and back
from the grave, blossoms oozed
like blood, loved
their way along the branches.
The sun's hymn woke the sap
and the limbs burned
electric around the mistletoe clump
each shock of pink froze
with life into May.

The first weeks scorched
and rained a plasma
of heat – the limbs purpled
the blossoms reigned
and leaves dull-coppered
but couldn't quite hide
the greening mistletoe.
You came just late
enough to miss the wake.
I tried to describe
and failed – and offered this.

Small Town Aphrodite

She headed for the city in the end
but found each swelling node
of light just numbed her more
surely than a lonely Christmas.
It might have broke her heart
if such a thing were possible.

The room reeks of it:
the heeled-up ashtray
full of butts that lop-sides
a blue stain of ashes across
the red map of Russia
where the claret seeps inevitably
towards the sheepskin rug.

She is across her unmade bed
looking not unlike the last piece
of installation art she did, the one
those bitches from her home town
up to the smoke on a day trip
pointed at and made a laugh of

and the last in a long line
of one night stands is not long
gone after demonstrating that desire
could be as keen as a hidden razor.
There is no need to ask her if it's true
the blue abstraction of her eye
affirms it.

Endymion

symbol of yourself on the wing
of the sea - no mirror exhumes you

wake on the further shore
the super-lucid heart of twilight

dream of death's chalk figure
emaciation sweetens on the tongue

the moon turns her back.

Lighting the Tree

Between us we carried the seven feet of fresh
cut tree up from the shop. You in front
with the butt and me behind with the tang
of sap sharp in my throat and the wind seething
through the needles, the smell of new wood
catching at my breath. When we reached home
you set to with the small hatchet and docked
the bottom foot of branches, squaring and skimming
fitting it to be wedged between the two half bricks
you held over from one year to the next.

You puffed and sighed and shouldered it
while I, your seven-year-old guide, narrowed
my eye and advised: left a bit or right.
It was manoeuvred or malafoostered
straight; and with one hand you trowelled in
a foot of sand, then lined the outside
of the bucket with Christmas paper. Paper
rasped from the scissors' cut and sand hushed
across the stones like a catch in your breathing.

That much done, the decorations were brought out
and strewed across the hours before dark
were wound around the entire house
footered and adjusted on the tree, until it danced
with a mass of coloured glass and ball, of tinsel
and crystal angels. By then the dark had settled
in and it was time to flick the switch. The corner
blazed and shone. I caught your hand
and we stood just long enough for the warm light
to catch at both our breaths, and I knew that if love
could have a sound, *that* was it.

The Science of Signs

Lightning strikes a tree
with all the love one jagged thing
can muster for another — out here
the sound cracks around the cavities
and the gap where the storm found me
where the wind searched
in every crevice and the rain clung
to the crevassed mountain.

Somewhere out beyond the hoop
of the fire — somewhere deep
in the ochre night I hear trees ramify
sway unstruck, enact the oscillations
between the sign of themselves
and what it is they signify.

Hours

I

There is not a breath.

Cobwebs lace the hedges together
and I part the frigid air
scraps of it grate their way in.

My chest is cold as the bow of a boat.
Nothing stirs. There is nothing
in my wake. Silence closes in like water.

Soon there will be lights and multi-coloured
curtains. Soon too the scrape of icy windscreens.
The rumble of engines will engulf me.

Life will take over. This is the last
hour before all that. I look up
catch a small face at a window

II

      it's thirty years ago
and the scream split my sleep
like an axe splits a log.

Up on my knees, elbows across
the sill and I pressed my forehead
to the glass. Outside, everything shone

leeched colourlessness and blinding in black and grey.
The streets were white, too cold for snow.
I watched their gropings in the frosty dark.

He had her half-stripped, her top and bra
thrust up exposing black nipples
that shrank like limpets on her skin.

I was hypnotised. She fought him off
and covered up, said something about
death and cold and going home. I juked down.

The day after, he boasted of his dry ride.
She denied all memory. My gran gave out
about the hole in her good hedge.

I never breathed a word.

III

The face at the window slips away
and I am left with the empty street
the five minutes to the bus stop.
The brief echo of my feet comes behind
like someone else. The light drifts across
and catches at the frost on the lichen
on the rooves, the odd dewy patch of moss
the milky webs on hedges. It liquefies.

I board the bus, flash my card. The driver
barely looks and looks away. We pull out
into the road and I press my forehead
to the glass. Stare out at the passing cars
avoid looking at the kissing couple opposite
although I see them in the glass. A lad of about eighteen
is draped across his girlfriend. She hugs his midriff
whispers something about death and cold and going home.

juked (Hib.) – pron: jooked – dodged or hid

Night Fire

and a frost of sweet winter air
goosepimples at the window
and my skin
             bitter-warm
coffee in the mouth bursts
in the gullet, sings like a glow
inside
             outside the moon
is just risen over the horizon
of a hedge, stars breakneck
above the yard-square
             hedged
eight feet high on all sides
the three-walled dark shadows
my claustrophobia
             the city
glows around the bowl of the sky.
I circle the bonfire under
the cone of starlight
             name
the familiars. Caolfionn
sees something else beyond
the rim of heat: an expanse
opening up full
             of planes
and helicopters, dark and twinkling
and rockets I don't see.
             He is
lifted up on the wing
of a cuckoo he invokes
at the end of each incantation.
He numbers us all on the wing

draws us all up

              where he stands
at my shoulder. Euan raises
one finger, points into the void
shouts out

          into the vowel of the sky
and that too is open lipped, hemmed
on all sides by the red horizon
that stretches out and rolls back
as we all stand amazed

                 raising
one finger Adam-like towards
a god as yet un-named

                trying
to guess what it is each other sees.
"Sky" I say. "Moon" says Caolfionn.
"Star" says Teresa. "O" says Euan
"O" he says again, but surer.

Aubade

the night balances
at quarter to three
and the boat rolls
my arm outstretched
my younger son
turns into me
his brother
and his mother
sleep in the other
bed
head to head
and breathe in unison
everyone sleeps except me
in the car
in the still-dark
I pass the lonely hour
composing this
I turn and turn
the verses over in my head
in the dawn
there is the dust of frost

it ungreens and thickens
to a covering of snow
the further south we go

and the morning is white
from head to toe
England is asleep
this morning's mine
this morning is all rime

Glenshane

coming across   out

                  of the fracturing

        night/day

                                   border

      the last   orts

of dark   strewn

            across   the shattered

                   mountain

black stone   grey stone

         white

           low cloud

                     peeling away layer

        by layer

           by layer

              under

the headlights

                   the air

       heaves up

              under the burden of light

we come home

                      again

           complete

another crossing   feel ourselves relax

         into the downward drift

come up the line   and cross

           never the same line

      twice

Iced Over

light shines   out   from

                    incandescent snows
    against

                an ever-darkening night
                                    where palls
                    of frost drape

        everything   in rime

the air is sharp   biting

                the throat   and sinuses

                        it hangs

                the last rites
                                    over a film
of life
                    left   barely clinging

                        to the land

        now   the long wait
                                        for rebirth

    the seeking   out of damp
                    and the slow
                                        sexing
            of a soft spring

Photograph

the shape

                                of a man

               is shouldering

                                     the shape

       of a child

           in the sun

                 and like all

         the other people

                      in the foreground

he is a shadow

              in negative

         the flash   that followed

           erased them

                  assumed them

shrouded them in white

News

today   the leaves cry

              three thousand

       green tears

                     for the leached out sky

                                   the sun burns

at a breathless fog   that winds itself

       until it becomes a shroud

                            around the trunk

       of a dead man

                     seeps and pools   spools
                                          like blood

                            in the hollows

              of his wounds

they found him

                            early and half buried

              hooded and tied

                     dispatched with five freshly

scabbed over

                 gunshot wounds

          one in the head

one in each limb

         at the joint

              Constable Hughes met her

face at the front door

          removed his hat

           brushed away the sweat

she wept

     out in the garden

           the young boy swung

    at the end of a rope

his shouts   hung on branches

    and in the house crying

   heart-sore   ripped bare   sighs

     words swept away

         by the wind

Poem

I have hunted something lean and hungry.
It has slipped the noose and dived
into a rat barrel brimming and over-
spilling. Light falls and ricochets
from the surface tension. Each drop
curls around an atom, lands and rolls away
tight as mercury, shape-shifting, oscillating.

Offer

          and I might take this small set
of random points in the web of your head
luminous as raindrops, instanter, present, gone.
A fizzle of bluebells in the brazen sun, a kiss
in another language, the helix of a forked tongue.
None of these need connect, no-one need take
any of them.

Love Song

Night. Chill. Clouds moon
a parting and midnight
blue opens out of white.
Moon-bathing in a rainbow
signifies the child of the wind
cutting, cutting under the skin
of my shirt. I could love you.

This is not flesh; not bleeding
every gasp freezes between us.
Kiss me. Taste: this is as strong
as a tongue unknown in ink.
It exists in the mouth. It passes
and my tongue catches
at ash, embers, spark, light.

Names of Things

Some things happen when your back is turned:
a thousand swans might freeze by their spags
and eight thousand feet of wing begin to beat.
Imagine the lift. The disc of spancelling ice
like a second moon diminishes upward, cracks
into a shower, pelting down like bones
in the white wind. None of this is mute:
imagine the rebounding whoops against each
other. The black feet free as cracks in a dome
shattering, and necks arrowing the great cross
of themselves onward to rest at Moyle
following their own ancestral map, more than
the sign of themselves, beyond metaphor
where language begins to disintegrate
into the frayed feathers of escape.

spags (Hib.) – large ungainly feet
spancelling (Hib.) – fettering or hobbling

Incendiary

1976. The lough had receded a good twenty yards
exposing the spurs of weed-coated, underwater piles
used to tether boats. They stank all through July
like something rotten. The skeleton of *The Wide Awake*
listed ironically, dry after sixty years. Everything waited
to catch in the heat. At the grocery shop a car is parked.

The owner has gone in to get a packet of twenty, locked
the kids in the car. It is just after 3 and a noise like an intake
of breath stops. The petrol, the vapour, the metal of the tank
all just hot enough that moment to go up. And who knows
as someone said after, why such moments are picked
those instants when we are most vulnerable and it all clicks
into place like the universe breaking a combination lock.

However it was, it was, and through the windows flames
ravelled and two kids are locked in a scream under glass.
Everyone stares. One woman drops her day's shopping
and a father hurdles out of the crowd. A man is busy
elbowing the driver's side rear window, drags a little girl
through in a flurry of fragment and flame.

                                        They run up
the arms in swarms; quick instinct drops, rolls a smoky blur
on the grass. A fraction later, having gone in again
and pulled the baby from the seat, smothered the legs
with a blanket, he stands and nothing moves that instant
until the child shakes in his skinless hands.

That's when you become aware of the panic.
Everything before happens in the time it takes
for the sound like an intake of breath to stop.

That's when you realise you have been holding yours
unable to break that strange calm where time
has concertinaed; when anonymous and unwilling heroes
happen. Like the man above, who turned down medals
and interviews after, asking "For what? What did I do?"

Synaesthesia

Barefoot morning steps it out on the grass. My glass feet break on the blades until I sit cooling them on flags and drink coffee and watch the early blurs of my sons. Caolfionn is at it full pelt with the blue train around the gravel circumference of the lawn. He pushes and stops at imaginary docks, stations, sheds; mends broken lines and babbles light-blue instructions. Sodor Island is somewhere between the aspen trees and his head. Euan is bouncing a straight cut across to me, coming directly out of the sun. His head is bathed in a yellow light refracted to a halo by his curls. His eyes gleam with devilment. The light is not just yellow – it's the colour of a 70's jumpsuit – Banana Blush, Electric Sunset, Blazing Sandstorm – the type of yellow that screams itself at you and his head is a'lowe with it. The pitch of his squeal as he rounds the picnic table for the fifth time is exactly the same colour.

a'lowe (Hib.) – pron. allow – on fire.

Catch 22

I

He had no intention of being snared:
he bridled up the horse and hit the fields
and when they came to Ithaca they found
Odysseus ploughing mad to dodge the draft

The fly boy caught on straight away.
Out in the field Odysseus clicked and hollered
looked right through him, ploughed rod-straight
until Nestor laid Telemachus across the furrow.

II

The Greeks knew how to handle the obscene:
a dramatic airbrush, a messenger reporting.
Very civilized, designed to prevent an audience
from seeing, demanding they trust the teller.

So several tellers tell their different tales, and we unpick
what truth might be: one or two have alluded to Odysseus
as the hero who did for Hector's son but Homer doesn't say.
And does it matter anyway who threw Astyanax from the
walls?

fly boy (colloq.) – clever or streetwise fellow

Exodus

I

That child hasn't made a sound
since he saw his mother
shot in the face.

Those eyes moon down
the lens of his fear
take him an inner circle deeper

unceasingly. He never sleeps.
A fly walks across his pupil
He never blinks.

II

The old woman
drilling the dirt with fingers
like stilettos is gathering

grubs to feed her family.
She arrived a week ago
just as the food ran out

with four children
and a husband
crippled by a mine.

III

The trains run regularly
crammed with refugees:
the dispossessed

the lucky ones, the not dead yet.
In the emaciated no man's land
between them and the camera

it could be 1943. By tomorrow
there might be no-one left.

Market

A brother bends to play with a little sister.
She shows off her new polka-dot dress.
Mother sits at the stall knitting from a red bag
trimmed with lace. Something is beginning.

In front four huge baskets offer peppers
crayfish, pumpkins, peas. Nailed to the wall
a yellow plastic bag holds money neatly folded.
A small basket of apples hides in the back.

Eight characters run down the wall
on a white wooden sign that separates
child-like graffiti from the dark entrance
to the slum stairs. Above, what remains
of a red poster announces its decay.
A soldier's face shines like a bright fruit.

At Bridge

A poodle is stuffed
on the Welsh dresser
and a pint of Guinness
yellows on the sideboard
while four fat fags slunge
in the mouths of the dowagers.
Two of them cheat at cards.

Pat prefers a holder
her sister Madge likes
to let her ash smoulder
and dangle shoulderwards
from a mouth corner.
She winks across at Red Josephine
who parts her lips for a draw

angles a fan of five cards queenwise.
Gladys leads with the ace of clubs.
Josephine reaches for her cigarette
makes a victory sign in reverse.
The conversation waits
for the flick of lamina on baise
the flush, the lift of glass
and a husband gone to the other room.
It starts again, as sudden as a gun.

Umbilicus

Clouds wave the old year in again over our heads.
Streets of shoppers gossip like jackhammers in the death
throes of the aftermath of Consumerfest.

Two lovers grip each other on their way to a coffee shop.
They sway like drunks and exchange a limping kiss, half-
connecting only. A hand is jammed in the other's pocket.

Ten naked cars rime themselves in the whitewashed light.
Lights dream of drowned shop girls while they burn. Soon
we will all wake in the waiting shame of daybreak.

Like a trip-switch turning off the weekend it will be Monday.
Holidays will end. Exhaustion will be a window we look
through like children wishing for life after warm rain.

Flat

After a week I needed to follow
Jackson Boulevard all the way
to Lake Shore Drive and look east.

Even from the 11th floor I miss
the jagged symmetry of rooves
black on a buttermilk band of sky

the sun coming up like the bole
of an alder cut. The gyroscope
in me won't settle. I get sea sick

on the rise and rise of office blocks
breathless with the stamp of the sky
and the all too sensible lineation.

I miss hills, and the effort of climbing
and squinting where the water misses
it's chance with the skyline. Somewhere

where the sun slips behind a thin band
of land that separates the two, a further
bank, an island that could be anywhere

a horizon, asperous, indistinct and inexact.

Topography

Caolfionn makes an esker
down the middle of the bed
to the far west, Teresa lies
shoulder skyward like the blade
of Muckish. Somewhere to the south
Euan hides himself like a drum
under the covers, punches the shape
of Cnoc na Rae from the duvet.
My knee is Ben Bulbin, the flat
of my chest, Upper Lough Erne.

In between us the bed sheets sink
into the valleys of Foyle, and Finn
and Derg. I play a game with them
pretend rivers and roads. The boys
climb the mountains of my knees.
I let them collapse under their weight
build again. Two giants striding across
the Ireland of the bed. This is Saturday
morning. By these tricks I teach them
their own geographies.

Rain

An only child traces where the rain
laces down the window of a bored Saturday.
Somewhere outside his father is drenched
and dark at one end of a road block.
He waits for the promise of games
of draughts by the fire.

The boy stares through the water
frosting, makes out lights and shapes
where the evening discolours. Not far
down the lane beside the gate, a jagged
oblong slips from a car, jumps over
and runs to the house. The boy makes
a rush for the door, hears the word
culvert. His mother falls to the floor.

From Paddington Out

The evening is mauve and black through the train window
yellow light after yellow light gleams like a butter heart
in between shadows and stretches where nothing moves
I speed backwards through trees, rooves and railway cuttings.
Out on the road the traffic is seized. Huddled in pale light
behind curtains, out in the country no-one moves. The fields
around the farm buildings concentrate on growing grass.
There are no cows. The white copse of beech shanks fluoresce
and grow at obtuse angles like the latter end of an alphabet.

Inside the train, people avoid people. One sleeps, one stares
judiciously upwards. *Metro*, puzzle book, novel, mobile, i-pod
laptop, progressively more complex ways of being on our own
avoiding eye contact, the threat of being spoken to. A young
woman struggles with a too-small mirror, applies makeup.
The train shakes – her eyes roll. Two more in their sixties
natter about the man who thrust a ticket in their face
demanded that they move. It is the only conversation.
Outside in the distance floodlights and a line of traffic are dulled.

The tannoy subdivides the hours by announcing that *we are now*
approaching Reading. This is Swindon. Mind the gap between train
and platform as you alight. The next station is Bristol Parkway. Please
change here for Gloucester. This is the First Great Western Service
to Swansea calling at . . .' Doors open and the train breathes out.
It empties as we get further west. The voice apologises again
for any inconvenience caused due to the fact that *the boiler's broke:*
and consequently no hot drinks will be served. The tic-tic of music
through earphones falls in and out of rhythm with the track.

Chora

The morning is vast and blank and nothing
moves in it. I open the door and enter it.
I make the shape of a shoeprint on the frost
and the weight of one person's heat cuts itself out
of the air. I step down the path towards the gate.

The air greens into mistletoe. Something
moves in my head. I open the poem and enter it.
It shapes itself and imprints its flux like the arc
of a spark fading through. The weight of a rhythm
cuts itself out of the place where forms form themselves.

It moves. The page in my head is vast and blank
and pregnant. I imagine choosing a green pen.
See the ink open and spill and enter the page.
A poem structures itself across the drafts. I hold
them all in my head until something cuts itself out.

The morning has not changed. The space where forms
are made has not changed. I reach the office, turn on
the computer. The page in my head empties itself
onto the page on the screen. This is the mother of all
creation. I shape what I need in it. I take. It heals itself.